T0276427

A QUIET LIFE

A QUIET LIFE

A NOVEL

WILLIAM COOPER
& MICHAEL McKINLEY

Arcade Publishing • New York

Arcade Publishing books may be purchased in bulk at special discounts for sales promotion, corporate gifts, fund-raising, or educational purposes. Special editions can also be created to specifications. For details, contact the Special Sales Department, Arcade Publishing, 307 West 36th Street, 11th Floor, New York, NY 10018 or arcade@skyhorsepublishing.com.

Arcade Publishing® is a registered trademark of Skyhorse Publishing, Inc.®, a Delaware corporation.

Visit our website at www.arcadepub.com.

10 9 8 7 6 5 4 3 2 1

Library of Congress Cataloging-in-Publication Data is available on file.

Cover design by David Ter-Avanesyan
Cover photo: Shutterstock

Print ISBN: 978-1-64821-033-4
Ebook ISBN: 978-1-64821-036-5

Printed in the United States

Dedication
WC: To Corynne
MM: To Nancy

If Tyranny and Oppression come to this land,
it will be in the guise of fighting a foreign enemy.
—John Madison

CHAPTER 1

TUESDAY, JUNE 21.

It was 2:15 a.m. and the stars glittered in the sky outside our window. A soft light entered the bedroom and blanketed most of the light-blue Persian rug lying atop the hardwood floor. The night was quiet.

My mind, however, was racing.

I kept thinking about Pam's sleeping pills. The ones she had started taking as work got more stressful. I had already opened the bottle twice and peered inside but was too worried that if I was sedated, I wouldn't be able to handle another surprise the right way. So I held back.

I couldn't get FBI Special Agent Weiss's face out of my mind. "Subpoenas are coming," she had told me about twelve hours before, her sharp green eyes unblinking as she looked right through me, as if envisioning me in a dark steel prison cell. What did she mean? Was I supposed to do something? I still didn't have a lawyer. How do you find a good national-security lawyer in the middle of rural Indiana? The way Agent Weiss said it—the cool, complete certainty in her voice—was deeply unsettling.

And as I heard her calm, cold warning, my boss's words pinballed in my mind again and again:

"You are a suspect."

"You are a suspect."

"You are a suspect."

I sat up in bed and turned on the television, quickly muting it. Pam, to my right, was finally asleep. I could hear the familiar purr of her soft snore.

SportsCenter came on, but I had already watched it. Up one channel was HBO. *No Country for Old Men* was on. But I was not in the mood for a movie—at least not one with the sound off. So I reluctantly punched the number for GNC into the remote and, grimacing, pressed ENTER.

The screen immediately lit up the dark room. Chicago was burning. Flames were blazing into the sky from several buildings downtown and giant plumes of smoke obscured the skyline.

My spine stiffened. I swallowed my breath.

The Chicago River, separating the two sides of downtown, was orange, reflecting the hovering flames. I turned up the volume just enough to hear the audio. The GNC correspondent, Janine Wood, stared into the camera with her deep brown eyes. I always loved her work because nothing frazzled her. Until now. She explained that a series of bombs had exploded only minutes before. Two separate buildings had been hit, she said, her eyes wet, her voice trembling.

The Iranian government had already taken responsibility.

One of the bombs, Wood continued, had been strapped to a man who reportedly was screaming "Iran is king! America no more!" before it detonated in the lobby of a fifty-five-story skyscraper on Wacker Drive.

Chunks of the nearby riverfront Davis Hotel—insulation, glass, and other debris—were floating down the river. The building was in flames.

Meanwhile, in Tehran, US and Israeli air strikes were intensifying. Wood reported that NATO's secretary general warned that NATO countries would participate in the United States' and Israel's illegal actions at peril of their membership.

GNC's footage showed billows of dark smoke engulfing the Iranian capital in midmorning. The bombs' pyrotechnics glittered in the smoke, and the sky filled with popping bright flashes of yellow. US fighter jets raced across the screen. Wood explained that the campaign had broadened beyond Tehran, with reports of air strikes in Ahvaz, Rasht, Qom, and Kermanshah. Her strong voice sounded like it was going to break in half.

And then I felt that familiar queasiness when I saw the president, Brian Davis, appear on the screen from the waist up. His black hair was slicked back, revealing an uneven, receding hairline above his scaly white forehead. While the forty-seven-year-old's paunch was a little bigger than normal, his shoulders and pectorals were typically awkward and oversized (rumor has it he takes cutting-edge synthetic steroids developed at one of his private company's labs). His thin lips were pursed in smug self-approval—as always. As his dark, shiny eyes danced around frenetically above dark and puffy pockets, one of his Davis Truths rolled out along the bottom of the screen like the punch line to a bad joke: "IRAN HAS LEFT US NO OPTION. IT WILL NOW BE TOTALLY DESTROYED."

Before Davis said a word the screen suddenly went black. After a few seconds he was replaced with a gray-bearded man in a white turban and a black robe, glaring out at the world through thick black horn-rimmed glasses, as if the Great Satan were before his eyes. It was Iran's Supreme Leader Ali Rhouhani, and as I read the subtitles, my stomach tightened into a rock-hard knot of fear:

"The United States' belligerence will not stand. These war crimes are predicated on a lie. It has chosen a path that will not destroy Iran but rather its own people. Every measure the US takes against Iran will lead to a more powerful countermeasure by Iran. The lessons of the last century—"

The speech was cut off. It was replaced by aerial footage showing large fires concentrated on Rodeo Drive in Los Angeles. Several buildings had been hit. Helicopters were landing on top of the Staples Center, and Disneyland was now an evacuation center. Janine Wood came back on the screen, barely holding herself together. "We have, moreover, learned from American intelligence sources that there are concerns Iran may have gained access to the US electrical grid through its cyber operations. President Davis will address the nation again in about ten minutes."

Pam awoke and slowly sat up. She looked at me, her soft and sleepy face illuminated by the television screen's light and clouded with worry as she saw the destruction unfolding on GNC. She put her left hand on my right shoulder and squeezed hard.

"Mikey, what's going on? Mikey?" she said softly, squinting her eyes.

I could feel her wedding band cold on my skin. She stared at me, then back at the television—terror and confusion in her turquoise eyes. Then back to me. Her long dark hair swung on her shoulders with each turn.

Another Davis Truth blazed across the bottom of the screen: "American people, hold tight. I have this completely under control. Total control. I am with our great generals right now. Iran has made a series of strategic miscalculations. First with its unprovoked cyberattack on our government and now with terrorist attacks on US soil. This will be a great victory for the United States—a great victory—and it will be over soon."

"Mikey, answer me," Pam pleaded in an alarmed, trembling voice. I wanted to speak to her, to tell her what I knew, but I was paralyzed by my own fear.

The GNC screen showed a photo of Russian president Igor Pryosnev, chiseled and stern, his black hair shining in stark contrast to his pale white skin. He was smirking, seemingly amused by the unfolding events. The ticker displayed his statement: "Neither Russia nor the world will stand for this dangerous American aggression. America has long been the central global player in cyber warfare. It is transparently using Iran's cyber activities as a pretext to meddle in the Middle East, yet again, in an impotent, embarrassing effort to cling to its ever-shrinking stature in the world order. Russia stands by Iran and—"

Suddenly, the television went black. The silent flat-screen disappeared into the dark wall behind it.

"Mikey?" Pam said, her voice trembling as I sat frozen with shock, staring ahead. "What's going on? Mikey? Answer me. Mikey. What's wrong with you?"

The alarm clock beside the bed came back on and started flashing "12:00."

"12:00."

"12:00."

"12:00."

The TV violently flashed on and off.

The streetlights outside flickered, bringing our neighborhood's dense rows of middle-American suburban tract houses in and out of view.

Then the alarm clock, the television, and the streetlights went out completely. Only the stars outside and the fully charged phones beside the bed emitted light. There were screams coming from several homes on the block. A chorus of barking dogs grew louder. A few neighbors were congregating in the street in their pajamas. Pam picked up her phone while I continued to stare at the blank television. She tried to go on the internet, but her phone rejected her: "no connection."

She reached across me violently and grabbed my phone. Same thing. She slammed it back down loudly on the bedside cabinet, knocking over my glass of water into the bed, and then shifted back to her side of the bed. I could feel the cold water seeping through my boxer shorts.

"Mikey," Pam whispered intensely, scared to raise her voice in the dark night. Trembling, she grabbed my shoulder and tried to turn my body toward hers. "Answer me. What's going on?"

Things kept spiraling faster and faster in my mind, and the worst part of it all was that I didn't know when—or if—it would all stop. I did not know how bad this would get. I felt like I was driving a race car in a thick fog and even though my foot had pressed the pedal all the way down, the car kept going faster and faster and faster.

"Mikey," Pam repeated, gripping my sweating face with both hands and pulling it to hers. Tears racing down her cheeks. Her lips quivering. Her hair draped across my bare, sweating shoulders. The right strap to her nightgown had fallen to the middle of her arm and her eyes, inches from mine, glowed frantically in the dim light.

"Mikey," Pam said, again, her voice rising. Her shaking hands tightened their grip on my face. Her nose mashed against mine.

I could see her eyes. I could hear her pleas. I could smell her breath. But the words were stuck behind a wall of my own fear.

"Michael Talbot Housen," she pleaded. "Answer me." She looked like I was breaking her great heart. And that look reached my heart and breached the wall. I could not let my wife suffer without me. We were together in everything, including this. So I told her. I told her that I—the most unimportant, the most anonymous, the most innocuous person on the planet—was responsible for this. "Pam," I said, my voice sounding like it was underwater. "I did this. The war is *my* fault."

CHAPTER 2

MONDAY, JUNE 20.

About eighteen hours earlier, I had woken up, showered, and hopped in my 2022 Prius—just like any other day. My commute sucks: an hour each way.

Driving on the long, straight highway, I was surrounded by a familiar panorama of dry Indiana flatland. The uneventful terrain—spacious pastures, modest homes, familiar fast-food joints—grew more visible as the summer sun rose above the horizon. The sea of oncoming, beaming-yellow headlights steadily disappeared into the maturing day. The sky became a bright, cloudless blue.

The Prius said it was eighty-six degrees outside. Already.

"President Davis this morning in a social-media message announced that he will be hosting next year's G8 Summit at an online resort created by his virtual-reality company Truth," the CBS News host explained through the Prius speakers.

The mainstream media doesn't like to call Davis's posts on his own social-media platform by their actual name: Truths. They instead call them "social-media messages."

"Participants in the event, Davis explained, won't have to travel anywhere physically but rather simply wear Truth goggles and participate through a Davis-owned and operated computerized virtual reality. In Congress, Speaker of the House Kathy Stewart and Minority Leader Nick Souza said doing so would be yet another blatant promotion of Davis's personal companies from the Oval Office and therefore a clear violation of the Constitution's Emoluments Clause and a high crime under the Impeachment Clause. They are adding this offense to the articles of impeachment in the ongoing House impeachment proceedings of the president. Davis supporters in Congress said they will oppose any plan to 'damage the greatest president the country has ever seen.'"

I shut off the radio when I reached Armor Security in Bloomington. We make internet-connected security cameras—the kind of high-tech video cameras that organizations use to monitor and secure their premises. I've worked here for a few years. The company was doing well before everything hit the fan later that day. Was the fourth biggest in Indiana. We had just made the Fortune 500, and our CEO had become somewhat of a celebrity in the business press.

Armor's new headquarters is eight stories of modern glass and steel. Plastered across the whole thing is the Armor logo: a red-and-black shield stopping a yellow lightning bolt. The building stood tall against the sky as I pulled up in the Prius. The sun's glare violently ricocheted down from the windows onto the parking-lot pavement.

The front doors are big, tall, thick, and wide. They boast reflecting glass, which the official version says is to keep out the afternoon sun. So I saw myself walk into work, as usual—just over six feet tall, ash-blonde hair, pale Scottish skin, and an emerging beer belly. I'm still pretty close to my college-baseball-playing weight (less muscle and more fat, but who's counting?). Pam says I have more than a passing resemblance to some action hero she loved when she was a kid. Rex Rockfield or Rock Rexfield or something like that. I was into baseball cards, not action heroes. She also says I've kept my baby face despite turning thirty last year and the salt-and-pepper stubble that now shows up if I don't shave for a few days.

When I get to Armor headquarters, I habitually grab some coffee in the kitchen on the sixth floor, where my office is. A wildly expensive and elaborate coffee maker is one of our CEO Caleb Wagner's transparent efforts to make the office Armor employees' "home away from home." The coffee is adequate, and the creamer is that fake carcinogenic stuff. So I bring my own carton of whole milk and keep it in the fridge, with a friendly note on it saying: "Hands off!"

My coffee in hand, I headed to my office, which is really a glorified cubicle, but at least it has a door you can shut. My trip was interrupted by my boss, Steve Velarde, who was standing in his office doorway, which is just down the hall from me. He motioned with his head for me to come to him. He had a serious look on his face—a slight frown underneath squinting eyes—that I hadn't really seen before. Steve's a nice guy who keeps things fun and light, so the serious look was a little jarring.

As I entered his office, Steve walked behind me to close the door. It was an unusual move. He usually leaves his office door open during meetings. It's part of his management style: open, friendly, collaborative. I'm not super passionate about my job or about Armor, but Steve is a great boss. He's the main reason I've stayed with the company as long as I have. Even though he's very busy, he takes time to mentor me and I've learned a ton about marketing from him.

After closing the door, Steve sat down behind his desk and looked at me. Forty-eight, he is tall, tan, and physically fit, really fit—squiggly-veins-popping-out-of-his-tan-arms-level fit—with wavy light-brown hair and soft blue eyes. He's unmarried, but if he didn't have an unusually large nose, he would be one of the more handsome men on the planet.

A red, white, and blue Davis-O'Neil 2032 campaign flag ("Keep America Great!") still hangs above his computer, even though Davis's reelection is already in the bag.

Steve is a big Davis supporter. It's annoying, but I forgive him given his other virtues. He's ignorant, not malicious.

Steve rose through the ranks at Armor through general charm, sharp business acumen, and—above all—fierce loyalty to the CEO. But he wasn't laughing or turning on the charm now.

I could tell something wasn't right. "What's up? Is this about the Game Changer?" I asked, as he had been bringing up his side project to me a lot lately. The Game Changer is this piece of software he was working on with a select crew of elite Armor software engineers. He told me once in his office that the Game Changer "will change the world forever."

He never said much more than that, just that it was "quantum defying." He made it sound like whoever had it would rule the globe. He didn't think I could understand it. Though, oddly, he said that Pam probably could. "She has the genes." Pam has great genes, making her the brains and the beauty of our family. Her parents had been academics. Pam isn't in academia, but she's brilliant, the smartest person I know.

"Thank goodness the Game Changer is safe. But we, and you, are not. We've been hacked." He was staring right at me. From that angle, and only that angle, you can't really tell how huge his snout is. "Our cybersecurity team working with FBI forensic investigators has determined the hacker got into Armor's computer network."

He paused and stared at me, like it was my turn to say something. All I could think to say was, "How?"

Steve smiled. "Don't feel bad Michael, I'm sure you didn't mean to do this on purpose." Then he said, "But they got in through your computer when you clicked on a phishing email in January, on, I think, January 25. It was a fake email purporting to be from Ad Supply. Odd because we haven't done business with them in over a year."

"Um," I replied, after a long pause. I have a degree from UC Davis—I know, I know, if he'd been president then I might have applied to UC Santa Cruz—in European history. I understand little about computers and virtually nothing about cybersecurity beyond what I read in the paper about hackers breaking into companies and government agencies all the time. "Okay," I said, wondering why our own cybersecurity products wouldn't have taken care of this phishing email.

"It was Iran," Steve explained. "They have huge cyber operations and have hacked into dozens of US companies. They got into our source code, created a back door, and, after we circulated a software update to our customers, used the back door to covertly get into the Treasury Department's computer network. We . . . you . . . we got hacked by Iranian cyberterrorists."

"What?" I said softly. "What does that mean?"

"It means Iran's state-sponsored hackers downloaded malware and got into your computer after you clicked on the fake link and then roamed around on the Armor corporate network and found their way into the source code we put into our cameras. Then they built a hidden opening in the code so after the Treasury's IT department downloaded our tainted software update, the hackers were able to get into Treasury's computer network through our cameras. We have forensic investigators looking into everything so we will know the full picture eventually."

"Okay," I said, desperately trying to understand where this was going, because surely Steve wasn't blaming me. "So I clicked on a link to a survey? I don't remember that."

He arched his eyebrows. "Really? Nothing."

I didn't know what he wanted me to say to that. I mean, I get so many marketing emails every day that they all look the same and become a blur.

"Well, even if you really can't remember," Steve said, shaking his head, "you opened it, Michael. The forensic team confirmed this." He paused again. I just stared at him, so he underlined things for me.

"This is not good, Michael. Again I don't want you to feel bad, and I have your back, but I can't sugarcoat this either." He looked at me with the deepest concern. "This means that Armor is on the hook for letting the Iranians into the US government's house."

I winced. "But don't we have internal security measures to stop that kind of thing?"

He smiled again, shaking his head. "We have internal security measures, Michael, yes. For example, if you tried to read my email, I would know. But we can't stop everything from getting in, no company can. And we don't have anything to stop hackers who get in because you let them in. There's a human element here." Then he said: "There's nothing Armor or any other company can do if you actually click on a bad link that gets through."

"But, Steve, I didn't know. I didn't know it was a bad link."

"And we don't know what the Iranian hackers did once they were inside Treasury's network," he said, ignoring me. "But from the limited information the Department of Homeland Security has been willing to share with us, it sounds pretty bad. Very sensitive information was accessed and exfiltrated. The Iranians may have encrypted some of it too, so that the government can't even access its own files. The Treasury is part of the National Security Council. The fallout is huge. The hackers apparently got into other government agencies, too, through Treasury."

"Okay," I said, disoriented, slumping in my chair. "I'm sorry." It was all I could think to say. It clearly wasn't enough.

"It's a straight line, Michael," he said bluntly, with a mix of agitation and disappointment in his voice. "The forensics team confirmed they got in through *your* computer, directly to the Treasury."

I just sat there quietly, looking down at my hands and then back up to Steve.

"Again, I have your back," he said. "Always have and always will. But this is serious. Caleb is pretty shaken up."

"I understand," I said, nodding slowly.

"We have a meeting with Caleb at eleven and the FBI will be here at two," he said, standing up from behind his desk and walking toward the door. He put his hand on my shoulder as I rose, and looked me square in the eyes. "See you in ninety minutes sharp."

"Got it."

But I didn't get it at all. I was going to meet with the founder and CEO of our company in ninety minutes and then with the FBI because I had clicked on a phishing link? They would want to know what I remembered about that email. In the time I had left before the meetings, I would try my best to remember anything at all.

CHAPTER 3

MONDAY, JUNE 20, LATER.

I went to my office, the tiny glassed-in closet—like a fishbowl for humans—and slammed the door shut. Then I went into my inbox, which, as usual, was overflowing with unread messages from all over the marketing universe. I searched for the Ad Supply email, in vain. I didn't think it would be there because I usually just delete emails like that, and Armor automatically empties its employees' email trash after sixty days. And, sure enough, it wasn't there.

I thought hard, and I kind of remembered the email. *Maybe.* But I wasn't sure. I get hundreds of emails a day and among them is tons of crap and I don't really pay attention to emails unless I get one that matters. Who does? A survey from a former vendor wouldn't qualify. And the emails that do matter, well, I can't always remember some of them, either. How was I going to remember this?

I closed my eyes and tried to take a deep breath. My heart was thumping fast and hard. I bit my bottom lip hard. This was bad, I thought. Precisely how bad? I didn't know yet. But bad.

Really.

Fucking.

Bad.

CHAPTER 4

MONDAY, JUNE 20, LATER.

"Mike, what's up, man?" my friend Bo said a few minutes later as I walked by his cubicle, trying to get some air, trying to think. He had a crooked half-smile and slightly bewildered look, his dark curly hair and tanned tubby cheeks perched just above the wall of his cube. I would never, under normal circumstances, just walk right by Bo's cube on a Monday without stopping by to say hi and see how his weekend was.

Bo, short for Bautista, is a manager in IT—a wonky techy. He loves Armor. He was employee ninety-two or something like that. So loyal to Armor, Bo has never sold a single share of Armor stock. And Caleb Wagner is his hero. His superhero. If Bo had a son, his name would unquestionably be Caleb. Bo is what us nonbelievers at Armor (that would be me, Kerry in customer service, and a few other brave souls) jokingly call a Caleb Bot.

When I first joined the company Bo was warm and welcoming, like he wanted to be my best friend. We'd have a beer after work, and talk about baseball, and sometimes watch baseball games at Duke's sports bar. Then he invited me to a Davis rally in Indianapolis. I wasn't sure if I could be around so many Davis bots all at once. But Pam said to go and keep an open mind and soak it all in as a learning experience. So I went. The whole thing was nuts. Thousands of people cheering wildly and laughing uproariously for Davis, no matter what he said. It was entertainment, not politics.

"What's up," I responded. "How are you?"

"I'm good. Adjusting to Monday. This one hurts." He tapped a hand to his head and grinned. "One too many mojitos, amigo."

I nodded with an absent smile.

"You okay? Mike?"

"Sorry, dude; yeah, I'm okay."

Bo could tell something was off. If something is going on in my head, it oozes out of my face. I'm as transparent as the air we breathe. Always been that way. The good side of this is that it makes people trust me. They know I can't fool them. The bad side, of course, is that it volunteers all sorts of things I would rather keep to myself.

"I'm okay," I repeated. Bo nodded gently, skeptically, more out of politeness than belief.

Bo had come to America from Cuba as a child, with his parents fleeing Castro and Communism. He gets his news from Davis's cable outlet called—what else?—Davis News, which delivers whatever "truth" Davis decides to convey.

More people watch Davis News than the other cable networks combined. A lot more. Davis started the network about six years ago, just before his first presidential run

At about the same time, he started Public Protection Centers, Inc., a corporate prison provider, another one of his conglomerate's subsidiaries. Since Davis became president, PPC's profits have quadrupled.

I think it was Aesop who said, "We hang the petty thieves and appoint the great ones to public office."

"So how was your weekend?" Bo asked me, just after my harrowing meeting with Steve. He was leaning against his glass cubicle wall in his brown suede suit, light-purple shirt, and pink tie. Bo is an eccentric dresser, to put it mildly. One of a kind would be more accurate. "Quite a game yesterday. Soderstrom is hot."

Bo loves baseball; I do too. Almost lost it when my team, the Oakland A's, nearly moved to Vegas before the owner's mom exercised some provision in his trust fund preventing the move. I was a pitcher in college. Had the kind of slider that could paint the black so well—break at the edges of the strike zone—that my teammates called me Michelangelo. Then I blew out my shoulder and that was the end of my major-league dream.

"Sure you're okay?" Bo continued.

"Yeah, just too much going on at once."

"Pam okay?"

"Yes. Thanks, she is. Working on a cool film." Pam is an archival producer on documentary films. I call her a history detective. She likes that.

Bo didn't ask about the film but instead said: "Let me know if there's anything I can do."

It was an odd thing to say. As if he already knew I was in trouble. Or was the look on my face so worried and shaken that he could just tell something was wrong? And why did he ask about Pam? He doesn't know her all that well.

Part of me wanted to tell Bo what had just happened with Steve. But I didn't completely trust him not to take whatever I said back to Steve or even Caleb. Maybe, the thought flashed across my brain, Bo had something to do with it. He's a manager in IT, after all. But why didn't he know about my email encounter with Iranian hackers? Or did he? Would all of IT have been in on the "forensic investigation"?

Those thoughts collided in my head. And until I could untangle the wreckage, I would say little. So I nodded and smiled and said: "Will do." And then I hurried to my office to prepare for my meeting with Caleb Wagner.

CHAPTER 5

MONDAY, JUNE 20, LATER.

About forty-five seconds after I knocked, the dark mahogany door to Caleb Wagner's spacious corner office swung open, fast and hard. I walked in, slow and hesitant.

I had never been in Caleb's office before. Without speaking, Caleb pointed at a lonely chair in the middle of the room, instructing me where to sit. Steve was sitting in the chair next to Caleb's large and well-kept desk. He looked at me and nodded. I could tell he was worried about me and nervous about what Caleb might do.

The rest of the office was a mess, with stacks of papers and piles of old, legacy Armor cameras. He had the same Davis-O'Neil 2032 flag ("Keep America Great!") that Steve had, also hanging above his computer.

Caleb is another disciple of President Davis. "A fellow entrepreneur," Caleb will say. He came to the USA as a kid from Poland in the late 1990s and became the classic successful immigrant. Living the American dream. Total assimilation, to the point of swapping out his Polish name, Kazmir Piechur, for an American one, Caleb Wagner. Caleb started Armor when he was sixteen years old in his family's garage in Bloomington, twenty-nine years ago. The company has occupied virtually all of his thoughts ever since.

Caleb is short and stout, with blue eyes and blonde hair aggressively slicked back with way too much gel. His cheeks are tan and puffy, and his eyebrows thick. He's got a fair amount of stubble on his face by

10:00 a.m. and nearly a full beard by the time he leaves the office at 8:00 p.m. or so. He's always clean shaven, though, when he goes on TV, no matter what time of day.

He can be ruthless. I remember how Caleb fired one hundred employees within twenty-four hours of his investment bankers saying he needed to reduce costs shortly before the Armor IPO. Someone handed him a list of Armor employees and he marched right down and crossed off one hundred names—a fifth of the company. My name was going to be one of them, but Steve stepped in and talked him out of it.

There's a bright, multicolored ticker just outside the kitchen, about ten feet long and five feet tall, flashing Armor's stock price in real time. If the price is going up (which it usually is) Caleb will walk by (he always walks fast, his thick thighs mashing together with each self-important stride) and give it a thumbs-up. If it's down for the day, however, he pretends the thing isn't there.

Armor began as simply a security-camera company but, in keeping with the times, became an *internet-connected* security-camera company. Our customers can watch the footage of their premises in real time from any connected device (computer, tablet, smartphone) in the world. Caleb is proud to explain to anyone who will listen—Armor employees, Wall Street analysts, his kids' friends' parents—that Armor now has over two hundred software engineers developing the cameras' cutting-edge networked technology.

Getting the initial sale to the Treasury two years ago was huge. The timing couldn't have been better: a few months before the IPO. Armor already supplied cameras to several federal-government agencies, including the FTC and EEOC. But a major department like Treasury? That was big. Caleb talks about it all the time. He met with the Treasury's head of procurement no less than six times. We had to cut them a huge discount. But it was "the best deal I ever made," Caleb often says. "If we can keep the Treasury secure, we can keep anyone secure."

Right now, with his eyes fixated on me in a highly caffeinated stare, he was making me feel very insecure.

"Michael," Caleb said in his baritone voice, "we're in trouble." I held my breath. "Do you remember clicking on a link in an email from Ad

Supply in January? It was purportedly a questionnaire asking for feedback on their services."

"Um. Vaguely," I replied. And "vaguely" was a stretch. I couldn't remember a damn thing.

"What can you tell me about it?" Caleb asked, taking a sip of coffee from his red-and-black Armor Security mug.

I took another breath before I spoke, aware that everything I said could be interpreted in ways I couldn't predict. "Not much. I looked for it after speaking with Steve this morning but it wasn't in my email. Must have deleted it."

"You've done all of your cybersecurity training and the module on phishing emails, right?"

"Yes."

"Does Pam know anything about this?"

My heart thudded faster. Why did my wife suddenly come into this conversation?

"No, she doesn't," I replied, hoping my pale Scottish cheeks didn't flash crimson with the anger rising up in me.

"You may want to check with her and let me know what she says."

I didn't respond, because I couldn't say anything that would advance my own position in this room. I looked over at Steve, who just stared at me, expressionless. Then I looked back at Caleb.

"Well, the investigation has been ongoing since we got wind of this six weeks ago from the FBI," he said. "It was leaked to a local reporter who called me this morning—I refused to comment, but—" He held his hands out, as if to say, the vultures are circling. "So, we are letting you know now before it's public. It could go viral. This will not be good for the company. We are, after all, a *security* company. Since you are a suspect, we did not tell you about any of this. The FBI wouldn't let us."

The words rang in my ears:

You are a suspect.

You are a suspect.

He then stood up. "Don't be late for the meeting this afternoon with the FBI."

"Okay," I said, my heart thumping harder now. Meeting with the FBI? As a suspect? What? "Why would I be a suspect?"

"Because . . . well . . . to be blunt: given who your wife is, since her family is from Iran, it looks like you knew the email was coming and clicked on it on purpose, to let Iran into our network. Why else would you have clicked on it?"

What? Whoa. My stomach fell through the floor.

"It was an accident Caleb. I didn't click on that link on purpose. People mistakenly click on bad links every day."

"Michael," Caleb said, pointing out his office window to the sea of Armor employees hard at work. "I have spent thirty years building this thing."

"I know," I said.

He just stared at me and touched his hair, making sure the gel was holding it in place.

A few seconds later the door to Caleb's office slammed shut behind me as I walked back to my office, shell-shocked. Now they had brought Pam into this and made it seem like she was part of some sinister foreign plot. I could sell my Armor shares and Pam and I could hightail it out of Bloomington before sunset, I thought. But that would be an admission of guilt. And the feds would surely find us quickly.

Did Caleb and the FBI really think I clicked that link on purpose? My father used to say to me, "Do not be afraid of the truth, Michael." I wasn't afraid of it now. I was terrified.

CHAPTER 6

MONDAY, JUNE 20, LATER.

"How's your day going, honey?" Pam texted me a few minutes later, at 11:46 a.m. No way I was telling Pam what was happening right now. Eventually, yes. Of course. But it would have to be in person. I needed to think this through first so she wouldn't freak out. Or at least so she'd freak out a little less than if I just blurted everything out in real time. Like I probably shouldn't respond with this: "I'm having a bad day because the FBI thinks you, me, and your family hatched a treasonous scheme to hack into Armor's source code and then into the United States Department of the Treasury. How are you?"

"Same ole, same ole," I texted back, instead. "You?"

"Good. Got some cool footage for the doc. Well not cool, exactly, but compelling."

"Got it," I wrote. I knew the kind of brutal footage that she had to view was a reason for the lorazepam.

"Miss you, Mikey. What time will you be home?"

"Should be normal. Will call you in the car. Cool?"

"Yes, love you."

"Love you too."

"Oh, I have a surprise for you." she texted.

"What is it?"

"You'll see. :)"

Pam has bright turquoise eyes, long black hair, a gentle aquiline nose, and soft pale skin, which all merge into a beautiful poem of Persian descent. It's hard on her, having lineage to Iran, a country that most Americans associate with violent extremists and failed armament agreements. She's defensive about it. So am I.

Pam's parents were from Iran. They were both young academics who fled the country in 1979. Pam was born Parvineh, which means butterfly in Farsi, in Los Angeles. The kids at school made her turn Parvineh into Pam in grade six just to stop the "getting it wrong on purpose" club. She grew up in a home infused with Persian culture—the philosophy, the science, the art, the food. The air was full of the sweet, rich scent of saffron and her mother singing radif, Iranian folk songs, and the floors had thick, heavy rugs so beautiful other people would have hung them on the wall.

Her father was a physicist and a mathematician. A double doctorate. He worked for Lockheed on their systems communications, and her mother was a poet and professor of Persian studies at UCLA.

We met at college and, yeah, we fell long and hard and fast in love. We met in Professor Vucinich's freshman class on Western Civilization at UC Davis. I was captivated the first day by her long, sparkling black hair and bright, multicolored blouse. Tall and slender with impeccable posture, she was sitting so serenely on the other side of the seminar room. I wanted to see her up close. It turned out she had noticed me, too, and we wound up in the same study group for a paper on the English Civil War, and before too long we were our very own two-person study group. And then it was her mind and her way of seeing the world and her great heart that got me.

"What do you like most about history?" I asked her on one of our first dates, at a little run-down diner in downtown Davis called Francisco's.

She gave me the cutest smile in response, showing off her bright white teeth and adorable little dimples. "I love how history has flash points, which frame the big stories."

"What do you mean by flash points?" I asked, taking a gulp of IPA, my favorite beer.

"I mean pivotal moments where one big thing changes and everything that follows is totally different."

"Ah, yes."

"But every story in history has several perspectives, too. And by adjusting the lens, the story changes. So you always have to ask yourself: What are all the stories that matter here? And what are the angles?"

I smiled and nodded, showing I was impressed.

"I know this deeply from my own history," she continued. "There's my own family's story of love and escape and success in a new world. There's the story of what the Iranian tyrants thought of them. There's the story of how American bigots hated them. And then there's the overall story of the revolution itself. How it changed the entire world."

"It's incredible everything your family has been through."

"Indeed . . . part of making a story true is telling it better than other stories. The aesthetic angle. So it stands out. That's what I want to do with my family's story. And it's what I want to dedicate my life to, to telling stories."

"And you will do so. And the world will be better off because of your storytelling."

She leaned over the table, smiling, and gave me a kiss.

We began a conversation the first day we met that has never stopped, and all I hope is that she outlives me because I cannot imagine this world without her.

When Pam wanted to test academia, we moved to Bloomington so she could do an MA in comparative literature at Indiana U. I got my job at Armor.

And just as life was looking good, Pam's parents were killed in a car accident on CA-1, that gorgeous highway that follows the California coast. The only consolation was that her parents had come to our wedding two months before. I was thankful they had seen how happy their daughter was.

After the accident, that was it for Pam's academic career. She turned inward and became an archivist and started working on documentary films, doing deep research to find whatever the filmmaker needed that was buried in libraries, or vaults, or hidden deep in the ether. She is, as I said, a history detective. Finding the evidence that makes the story.

She's so good that she gets work from all around the world. She has been working on a documentary about the Iranians, like her parents, who left in 1979 and changed the world. A lot of the material from Iran that she had to view showed how Iran's government brutalizes its own people.

Pam is the kindest person I've ever known. She treats me like I am the biggest rock star on the planet even though I only know three chords on the guitar and two on the piano. And I can't sing. She's the only person in the world who really, genuinely cares what I have to say. She always does. Always has. Most people's eyes wander behind me or drift down to their phones after asking me a question about my life. Pam hangs on my every word. Makes me feel like a king.

Pam is, quite simply, the glaring exception to my inability to mold the world into what I want it to be. Most everything else is hard. Everything with her is easy.

My favorite thing in the world—by a mile—is sitting on the couch with Pam, watching sports, drinking beer, and talking. Just us. We're pretty frugal but we splurged on our couch and TV. The couch is long and wide, with light-brown, soothing leather; your whole body melts right in. We've got big, colorful, comfy pillows and soft, bright blankets all over the place. The TV is eighty-eight inches wide—no joke—a gorgeous, beaming flat-screen. And we have surround-sound speakers (of course).

When we're together on the couch, the rest of the world—the entire solar system—disappears from consciousness. It's just me and Pam. We laugh. A lot. We gossip. We tease each other. We make fun of people we know. We don't need anything other than each other. Lots of other things usually just get in the way. It's so simple and easy, and that's what you want: the best things in life to be low-hanging fruit.

We have a quiet life, just the way we like it.

The night before shit hit the fan at Armor, we were on the couch together. Two small pillows were stacked beneath my left arm; my right arm was draped around her shoulders. Our legs were resting on our big, rectangular, light-brown-leather ottoman. She had a beige blanket draped over her legs and lap.

We were watching a big game at the A's new waterfront stadium in

Oakland. They were playing the Kansas City Royals, who are really good this year.

"Huge game tonight, hun. We need this win," I said while cracking an IPA.

"We do. Hey, you know what? Fact of the day, husband. Baseball is getting big in Iran," she said with a soft smile, putting her hand on my knee.

"Really?" An American game getting popular in Iran?

Pam read my face. "They don't think it's an American game. They think it's Japanese."

Then she laughed, and I laughed, and the A's went down 1-2-3 in the first.

Baseball in Iran.

I'm pretty light-tempered and I *hate* confrontation but I get angry if anyone suggests something negative about Pam's family background. It happens. A friend of mine from college, a baseball teammate, refused to come to our wedding because of something the Iranian president said about Davis after he was elected the first time, in 2028. Davis brought up Iran several times during the campaign, claiming they were an unacceptable threat to the world order and had to be dealt with. My friend's wedding RSVP card checked the NO box and read "Sorry Housy, I can't get on board with you marrying a foreign adversary."

He had never met Pam. I haven't spoken to my friend since, all because of what some stranger said about some other stranger.

It's weird if you think about it. There are eighty million people in Iran—tens of millions more with family ties there—and you get all the big and complicated variation in that group that you would in any other large group of humans. Without exception. A simple family dinner of five reveals stunning differences between blood relatives under one roof. Yet to most outsiders, all Iranians are crammed into one monolithic category defined by a handful of zealots who happen to have seized the government.

How's that any different from thinking all Americans are like Davis and his cronies?

I'm guilty of oversimplifying, too, of course. Everyone is, to some degree. It's hardwired into the human mind. But at least I'm aware of it, which helps.

Outside of most Americans' field of vision when it comes to Iran is a country filled with great traditions and beautiful people. Not to mention wonderful food—Ash-e jo, Naan berenji, Kuku bademjan, Kuku sib zamini, Naz khatun—which I enjoy, thanks to Pam, on a regular basis.

Pam introduced me to the Iranian poet Hafiz, who is a national hero. I love Hafiz. He said: "Who laughs the most knows the most, if that laughter is sincere." I think of this often. The more you laugh—the more you *really* laugh—the more you understand the world. What a beautiful correlation.

We've learned to live with all the misunderstandings about Iran. And the consequences tend to be only occasional hurt feelings. But now, with shit hitting the fan, that could all change.

Ignorance and power is a bad combination. And it just landed in my house.

CHAPTER 7

MONDAY, JUNE 20, LATER.

At 1:59 p.m. I entered a large conference room—the place where Armor's board of directors meets each quarter—and found four strangers along with Steve and Caleb. Two women and two men. The woman sitting at the midpoint of the long rectangular table seemed to be the leader. She seemed to be about forty. The guys looked a few years younger, one Black, one white, and the other woman, also younger, was Latina looking. They all sat on chairs along one side of the long conference table, along with Caleb and Steve. I heard talking as I opened the door, but once I entered, things went silent. Everyone was already seated, and the three strangers had yellow notepads in front of them with pens in hand. Their boss did not.

The group stared at me as I reluctantly walked to the lone chair on the other side of the table. In the middle. The room was so quiet the sound of my loafers shuffling on the short-pile industrial carpeting was achingly loud. The sun was trying to enter, but the shades were mostly closed, and the low light only made things grimmer.

Directly opposite me was the boss: a slender blonde woman with eyes like pale emeralds and a strong face with a cleft chin. She gave me a thin smile. She was sitting up ferociously straight.

"Are you Michael Talbot Housen?" she asked.

"Yes, I am," I said.

"I am Special Agent Jo Weiss with the FBI Cyber Division," she replied proudly, confidently, and a little softly, as if to convey the power was in who she was, not how loudly she proclaimed it.

Then she swept her hand across the trio sitting to her side, like a conductor landing on the instrument to play when she pointed at it. "This is my team, Special Agent McGarvey"—and the white guy nodded once—"Special Agent Ortiz"—and the Latina woman nodded once—"and Special Agent Cole." The Black guy didn't nod. He just gave me a slight smile. Like he knew what was coming my way.

I noticed Weiss had a Davis pin on her black suit jacket. It had 48 (the number of his presidency) superimposed on top of an American flag.

Davis had issued an executive order requiring federal employees to wear the pins, replacing the traditional American flag pins that many bureaucrats chose to wear. Only about a quarter of federal employees did so. I noticed that McGarvey, the young white guy, had one as well, but Ortiz and Cole did not.

"First and foremost, everything we talk about today is strictly confidential and may not be shared with anyone," Weiss said to me. "Do you understand?"

"Yes," I replied. I have always hated speaking in front of groups of people and being the center of attention. As everyone continued to stare at me, the knife twisted in my gut.

"I understand you are aware that our forensics team has determined that hackers entered Armor's computer network through *your* computer," Agent Weiss continued softly.

I fidgeted in my seat and nodded.

"Do you remember this email from January 25 of this year?" Agent Weiss asked, gently placing a color printout of the Ad Supply email on the table, like it was the ace of spades.

That thin little smile played on her face, and she didn't blink her green eyes.

I looked at it, stunned. There it was. In my inbox. "Very vaguely, I think. Maybe." I said. "I went back through my emails this morning and couldn't find it. I must have deleted it. I get several hundred emails a day."

She nodded, and Ortiz jotted down a note on her yellow binder. Following her lead, the two male agents likewise jotted something down on their notepads. Weiss then looked at me again with that chilly blonde stare of hers.

"We were surprised to see that your computer was the point of entry," Agent Weiss said with a touch of exaggerated sadness in her voice now. "You're a smart guy with good experience working at a technology company. I can't understand why you would have clicked on that link. The sender's email address has only a single 'p.' See?"

She took her pen and tapped each of the letters in the email: "A-D-S-U-P-L-Y."

"I honestly can't remember," I said.

Weiss leaned back in her chair.

"Your wife, Pam, is of Iranian descent, is that right?" It wasn't so much a question, as the dealing of another face card.

I stared at Weiss for several seconds before responding. What a fucking joke, I thought, as if Pam had anything to do with this. I'm just some dude that works at a company that does business with the federal government, one of hundreds of thousands. Iran hacks everyone. And millions of people have family connections to Iran. Pam was not in cahoots with Iranian-government hackers. She is smart and kind and works for the greater good of us all with the films she makes and she is the last person on the planet who would use her husband as a pawn in a treasonous cyber espionage campaign.

"Her parents were born in Iran," I said. "She was born in Los Angeles."

Agent Weiss seemed to interpret that as if Pam's American birth made her doubly dangerous, a sleeper agent. Her eyes hardened into diamonds of suspicion. "Does she or her family have any connections to the Iranian government?"

Now *I* was mad. And Weiss could tell. "No. She does not."

"Michael, you need to be fully transparent with me, do you understand?" she said.

"Yes," I said.

"Does her family have any connections to the Iranian government?"

"They left Iran in 1979 because of the Iranian government. No, they do not."

Agent Weiss looked skeptical. "But Pam's work as a documentary film archivist would connect her to such people, would it not? Especially the film she's working on now, with that Iranian dissident."

I was stunned. How did she know that? Clearly, they had gone deep into our world, over some meaningful period of time, and we hadn't noticed a thing.

Weiss crossed her arms. "You guys live in Bloomington, is that right?"

"Yes."

"3455 South McDougal Street, is that right?"

I looked over at Caleb, and then Steve. They sat to Weiss's left. Caleb just looked at me and gave me a go-fuck-yourself blank stare. To him I was just a dipshit in marketing whose negligence was jeopardizing his life's work. Steve looked down at his notebook and pretended to take notes. His nose almost touched the table. I knew he felt bad about all this, and powerless to help me. The three agents just watched me. Silently. Judging.

"Zip code 47403," I replied.

"Okay," Weiss said, smiling again at the edge in my voice, her unblinking green eyes fixed on me. I stared right back at her. Also not blinking.

She moved on.

"What's your relationship with Ad Supply?"

"We used them for about six months to help us place ads on the internet. The results were mixed. So we stopped. I haven't spoken to anyone there in at least six months."

"Have you noticed anything funny about your computer in the last several months?"

"Um. No."

"Are you sure?" Caleb interjected. "Nothing?"

"Yes. Nothing. I haven't noticed anything funny about my computer."

"Okay. You can leave now," Weiss said to me abruptly, looking miffed that Caleb had interjected into her show. But she had a piece of parting advice for me. "We recommend that you hire an attorney immediately. Your wife, too. Subpoenas are coming."

Subpoenas are coming?

I looked around. No one else was getting up from the table. I looked at Caleb and Steve: blank stares came back at me. I rose and walked out of the room, turning back to the group before closing the door behind me. The room was quiet again. They were all staring at me as I left. They looked like they were staring at a guilty man.

CHAPTER 8

MONDAY, JUNE 20, LATER.

"Can you pick up some asparagus and parmesan cheese on your way home?" Pam texted me about fifteen minutes later, at 2:45 p.m.

"Yes."

"You okay?" she replied.

Pam could sense I was not okay in my abrupt reply.

"Yes, why?" I texted back, trying to seem normal.

"Just checking."

"See you later 😘."

Pam texted back with an emoji of her own: ♥

I knew she loved me. And I also knew that I had absolutely no idea how I could tell her what I had done.

CHAPTER 9

MONDAY, JUNE 20, LATER.

"Cliff," I said while pacing the Armor parking lot with my phone latched hard to my ear. The sun was beating down on my head through my thinning hair. It was 3:05 p.m. "Are you alone?"

"What?"

"Are you alone?!"

"Calm down, Housy. Yes. What's going on?"

Cliff is my best friend. We grew up on the same block in El Cerrito, a small city just north of Oakland, California. He's a lawyer. Does corporate transactions at Cravath in New York. They're a famous, white-shoe firm with lots of Wall Street clients. "We have big swinging dicks everywhere you look," Cliff once said. He makes like $450,000 a year but, as I like to remind him, that's just over minimum wage per hour. I ask him legal questions all the time and he almost always says, "I don't know, that's not my area." He specializes in "capital markets," whatever that means. He's given me about six seconds of legal advice since he got his law degree from Georgetown, and that was when we were buying our house and his legal advice was "It's a money pit." I had expected more.

We've had a loving rivalry since we were kids. It occasionally gets heated—especially on the basketball court. When we were kids, fisticuffs were fairly common. We had a falling-out in high school, over a girl of course. But we got past it and by senior year, everything was back to normal. He's definitely more successful, but I'm better at sports and kick his ass in fantasy football. Biggest of all—he's single and I have Pam. I can live with that balance.

"Some really gnarly shit's going on at work and I need your help," I said.

"Okay." He sounded surprised.

"Are you sure you're alone?"

"Yes."

I took a breath and looked around to see if I could spot any black vans in the parking lot listening in. I didn't see any.

"I just got out of the meeting with the senior leadership of my company including Caleb fucking Wagner and some special agents from the FBI Cyber Division. Iran hacked into our corporate computer network through *my computer* because I clicked on a link in a phishing email. The hackers got into our source code repository and implanted something into our software, and when the Treasury Department, one of our customers, updated its Armor software with the corrupted version, Iran's hackers got into their network and caused trouble. They won't tell me what the Iranian hackers did, but it sounds like a really big deal."

"What?" Cliff replied.

"*Seriously?* Do I need to repeat that?"

"No. Hold on," Cliff said. I could hear his office door closing in the background. "Have you confronted Pam about this?"

"No! Dude!" I shouted. "You too? Pam has nothing to do with this. Are you serious? Iranian hackers sent me a phishing email and I clicked on it. Do you read the paper? Iran does this to everybody. She didn't make me click on the link."

"Okay, okay. Sorry. Did the FBI say you were a target of the investigation?"

"They said subpoenas were being drafted and I should get a lawyer. The FBI agent was a total jerk to me in a very controlling way. Pam needs to get a lawyer, too, apparently. Caleb said I was a suspect. So yes. I am a target."

"Okay, hold on. Let me get a notepad." I could hear a change in his voice.

"Cliff, dude, I'm just trying to earn a living, man. Pay the mortgage. That's all I'm doing here. It's just a job. My life is simple—on purpose; a wife, a dog, baseball on game days sitting on the couch with some tasty IPAs. I majored in history and, hey, wound up with a good marketing job. It's a small life. It's cabined in. Protected. *On purpose.* That's all I've asked for. That's all I've sought from the beginning. Minimal upside and minimal downside—they're supposed to travel together. I don't want anything to do with this sorta big, geopolitical thing, man."

I took a breath to calm myself down and let Cliff help with that, but he was silent.

"We were supposed to make the bigs, Cliff! I threw ninety fucking miles per hour as a sophomore. Had pro scouts coming to our games. Remember that? And now I'm the reason the Iranian government has hacked the United States Treasury Department and stolen a bunch of sensitive information? Cause of my carelessness. I'm under investigation by the FBI? What the fuck? If I wanted to be entangled in this shit, I would've joined the CIA. I'm not wired for this. It's one thing not to achieve your dreams. Fine. Most people don't. But you should at least be able to *choose* a quiet life. And here—"

Cliff had heard enough. "Stop. Dude, stop. You will drive yourself mad. I know, I know. I get it."

"But you're not being investigated by the federal government for treason."

Cliff didn't respond.

"What is gonna happen to me? What is going to happen to Pam?"

"Let me think about this. This is not my area of the law," he said.

Of course it's not his area of the law.

"Cliff, dude, how could this happen? I clicked on my mouse and hackers from thousands of miles away ransacked the federal government in Washington?"

"I don't know," Cliff said after a long pause. "They say the world is flat now."

"The world isn't flat, though. No. The world is combined into one, I don't know, one dense, interconnected thing."

"I hear you."

"And it's not just combined in the fun exciting ways it used to be like surfing the web and reconnecting on social media. Now anyone with a computer can wreak havoc anywhere in the world. And anyone, anywhere, can be a victim even if they are just innocently going about their life. And I am the fucking exemplar."

"I'm sorry, Housy."

Cliff had run out of things to say.

"What can I do to stop this?" I asked.

"Let me talk to some people. I have a meeting but will call you back in under two hours. Do not talk to anyone else about this until I get back to you. Don't call anyone; especially not Pam; your phone could be tapped. Probably is. Okay?"

"Great. Well, if anyone's listening, I'm innocent! Okay, just leave me alone so I can watch the A's this weekend. Just leave me alone."

He didn't respond.

"Okay," I said. "Okay, I will talk to you soon."

The sweltering sun continued to pour down onto my head, softened slightly by a mild breeze. It was ninety-five degrees. I could feel my pale skin starting to sizzle. My nose was pink. I paced, trying not to appear nervous to the Armor employees nearby heading to their cars. My shadow was short and dark on the scalding-hot parking-lot pavement.

I thought about Pam's sleeping pills in our bathroom cabinet. Lorazepam. She took them because of what she was learning about Iran for her documentary, seeing things she couldn't get out of her head. I was going to need some lorazepam tonight if I wanted a wink of sleep.

My heartbeat, throbbing, expanded throughout my body. I could feel it in my fingertips as I pressed the phone to my right ear. I kept hearing Caleb say, "You are a suspect." An act of war had been perpetrated against the United States by a rival nation state and *I* was a suspect.

Me. Michael Talbot Housen. A thirty-year-old, mid-level marketing guy in Bloomington, Indiana.

I was nauseous. Numb.

"You are a suspect."

I felt like I was floating.

Heading back inside the office, I remembered being in a park once when I was ten years old. In the memory, there was an odd-looking tree ahead of me, about twelve feet tall with dark-green leaves and five or six interwoven branches reaching up to the sky. I was walking in the tall grass toward it, alone. To my left was a still pond with quiet water. To my right, several acres of open field. After reaching the tree, I grabbed its trunk with both hands. What had been the present at one moment—walking toward the tree—had become a memory. Then moments later, touching the tree became a memory, too.

Everything that has happened in the last twenty years blends together with my time at the park that day. Just memories. Unlike life as it unfolds, you already know what happens with memories—the good and the bad.

I like that. Already knowing what happens. There didn't used to be such a gaping divide between the past and the future. When I was young, I just lived. That's all. I was curious about the future. Not scared. I thought I would come to know a different world as an adult—a world where reality was better friends with intentions and desires.

As I reached the door to head back inside, Kerry, my colleague, came out for a cigarette. They are tall, maybe six-two (a couple of inches taller than me) with kind green eyes and red hair that falls just below their shoulders. Thin and athletic, they have a round face, a warm smile, and are transitioning from male to female.

Like me, Kerry doesn't bend their knee to Armor.

Kerry manages customer services and is aces at their job. In this business, you get a lot of twitchy paranoid types, but Kerry somehow defuses them and allows the conversations to go forward in the spirit of happy resolution.

Kerry ran a hand through their long auburn hair and offered me a Marlboro. I don't smoke, but for a moment, it felt like I should. A cigarette before the firing squad.

"No thanks, Kerry," I said, and they smiled.

"I should stop, Michael, I know, but it's either suck Marlboros or mainline heroin in this place, so I choose the path of least resistance."

I smiled back. "You mean Armor or the country?"

Kerry laughed. "The country is totally and utterly fucked so long as

Davis is in the White House. But I don't think he's going to jail. He has too many loyalists in the right places. If it were you or me on the other hand . . ."

I nodded.

"You look like you've seen a ghost, Michael. Or I'm having a bad hair day."

I smiled back. "Just feeling things are a little out of whack here, you know?"

Kerry looked around to see if anyone other than the Armor security cameras that watched the parking lot were watching us now. "These are indeed strange times, Michael. Lots of official types poking around today. Of course, my team doesn't connect directly with them because they are not customers, but it makes me wonder."

I knew who they were. But I went fishing. "And what do you think?"

Kerry shrugged and took a drag. "Maybe Caleb is selling the company. Maybe they're here kicking the tires."

No, they were cybercrime agents from the federal government. Investigating a crime. Investigating me.

"I need to get back to work," I said.

Kerry nodded and took another drag. "If you hear anything, let me know"

I nodded. "Sure. Same with you?"

Kerry nodded back. "Same with me."

I walked by Steve's office at 2:17 p.m. His door was open again. He was talking to someone in product development, his right leg casually crossed atop his left. He looked completely happy, normal. *Normal.* He laughed—a tilted head, then a loud burst. He had an immediate subordinate, me, who had opened the door to the US Treasury Department's classified files to Iranian hackers, and he looked totally normal. I wished I had that skill. Steve has taught me a lot but he couldn't teach me how to keep my calm like he could.

A few steps ahead I saw the giant Armor stock-price ticker Caleb had mounted outside the cafeteria: $188.95. Another all-time high. Apparently, the market had not yet learned that a company whose mission is to protect its customers had been used as a vector allowing a hostile nation-state to enter the federal government's computer network and ignite a national-security firestorm. How much Armor stock did I have? I needed to check. It was toast. Gone. Destined for zero.

"DUDE WHATS UP," I texted Cliff at 4:55 p.m. All caps. "It's been two hours."

"Sorry dude," he replied within seconds. "The IPO is tomorrow. I'm in a meeting. Hold tight. Don't talk to anyone about this until you hear from me."

CHAPTER 10

MONDAY, JUNE 20, LATER.

"DUDE WHAT'S UP?" I texted Cliff an hour later.

He didn't respond.

CHAPTER 11

MONDAY, JUNE 20, LATER.

I walked to my car to drive home at 6:16 p.m. The shadows had relaxed and become long. The day's heat had barely relented, though, displaying a stamina I wished I had. Tired and disoriented, I grabbed the piping hot handle and opened the Prius door. It felt like I had last gotten out of that car many years ago. I had aged.

I pulled out of Armor's parking lot, nodding at Bo, who was getting into his vintage Ford Mustang—bright white with two crisp blue stripes down the middle—a few parking spots away. Bo nodded back, but not in his ordinary, smiling way.

He looked concerned.

As the evening sky got a little darker each minute, I drove ahead on the long freeway, replaying the day in my mind.

Processing.

The last time I was in trouble with an authority was when I got a detention in high school for talking to my friends in Mr. Schulz's history class. I avoid trouble. Consciously. Feverishly.

Trouble is unpredictable.

And now the FBI was investigating me for treason.

I wanted to call my father and ask him what I should do, but we had stopped talking when I was twenty-one. He was a civil engineer who worked in construction, and they were building an overpass on the 580 and a block of concrete fell from a crane and hit him on the head. And that was that. He was rushed to the Summit Medical Center, and it was touch-and-go for a month. But he came out of the coma. He just couldn't speak or write. He wasn't a vegetable; he was just trapped in his own body. He's in a hospice in El Cerrito. Workers' comp has paid everything, forever. The doctors say he could speak again some day, but I doubt it. I know he loves me. I saw it in his eyes the last time I saw him. About a year earlier. I could call my mother, but she bailed on me when I was a sophomore in college for some louche rock and roll guitarist from New Zealand and went on the road with him and his band. No looking back. Ten years ago was the last time I had spoken to her. This didn't seem like the day to reconnect.

I turned on the radio. "President Davis will soon address the nation regarding the escalating situation with Iran," the radio host announced, in a deep and sober voice.

I squeezed the steering wheel tightly with both hands. I could feel my pulse pounding the wheel through my hand with the escalating cadence of a drunk, angry table drummer at the local bar.

I clenched my teeth. My stomach hurt.

"As reported by GNC," the host continued, "the Iranian government has hacked into the United States Treasury Department through an internet-connected security video camera at Treasury's Washington, D.C., headquarters. The hackers accessed and exfiltrated voluminous data relating to the Treasury Department's multibillion-dollar Iranian sanctions program. This includes highly classified information involving the United States National Security Council and numerous US allies. The sensitive, proprietary information of numerous leading global financial institutions has been compromised. There are concerns this has led to the theft of billions of dollars of assets from banks around the world. Politicians from both parties on the Hill are calling this an act of war."

I felt like I needed to throw up. I considered pulling over.

"My fellow Americans," President Davis began, clearly reading prepared remarks, his voice sounding tired and haggard. "On my orders, the United States military has . . . excuse me . . . the United States military has begun strikes against key political and military installations in Iran. These carefully targeted actions are in response to Iran's highly destructive cyberattack on our nation. They hacked into our Treasury Department, after they hacked into the vendor who supplied our Treasury, a video-camera security company in the Midwest. As always, we will defend America first! Cyberattacks are no less hostile than any other form of warfare. And Iran's denials mean nothing in light of its long history of deceit. This is not a confrontation we sought, but is a confrontation I will decisively win. America will win."

I turned off the radio and kept driving. All I heard was the soft, efficient hum of the Prius's hybrid engine.

I thought about the pond at the park I went to as a kid. Ducks were floating on the surface, birds flying effortlessly overhead. Everything was so under control. There were no waves. The water was still. Clear. Quiet. Then I thought about the odd-looking tree, with the branches reaching to the sky. Walking toward it I did not know what it would feel like, what the texture would be when I grabbed it. But I knew it was just a tree. The future was so simple. Seemingly so predictable.

Driving home from the office, I had no idea how bad this would get. Iran was no pushover. They had technical sophistication and decades of creating a dangerous army focused on asymmetrical warfare.

How big would our invasion be? I wondered. Targeted strikes? Or shock and awe? Just Tehran? Or nationwide? Would Iran fight back? How? Their military was tiny compared to ours but big enough to land some blows. And as we had seen in the Ukraine-Russia war, bigger armies didn't always win. The heart of those under attack still mattered.

Did Iran have terrorists in the US who would cause harm?

Would Iran come after me?

Did they know who I was?

Was I in trouble? Would I go to jail? Would I wind up dead in some ditch? With Pam?

"You are a suspect," Caleb had said. What did that mean?

"You are a suspect."

You are a suspect.

You.

Are.

A.

Suspect.

My head was buzzing with questions.

Was I going to get arrested when I got home? Would Pam get blamed? Would her family in Iran be okay? Would I get fired? I almost *had* to get fired. But when? Was Armor toast? How can a security-focused company continue to do business if it's associated with the largest security lapse in US history? How much would Steve lose from the stock hit? How much would Caleb? His whole life was being shattered—decades of building Armor, his "canvas," soon to be gone.

Poof.

Gone.

And he was not an enemy that I wanted to have. Rich. Ruthless. And injured beyond repair.

I couldn't see around any corners. I was driving blind at a thousand miles an hour, violently thrust into the epicenter of a harrowing geopolitical flash point while going through my email at work.

The click of a mouse. One. Single. Click. One simple click. Among thousands. Millions even.

I tried to remember the click. What it felt like. What I was thinking? Why did I click on that damn link? Why would I even waste time filling out that questionnaire?

The mundane had triggered the breathtaking in an unimaginable—yet crystal clear—chain of causation. A seemingly normal moment had, beneath the conscious surface, been a pivot point not just in my life but in human history. The whole world was on edge, anxiously watching what would happen.

All because of me.

Me.

It wasn't a memory. This. *This.* No. It wasn't cabined in with any boundaries. There was no protection. No limits. It was real life.

Unfolding.

Unrestrained.

And very loud.

Then the car suddenly filled with the jarring sound of my phone ringing through the speakers, reverberating through the Bluetooth-juiced airwaves. The car zigzagged.

It was Cliff.

"It's been five hours, dude," I said.

"I know. I'm sorry."

"What's going on?"

"So I talked to two of the partners in my office who have national-security experience. One used to work for the counterterrorism unit in the DOJ and is on TV sometimes. MSNBC."

"Okay?"

"He said to talk to Pam. See if she knows anything at all, heard anything in her work. Don't talk to anyone else. Get a lawyer in your area who has relationships with the local FBI field office in Indianapolis. I will try to get you a referral. But first talk to Pam when you get home. Find out if she knows anything. Once you have ruled that out—if you rule that out—work closely with your lawyer."

"Okay," I said. But for fuck's sake. What was it with these guys and Pam? My wife is one of millions of people with family ties to Iran.

"Thanks, dude."

"Sorry, man. I know you were looking for more than that. But you really need a local lawyer who knows the right people in local law enforcement."

"I understand," I said, pressing the bright-red END CALL button on the Prius touch screen.

It was quiet again. Just me, the Prius, and the road.

I thought that Cliff might come through *this* time. But no. So I found myself completely alone: the suspect in an FBI investigation; my best friend unable to help; my wife not yet aware of what was happening to me, and to us. Completely alone. And yet at the same time an accelerating chain of events that I started with the single click of a company-owned mouse had the potential to impact every human being alive.

Brian Davis was leading the United States into war because I didn't notice Ad Suply was spelled with one p instead of two.

Then the phone rang. The car swerved again. I didn't recognize the number. 202-245-9561. The area code was Washington, D.C. My heart lurched. Who would be calling me from there?

"Hello?"

"Is this Michael Housen?" The caller was female. I thought I recognized her voice.

"Who's calling?"

"This is Janine Wood from GNC. I was wondering if you had a few minutes to talk about the phishing email that allowed Iranian hackers to get into Armor's computer network. There's lots of misinformation flying around so I want to give you an opportunity to set the record straight."

Normally, I would be excited to be called by Janine Wood. I knew her work and liked it a lot. A guy like me doesn't get calls from someone like her. But now the media knew that it was Armor, and I was the victim? So I wouldn't just be fired, and I wouldn't just be the reason that thousands of Armor employees' stock tanked, and I wouldn't just be the subject of an FBI investigation. I would be plastered on the cover of magazines and websites as the doofus who got bamboozled by Iran and caused our nation to go to war.

Awesome.

"Michael? Are you there? Is this Michael?"

My shaking hand reached slowly for the touch screen again: END CALL.

The evening sky got darker still, the ruby-orange sun sinking in a cloudless sky. A few stars had introduced themselves in the twilight. Surrounded by fading Indiana flatland, I drove.

I thought.

I melted down.

The highway stretched out before me in an unyielding straight line as far as I could see. The Prius engine purred.

I placed a half-pound of asparagus (*thump*) and an awkward-shaped block of Parmesan cheese (*thud*) on the counter at the local convenience store a few miles from my house.

A clock on the wall said it was 7:05 p.m.

On a small, dusty, old television behind the counter, GNC blared.

The audio crackled. A *Washington Tribune* reporter was on. "This is a transparent attempt by Davis to deflect attention from the relentless onslaught of daily scandals rattling this administration," the reporter said. "Cyber hackings are commonplace. The US is the worst offender of all. Davis and his cronies have been wanting to strike Iran since before the inauguration. It's a reflexive, partisan move to undo the progress made by President Mulder with Iran. Davis and his gang just can't stomach operating under an agreement with Iran put in place by a 'socialist' administration. So this action kills two birds with one stone: it's an attempt to divert attention from the administration's scandals and, finally, to get Iran."

"That may be true," the host replied. "But setting aside the intentions, what will be the consequences of this attack? How serious is this?"

"Our sources in the military believe this will be limited to strategic targeted air strikes. They caution, however, that you never know once hostilities begin. Anything can happen. Especially with an unhinged commander in chief who's actively trying to put nuclear missiles on Mars."

The cashier gave me a soft head nod. We typically banter about baseball (he's a Cubs fan). I wordlessly nodded back. He could tell by looking at me that I didn't have a lot to say tonight.

He swiped my card.

The food cost $16.19. Davis's initiative to stop inflation was still a work in progress.

CHAPTER 12

MONDAY, JUNE 20, LATER.

I pulled into my driveway a few minutes later. The sun had finally slipped away beneath the horizon. It was dark. Now only eighty-four degrees. More stars had appeared. Their glow amplified as the night took hold.

We live on a quiet, unassuming block in suburban Bloomington. Our house is a two-story white stucco bungalow, with a pair of lilac hydrangea bushes flanking the doorway. Just over 2,000 square feet. We bought it two years earlier, scraping together every penny we had for the down payment.

It looked calm and safe.

I grabbed my gray Patagonia backpack, along with the half-pound of asparagus and unwieldy block of Parmesan cheese, and walked to the front door.

The FBI was not waiting for me.

And neither was Pam. Usually she'd be at the door with a cold IPA. The only greeting I got was from our dog, Cecil, a rescue hound who was part German shepherd, part Rhodesian ridgeback. We named him after Cecil Rhodes, the man who painted Africa red, the colors of the British Empire. None of our neighbors caught the reference.

"Where's Pam?" I asked Cecil, and he kept wagging his tail. After a few steps I heard her sobbing in the living room. My first thought was what an idiot I was for not calling her when news broke about the war. Then I wondered why she didn't call me.

She was sitting in front of the TV, with her phone against her ear, watching GNC broadcasting live footage of US air strikes lighting up the sky in Tehran. She was wearing comfy gray sweats and a white V-neck T-shirt. Her black hair was long and silky, and a thin silver necklace bounced when she turned after hearing my footsteps. She wiped her eyes, red and puffy, and gave me a smile of both relief and devastation. "Mikey's home, Zahra," she said into the phone. "Let's talk later."

She ended the call, put the phone down on the coffee table, and picked up a glass of wine, pinot grigio. Then, as if she'd forgotten the most important thing in the world, she rose and said, "Mikey my love, let me get your surprise. I think you'll need it."

She disappeared into the kitchen and returned with a cold IPA and handed it to me. It was the brand-new IPA from our local brewery, Blair's. She knew I'd been waiting to try it since they'd announced it was coming weeks earlier. It was the perfect example of how Pam treats me like a king: nourishing my little passions with conscientious love and attention.

The IPA was crisp. Hoppy. Protective. The bottle was sweating, with cold water droplets working their way down the curves. The taste was potent, my first sip a welcome but fleeting antidote to the harrowing reality that was enveloping my life.

I put my arm around her, and she leaned into me, tears gently falling down her face.

"Sorry I didn't call babe," I said.

"It's okay, I was just processing everything and then started calling people in Iran."

"Have you been able—?" I began.

She shook her head. "Haven't connected with any family. I was on WhatsApp with Foad," her friend in Tehran helping her get footage of the basij beating up teenage girls for not wearing the hijab. "The call just went dead. I called Uncle Behzad in Shiraz, and he said he couldn't talk and hung up."

"How is Zahra?"

Pam took another sip of wine. A gulp, rather. Kind, brilliant, and beautiful, Zahra is like Pam's second mother. They have a powerful bond rooted in respect, affection, and love. Zahra was the director of the documentary Pam was working on. She lives in LA. She had been a high school classmate of Pam's mother, and while Yasmin had been a poet, Zahra had turned to film. She had won top honors at Cannes for her documentary on the 1979 revolution and an Oscar for its sequel, a documentary about the US involvement in the Shah's corruption. The film she was making with Pam was the third one in that trilogy, looking at what those Iranians who had fled in 1979 had done for the world, things that they might have done for Iran had they not been forced to run for their lives.

"The worse it gets, the calmer she is. But she can't reach her sister in Tehran. All the communications have been shut down. What is that maniac doing?"

"Just letting loose his sadistic cruelty on the world," I said.

And he was doing it because of me.

"Davis, of course, didn't give the Iranian people any time to flee Tehran," Pam said. "General McCluskey, chair of the joint chiefs, was on GNC, and he said this will be limited and targeted air strikes focused on specific military installations in Tehran. He said it would be similar to the first Gulf War where we had targeted strikes in Kuwait."

She squeezed my hand, and I squeezed hers back. I wanted to tell her that her family would be okay and so would Zahra and Foad. She was probably thinking the same thing, trying to convince herself that this was true. But we didn't dare say it. We had no idea if it was true.

She apparently had not heard that her husband was responsible for this.

Yet.

"Everything will be okay, hun," I said. I rarely lie to Pam because she can spot my fibs from a great distance. "We've bombed Iran before. We also bombed Syria a few years ago. This is just another round of air strikes. Same thing. It's all under control."

"And there's still some competency in the military, which hates Davis," Pam added, nodding. "As long as they stay in control, everything should be okay."

"Yes," I replied, hugging her and kissing her on the forehead. "And they will."

A Davis Truth ran across the GNC news ticker:

"Iran must learn its lesson as it faces our great American military and our great generals. Cyber warfare is just as serious as any other act of war, and Iran's actions will not be tolerated."

Then the screen showed President Davis, wearing an army jacket in some kind of central command room with generals around a table as he waved his hands in the air. Vice President Gus O'Neil was sitting next to him. O'Neil is in his late forties, packing about thirty pounds over his playing weight as running back at Army. His nose leans to the right, having been broken more than once. He had a finger twirling his dirty blonde hair and a look of glee in his hard black eyes at the mayhem Davis was unleashing on the world.

My stomach tightened even more.

"How was your day, other than, uh, this?" I asked her.

She smiled. "I made great progress with Foad. He has the footage we need, and Zahra was thrilled."

"That's great," I said. Zahra had helped Pam so much. Having Zahra happy would make Pam happy. But she'd probably still need a sleeping pill after seeing whatever Foad was sending of thugs pounding on schoolgirls. And now, because of Davis, she'd need two.

"Anything exciting happen at work with you?" Pam said, attempting to establish our old order of a daily check-in. I wrapped an arm around her shoulder.

"Nah," I replied, hugging her tighter. She couldn't see my face when I answered. "Just another day at the office."

I couldn't tell her everything yet. Pam needed to sleep, and this might be the last sleep of the innocent. I would tell her everything in the morning. But I needed to do it the right way. For both her and for me.

CHAPTER 13

TUESDAY, JUNE 21.

So there we were, awake in the middle of the night in our bed with the world collapsing around us, the power out and only the faint light of the stars and our smartphones separating us from darkness. As I looked into Pam's eyes, I didn't know how our lives could ever be normal, could ever be quiet again.

"Mikey," Pam said, squeezing both my shoulders and pressing her nose against mine. "What do you mean it's your fault?"

I could see in her eyes that she thought something terrible had happened to me. I just kept thinking that this whole terrible conflagration with Iran was my fault—directly, unmistakably. I clicked the link. I let the Iranian hackers into Armor and then Treasury. I caused this. I looked at her with tears in my eyes, but I could only repeat myself: "This is my fault."

She simply hugged me. Hard. The enormity of what I was in the middle of—what I caused—was enveloping us both.

More neighbors were congregating outside. I could hear their nervous chatter—punctuated by the occasional laughter—growing louder. I could hear the stern choppy diction of Grant Woollard, a former Indiana state trooper who lived across the street. He never liked us.

More dogs were barking. Our dog, Cecil, didn't bark thanks to his Rhodesian ridgeback genes, and he just stood there wagging his tail and looking at me, as if it was time for an early breakfast. It was this intrusion of ordinary life—the dog wanting his breakfast—that unlocked me from myself.

"I'm sorry, baby," I said, finally gathering some composure and able to elaborate. "I did this."

"What do mean, Mikey?" she replied, her voice shaken, her eyes wide with alarm.

"What's happening. This. With Iran. It's my fault."

Pam looked at me as if I might be really ill. She put her hand on my forehead, to check for raging fever. Her touch was soothing, making me feel for a moment as if it would all be okay.

"I wanted to sleep on it before I told you what happened. I was going to tell you about this when we woke up this morning."

Pam kept her hand on my forehead. "What are you talking about, Mikey? You're scaring me." The sweat on her brow glistened faintly in the soft light. She was deeply concerned, her eyebrows scrunched in disbelief.

I took a breath. "I clicked on a bad link at work. I got a fake email from Iranian hackers. A phishing email. They got into Armor's computer network because I clicked on it. The United States Treasury Department is one of Armor's customers and the hackers got into the Treasury through us, through a back door the hackers put into our video camera's source code. That's what Davis was talking about in his speech today announcing the war. The government vendor that he was talking about in his speech today is Armor. I'm the Armor employee that Iran tricked into clicking on a phishing email. Me."

Pam's head tilted to the left and she looked at me as if she was seeing me for the first time. I was scaring her.

"Mikey, this isn't funny," she said, taking her hands off my shoulders "What's wrong with you? Why are you saying weird things?" Her eyes bunched into a confused squint. Her head then tilted slowly to the right.

"I'm sorry, baby, but it's true. This really happened. It was an accident, but it was my fault. I'm not making this up."

"What . . . Mikey?"

"It's true, baby. I'm sorry, but it's true."

Her facial expression changed, and her fine features softened from hardened fear into something resembling understanding. She knew me, and she knew I wasn't kidding. Her lips moved, but no words came out. Then she asked: "Are you okay?"

"I'm okay," I said reflexively, wanting to make her feel better. And yet, there was worse to come. "There's more, Pam, though. There's . . . more. The FBI is looking into this. They think that you and your family had something to do with it since the hackers were Iranian."

Her head moved back several inches. Her face flashed with anger. "What?"

"Yeah, I know."

"What do you mean?"

She got out of bed and walked to our window. I followed her. The noise on the street was louder, the neighborhood congregation bigger.

"I'm so sorry, Pam. They're wrong. They are a bunch of racist idiots. Davis nutsos. They think that because you're from Iran and I was hacked by Iranian hackers, there must be some connection there. Like I knew the email was coming and clicked on the link on purpose to let the hackers into the network."

"That's crazy, Mikey."

"I know. I'm sorry."

Pam went back into bed and sat in silence, processing this mess. She started to cry.

Then I did too. She kept telling me sorry, sorry for her family, sorry for making everyone think I did this on purpose. I, of course, said that was insane and that it was me—the one who actually clicked on the link—who got us into this mess. I was the one who started this war, who caused Chicago and LA—and who knows what other cities by now—to get bombed.

She was mad, too—mad that the FBI thought she was involved. "Those bastards. Screw those bastards," she said, before bursting into tears again.

She wanted to call her family and friends in Iran again, but I told her that the FBI could be listening.

I peered out the window and saw Grant Woollard with one hand on his beer gut and the other pointing at our house. He always looked at me and Pam as if we were liberal smog that had blown in from California.

Even when he waved hello in the driveway, there was always the whiff of the highway stop about to go wrong with that guy.

"I think the best thing we can do is try to get some sleep if at all possible. I have a feeling we will need all our wits tomorrow, or today."

"How do we sleep in the midst of . . . of . . . this?"

"I know. I know. But we should try."

Pam sat on the bed, sobbing, and I held her close. I held her as she—my wife, my innocent, smart, good wife—cried and cried and, eventually, fell asleep.

Not me, though. I couldn't sleep. I was lying in bed, still in my boxers, as the rising sun slowly brightened our room. Other than two very large and very loud helicopters that had flown overhead, it had been a normal hour or so since she fell asleep. Most of the neighbors had gone inside.

I looked out the window, watching the electricity-free morning unfold. Processing all that had happened to us. Our phone batteries were slowly draining. It was eerie not having any power or connection to the ether. I knew the US was at war with Iran—because of me—but I didn't know anything else. The basic comfort of knowing the general state of the world that could be accessed online on a whim had vanished.

Suddenly a motorcade of four or five large, striking black SUVs with huge tires and shiny rims appeared on the street—their engines emitting a steady roar—heading straight toward our house. One by one, each SUV stopped in front of our house and men—in suits, SWAT-team gear, and military fatigues—leapt out and beelined straight for our door.

"Honey . . . honey . . . you need to wake up," I said to Pam, pushing her on the shoulder.

"What?" she said in a groggy voice.

"I'm sorry, baby, you need to wake up now and get dressed."

"Why?"

"Now."

Suddenly there was a loud smashing sound downstairs. I could hear our wooden front door crack and burst and fall to the floor in splintered chunks.

"FBI! Michael and Pamela Housen, are you here?!" a man screamed in a deep Indiana twang. "Michael and Pamela Housen, are you here? Come out with your hands up!"

Pam's eyes widened and her face went pale. She grabbed my hand and squeezed. A tear ran down the left side of her face. I threw on a pair of blue jeans and a green-and-yellow A's T-shirt and walked out of our bedroom and stood at the top of the stairs and saw the men spreading across the downstairs of our home with guns ready to cut us to pieces if we did anything other than obey.

"On the ground now!" a large man wearing sunglasses and a bullet-proof vest screamed, looking up at me. He pointed his gun right at me.

"Good morning, Michael," said a cool female voice, as I stood there in shock. I looked down and saw Agent Weiss, her blonde hair still damp from her morning shower, smiling up at me.

"Get down on the floor!" the man screamed at me again.

I looked to my left and saw Pam, standing just inside our bedroom, dressed in a T-shirt and shorts, holding her phone. Terrified. They couldn't see her yet.

"Get down on the floor!" the guy yelled again. So I did.

Two men in full SWAT-team gear climbed up the stairs, guns blazing, screaming like they were part of some demented choir. "Get your hands behind your back! Now!" So I put my hands behind my back.

They marched up the stairs toward me. Upon seeing Pam, they yelled the same thing. "On the floor! Now! Hands behind your back!"

They put us both in handcuffs and walked us downstairs.

"You must be Pam," Agent Weiss said, smiling and peering closer to my wife's face.

Pam looked at Agent Weiss and said, "And you must be . . ."—she looked around at all the guns pointing at us—"the people who keep us all safe."

I had a feeling that Pam's retort would be dealt with later.

They marched us outside and put us into separate cars. I kept trying to see Pam's face in the violent commotion but caught only one fleeting glance at her turquoise eyes welling with tears and fear. The man holding her cuffed hands behind her wore a military uniform and was five times her size. I wanted to wrap my arms around her and never let go, and that thought sent a shudder through me. Would I ever hold her again?

Several of our neighbors were outside watching the whole thing. I saw Grant Woollard meet my gaze. And the way he looked at me now, a satisfied little smile turning up the edges of his gray mustache, as if to say justice has been done.

The SUVs then left as abruptly as they had come. I rode the same highway I had been driving the Prius on about twelve hours before. Pam's car was right behind me. We were vehicles two and three in the five-car motorcade. Agent Weiss was in my car, riding shotgun. She turned to look at me and I could see her Davis pin—glittering in the morning sunlight—latched to her bulletproof vest. And she gave me that smile, telling me: "Your entire life is in my hands, and I am squeezing them shut."

A young man, maybe thirty, in army fatigues and Oakley sunglasses and who had obscenely large triceps was driving. His buzz cut was almost as blonde as Weiss's hair. No one spoke. I didn't know where we were going.

Sitting in the back seat of the SUV I thought about the last twenty-four hours. For the first time since Steve told me about the hack in his office the day before, I had some clarity of thought. The blizzard of stress, fear, and confusion finally started to subside. And as I sat in the back of the quiet car speeding down the familiar highway, something rose to the surface of my mind: I had no memory of clicking on that link. None at all. I usually don't do things like that. I'm nervous, cautious, afraid of hackers. I didn't remember taking any survey. I probably wouldn't have done that either—a waste of time. I did, apparently. In the haste of a busy day at work, apparently, I did in fact click that link. But it felt odd that I had no memory whatsoever of doing it.

The sun was mostly above the horizon. Familiar Indiana flatlands spread out to my right and a concert of oncoming headlights whizzed by to my left. The sky was a cloudless blue. We were driving north.

CHAPTER 14

TUESDAY, JUNE 21, LATER.

After about half an hour heading north on I-69 my wrists were hurting from the handcuffs. I was shaken by all the cars on the road this early, many of them fully loaded with families and luggage, heading north as well. It did not look like they were getting a jump on the summer holidays. It looked like they were getting the hell out.

We passed three buses with "Public Protection Center #17" plastered on them. It was one of Davis's most wretched prisons, located in Indianapolis. I had read about it when he opened it as "a special detention center for the incorrigible" and the piece made it sound like some medieval dungeon. Was I going there? What about Pam? Would we be kept together or separated? My stomach churned in anger and fear as I contemplated the likely answer.

I kept turning back to see the SUV that Pam was riding in, to make sure she was still near me. It was there, following a little too close.

I took a breath and thought about where they would take me. We were probably heading to Indianapolis, I thought, and we'd wind up at the FBI HQ in downtown Indy. But instead we veered off I-69 into the Morgan-Monroe State Forest. I turned again to see Pam's SUV, but it did not follow us. It kept going straight on the highway. My harrowing nightmare exploded into a blizzard of emotion.

"Where is Pam?!" I screamed. "Where is she going? Why isn't her car coming with us?"

No one answered.

Weiss smirked.

I wanted to smash the thick glass separating me from Weiss and her driver, but the cuffs keeping my hands behind my back wouldn't budge. I could feel the blood emerging on my wrists and dribbling into my fingers as I tried to yank my hands free.

Soon the sunlight of the flatlands turned into the cool shade of the big trees. Why were they taking me into the forest? To shoot me? After everything that had happened, I knew that anything could happen next.

Shortly thereafter we drove out of the trees and into a clearing. We rolled up in front of a windowless building that looked like a big boxy warehouse. It seemed to have just one way in—through a checkpoint outside a tall steel gate, topped by barbed wire. Then I saw something that gave me chills: Armor security cameras, with their red lightning bolt and black shield domes, looking down at me from the top of several tall wooden poles.

The scene was surreal. But all I could think about was Pam. She was all I had in life—everything—and I didn't know if I'd ever see her again. As long as Davis and his thugs like Agent Weiss thought Pam and I had colluded with Iranian cybercriminals to hack into Armor, then I probably wouldn't see her again.

Agent Weiss showed the guard at the checkpoint—maybe nineteen years old, wearing camouflage and heavy body armor—a sheet of paper. He took it and held it like it was some kind of hieroglyphic. Then he handed it back and saluted Weiss, and the gate slowly opened. We drove in. As we passed the checkpoint, I could see another guard inside, in front of a laptop, jiggling a joystick. What could that be for, I thought. That's when I noticed a big machine gun on top of the checkpoint, its barrel following us in.

I could soon see that behind this first building there was another big box without windows, and the SUV rolled up in front of it. There were bars on the entrance and blast blocks flanking the doorway. This didn't look like a Public Protection Center. This looked like one of those secret places that governments—or the Davis government—have when they want to do things in the dark. There were no signs, no American flags, nothing outside to identify this place.

The driver of our SUV opened the door and commanded me to get out. I slid across the seat and swung my legs out the door, then tried to stand. With my hands cuffed behind my back, I was off balance and fell forward, landing on the asphalt parking lot face-first. My head hurt and blood trickled out of my nose, and Agent Weiss was angry.

"Hey soldier, you want to get better at that. We don't want to leave any marks on the merchandise."

"Yes, ma'am," he said, then he hauled me to my feet. I couldn't see his eyes through his Oakley sunglasses, but the snarl on his face looked as if he wanted to punch me for making him look bad.

I looked around desperately, to see if Pam's SUV might have shown up, but it was not in sight. And then the soldier grabbed my arm and shoved me forward and through the entrance door, with Agent Weiss behind me.

"Where is Pam?!" I screamed. "What are you doing with her?!" Again they ignored me.

Inside was a reception area with thick bulletproof glass above a steel counter. The glass had a voice plate, those perforated circles that allow the person behind the glass to speak to those on the other side. Behind the glass was another young soldier in camouflage, again with no insignia patch.

"We processing him, ma'am?" he said, his voice sounding robotic.

"Not yet," Agent Weiss said.

He nodded and pressed a button and a heavy door to our left clunked with the sounds of a lock being shifted.

What does that mean, "Not yet?" I thought.

The soldier pushed me toward the door, and holding me with one hand, opened it with his other. The one thing that was clear to me was that I had to get out of this place. Somehow. I had to find Pam. My stomach hurt at the thought of Pam going through all this because of me.

Agent Weiss and the soldier marched me down a cold gray hallway, its nauseating fluorescent ceiling lights protected by steel grates. All I could hear was the chilling pitter-patter of our footsteps echoing off the walls. The place was silent, as if no one else was there.

Then the soldier opened a door to a room at the end of the hallway. Inside it was a table and two chairs and Armor security cameras planted diagonally—one on the left of the rear wall, and one on the right of the front wall. The gray walls were padded with soundproofing and ringed with blue LED lights.

The only other light in the room came from the blue glow of a laptop screen on a small desk.

The soldier pushed me down in one of the chairs, and Agent Weiss sat opposite me, at the desk, the glow of the laptop shining up on her face like she was a sculpture in a museum. The soldier retreated to stand guard against the wall behind me.

Agent Weiss tapped something into the laptop, then looked up at me.

"Why did you lie to me yesterday at Armor's office?" she said calmly.

"What?" I hadn't slept in more than twenty-four hours, eighteen of which had been beyond harrowing. My tank was empty. "What are you talking about?"

"Why did you lie?" she said louder, her voice rippling throughout this secret blue room in the woods.

"I didn't."

"You said Pam's family had no connections to Iranian government."

"Where is Pam?"

"You don't get to ask the questions."

That sent a hot flare of anger through my brain. "Then you won't get any answers. Not until you tell me where Pam is."

Agent Weiss looked at me with curiosity, as if I was an experiment that she was conducting. As if I needed a tweak, this way or that way, to come out the way she wanted.

"She's in our custody," Agent Weiss said.

"Where?" I asked, my voice hot to her cold.

"Somewhere for her own protection. You don't want anything to happen to her now, do you?"

That sounded very much like a threat to me. I realized it was useless, from where I was sitting, to try to help Pam. Weiss enjoyed tormenting me. So I decided to try another tack and see how far we had slid into fascism.

"I want to speak to my lawyer."

Agent Weiss smiled. "Those rules don't apply now. Why did you lie to me about Pam's family in Iran?"

"I want to speak to my lawyer."

"You don't seem to understand. You are in my jurisdiction. The nation is at war and those comforting rights you see defendants get on television do not apply right now. I ask the questions. If you give me answers, then we can see about that lawyer."

"I won't give you any answers without my lawyer present. It's the law. You have to do it."

I had barely finished saying that when I was hit hard on my back between my shoulder blades with a thick rubber club. The pain shot through my body, and I gasped. Agent Weiss didn't blink. "I am the law. And you have to do what I say. So . . ." She looked at the laptop again. "Why did you lie to me and tell me that Pam has no family in the Iranian government?"

"I didn't lie. Her uncle works for a local municipality in Shiraz; he doesn't have connections to the people running the country."

"So the answer is yes—not no!"

"What? He's a low-level bureaucrat in a small town. That's like saying the deputy press secretary to the mayor of Bloomington is connected to President Davis and somehow played a role in yesterday's air strikes. There's no connection."

Agent Weiss looked back at her laptop and shook her head. "That's not what our information tells us."

A buzzer sounded, and Weiss looked up at the camera on the rear wall and nodded once. Then the door unlocked and in came a tall man, about sixty, with a silver-gray buzz cut and deep, haggard bags under his eyes. He was thin, all bone, and wore a black suit, white shirt, and no tie. He looked tired. He didn't say anything. He just nodded to Agent Weiss and gave her a crooked smile. He walked to the back of the room and sat in a chair. But I could see that Weiss's demeanor had changed. She had a sparkle of ambition in her eye, like she was performing before someone who could elevate her to a level where she believed she should be.

"What does your information tell you?" I asked.

Agent Weiss smiled at me. She ignored my question. "Why did you click the link, Michael? Why would you waste your time on some stupid survey?"

"I don't even remember clicking that damn link or filling out an online survey," I said, agitation in my voice. "I get hundreds of emails a week. What do you want me to say? Do you want me to lie and say Pam's family is entrenched with the ruling mullahs in Iran? Do you want me to lie and say I remember that stupid email? That I clicked on that link on purpose?" I felt blood dripping down my back and settling into a little pool where my butt met the chair.

Weiss looked at the man at the back of the room, then back at me. "You need to start telling the truth, Michael," she said in a voice of puritanical reason. "I am responsible for the safety of the American people and you and your wife pose a clear and present danger to this country. This will only get worse if you keep lying."

Worse? How could this get worse? I was sitting in an interrogation room in a secret prison after having started a war between the US and Iran by clicking a phishing link. I didn't know where my wife was. Worse?

Agent Weiss tapped something into her laptop. "May I have some water, please?" I said.

Weiss just stared at me. Then the door buzzed, and a guard brought in a plastic bottle of water. He put it down on the table in front of me, so I could see it but couldn't drink it with my hands cuffed. Then he left.

"So, here's how this works, Michael. You tell me the truth, and I will open that bottle of water for you."

I looked at the bottle of water and blinked hard. The bottle had already been opened. The plastic seal around the top was missing.

"I want to see my lawyer," I said.

Agent Weiss sighed and shook her head. "There are too many coincidences here, Mr. Housen. Far too many. You can either start to cooperate and maybe—just maybe—get some leniency. Or you can keep lying. We'll get the truth either way."

She glanced toward the quiet older guy again, and then turned back and smiled at me.

Then she opened the bottle of water and put it to my lips. I squeezed them shut.

"Open up, Michael. You said you wanted water."

"I'm not thirsty anymore," I said.

"I want to see my lawyer," I said again.

Weiss just smiled.

CHAPTER 15

TUESDAY, JUNE 21, LATER.

There was no processing of me at this secret prison. No grim mug shot against a white height board with black stripes, no filling out of forms or handing over shoelaces. The guards just took everything and, leaving me naked in a cell about the size of a walk-in closet, pointed to the bundle on the bed. "Put it on."

I unrolled the bundle and saw that it was a blue jumpsuit and blue slippers. I put them on.

The guards, satisfied that I had followed their orders, turned and left, slamming the heavy metal door shut. The room was windowless but had those damn grated fluorescent lights on the ceiling, so I was awash in sickly yellow light. There was a sink, and I turned on the water to get a drink. The water was brown and thick. I didn't drink it.

I laid down on the steel cot that passed for a bed. There was a rough wool blanket covering the board they had apparently used as a mattress, and that was it. No pillow.

It didn't matter. All I could think of was Pam. I started to drift to sleep, the exhaustion of over twenty-four hours awake taking hold. Was she in a cell somewhere? I could see her face in my mind's eye, smiling at me, telling me everything would be okay. Could she see mine? What was I telling her?

I was telling her that it was my fault, that I deliberately clicked on that link to allow the hackers in because I hated the Davis government so much that I would do anything to destroy it. If thousands of people had to die to save democracy, to save us, then so be it.

Pam started to sob. We were in a courtroom and the foreman of the jury entered and hollered, "Guilty! Guilty! Guilty!"

A wave of applause rose up in the courtroom and then got louder and turned into screaming. Then a symphony orchestra played "The Star-Spangled Banner"—with a lot of cymbal action—as I was wheeled past the Lincoln Memorial reflecting pool in a cage. Thousands of people were frothing at their mouths as I went by, screaming obscenities at me, throwing things at me. Caleb was there, and so was Steve, both of them hollering that I deserved to die.

Someone threw an egg, which made it through the bars of the cage and smashed into my nose and burst on my face. Blood from my nose and egg yolk ran down my face and onto my blue jumpsuit. At the foot of the Lincoln Memorial stood a construction crane, festooned with stars-and-stripes bunting.

Guards in black body armor and masked black helmets marched me from the cage to the crane, and they looped the metal noose around my neck and cinched it tight. Just like the mullahs do to enemies of the state in Iran.

One of the black-helmeted guards held Pam's head and made her watch. Agent Weiss raised her hand, then lowered it, like a chop, and the crane's gears groaned to life, as I headed toward death. I started to rise up into the bright and clear Washington morning, the noose cutting into my windpipe, and my life flowing out of me. Pam shrieked my name . . .

"Mikey!"

"Mikey!"

Then I sat up sweating, having been woken by the sound of Pam's voice. But we were not in our bed, enjoying an uncomplicated world. I was still alone in this cold, ghoulishly lit cell in this secret Davis prison with Armor cameras everywhere. I was hungry and thirsty and afraid. I knew that no help was coming. Not until Special Agent Weiss decided that the law was not her law, but our law. The people's law.

I closed my eyes and tried not to think of Pam or of what she was enduring because of me. And of course, Pam was all I could think about. After about thirty more minutes of lying on that rock-hard steel cot, exhaustion set in again. For the first time since my father was injured in his accident eight years ago, I cried myself to sleep.

CHAPTER 16

WEDNESDAY, JUNE 22.

I woke up an hour or so later with a shudder. As if I had been shocked. For a second, I didn't know where I was. Then it all came rushing back like some tidal wave of terror.

The door to my cell clanked open and a guard stepped in. He was white and blonde, with the sharp blue eyes of a killer, no older than twenty-one or so, like some kind of Davis Youth brigadier in his camo. He was carrying a blue plastic box, about the size of a book.

"Stand up!" he shouted at me.

I stood up.

He got louder: "Face the wall, hands above your head, legs spread."

I did as he commanded. What was he going to do? Search me for weapons that I had acquired in a nightmare?

I heard the box land on the floor.

Then I heard him step away and out the cell door. It clanked shut.

I waited to see if this was some sort of trick and he hadn't really left and would beat me to oblivion for disobeying an order. But I could only hear my own quick breathing and nothing else, so I turned around.

The cell was empty, except for me and the box.

I stepped over to it and then knelt next to it, leaning down to see what it was. It had a latch on the front and hinges on the back, so it was some kind of container. I carefully released the latch and gently lifted it.

Inside was a bottle of water, a small carton of orange juice, and some sort of bar that looked like melba toast covered with thick brown goo.

This was my breakfast, apparently.

I ripped off the sealed cap on the water and drank it in two gulps. Then I yanked back the pull tab on the carton and drank the orange juice. I left the bar alone. If I was going to send any messages, this was my only way to do it. I will drink but not eat. Not until you let me see a lawyer. Not until you let me see my wife.

CHAPTER 17

THURSDAY, JUNE 23.

I was awake when the guard arrived the next morning with the blue plastic box. I had not eaten the liquid in the plastic bowl labeled "Soup" when he dropped it on the floor last night. I was curious to see how they would respond to my refusal to eat. I was starving and lightheaded. I knew that I couldn't sustain this for much longer, yet I had no sense of how much longer I would be here.

We went through the ritual of me with my face against the wall and hands raised while he put the box on the floor. After he had made his noisy and angry exit, with the cell door slammed shut, I walked over to the box. I opened the latch.

This time it was empty.

CHAPTER 18

FRIDAY, JUNE 24.

I had lost all track of time, so I didn't know if it was day or night when I woke up the next day. All I knew was that my stomach hurt and my head hurt and two guards were now in my cell: my food delivery guy, without the plastic box, along with another young guard with the same kind of muscular build and mean stare. He was holding ankle chains the way you'd hold out a jacket for someone to put on. They chained my ankles together. Then they cuffed my hands in front of me.

Then, without speaking to each other or to me, they marched me down the hall and through a set of steel doors. We entered another gray steel corridor and walked halfway down it. Then we stopped in front of a door that I guessed wasn't a cell door, because it was open.

The guards shoved me inside. Sitting at a table and looking at me as if I was somehow more complicated than she expected was Special Agent Weiss.

"Do you want us to stay, ma'am?' one of the guards asked.

Weiss shook her head, never taking her eyes off me. "I'll let you know when we're done."

The two guards turned and left the room, and my food-delivery guy took much more care in how he shut this door. Almost as if he was being polite.

Weiss motioned for me to sit in the chair opposite her. I slid into the chair and swung my shackled legs in front of me. The chains clanked on the cold cement floor. My hands were cuffed in front of me and—looking her directly in the eyes—I thumped them down on the table between us.

Weiss nodded. "I know. It must be uncomfortable." She paused. I said nothing.

"Why aren't you eating?" She had a touch of concern in her voice.

"I'm not eating until you let me out of here," I said.

"I see. You could die."

I smiled weakly. "Well, I have heard that no one gets out of this life thing alive, so I have accepted that eventuality. I just think that if I died while in your custody, you would have some explaining to do."

It was the most I had spoken in three days.

"I don't want you to die, Mr. Housen," Agent Weiss said, in her soft voice, this time edged not with understated power but with what perhaps was hope that maybe we could find a way out of this.

I was surprised at her new tone. "Let me see a lawyer. Please."

Special Agent Weiss leaned back in her chair and looked up at the ceiling. I said nothing, just waited for her to come back to me, but she stayed like that for a long time. Maybe a full minute.

"I need you to eat something," Special Agent Weiss said, her voice still soft.

"If I eat, will you let me speak to a lawyer?"

Weiss smiled. "Do you really think a lawyer can help you?"

She was telling me that I was beyond the law. Or there was no law anymore. So with my head throbbing and my eyes straining, I said, "Yes I do."

Weiss smiled at me again, though this time she seemed pleased with my answer. Maybe I was delirious, but she looked like she was going to agree. And then she said, "You eat."

I shook my head. "I won't eat until you let me see a lawyer."

"You're guilty, Mr. Housen. You clicked that link on purpose. You and your wife worked with Iranian hackers to attack the United States. And now we're at war. You don't get to make demands."

"I don't recall having a trial," I said. I felt like I was going to fall off my chair. But my words got a reaction out of her.

"No, we need you to be alive until your trial."

"Have I been charged?"

She looked at me with those sharp green eyes. "I'll make sure the chef whips up something good tonight," she said, then she rose and called for the guards.

"Take him back to his cell. And bring him a special meal."

CHAPTER 19

FRIDAY, JUNE 24, LATER.

I stared at the blue plastic box in front of me on the floor of my cell. Weiss had called for a special meal, but I couldn't smell anything special coming out of this thing. It was tall and thin, the size of container you might put a water bottle inside and not, say, steak and lobster.

I opened the box and saw a blue plastic thermos. I picked it up and felt the weight of the liquid inside. Heavier than water. Maybe it was a vat of truth serum.

I opened the bottle and looked down on what seemed to be a strawberry smoothie. It was pink and had a thin froth at the top. I poked a finger in and smelled the liquid on my finger. It smelled sweet and fruity, so if it was laced with drugs they had disguised them well.

I had not eaten in a long time. I felt like I had just enough strength to lift the thermos and hold it to my lips, but I didn't know what would happen next. On the other hand, I knew what would happen if I didn't drink the liquid inside the thermos. I would grow weaker, and Weiss could use that to her advantage. It was better to take the risk now. Besides, the liquid smelled so sweet that I was licking my dry, parched lips.

So I lifted the thermos and drank. A little sip at first. It was as if I could feel the glucose hit my stomach. I immediately felt more alert. I sipped the rest of the contents of the thermos. Slowly, so as not to shock my system, but happily. The more I drank, the more at peace I felt. I felt laughter rise in my chest. I saw Pam's face, smiling at me. Then she was laughing, too. She was walking toward me, her arms extended. I reached out to her and took her in my arms. We were free. We were happy. We were home.

Then everything went black.

CHAPTER 20

SATURDAY, JUNE 25.

I felt Pam shake me awake and tell me it was time.

Time to get up.

Time to tell the truth.

Time to get the hell out of here.

I opened my eyes and saw that the person who was shaking me awake wasn't Pam. It was a guard I hadn't seen before—male, again not much beyond a teenager—looking down on me.

"You have a visitor," he said.

My groggy brain started to revive. A visitor? My first thought was that maybe Weiss had brought Pam to see me.

"Okay," I said. I swung my legs over the side of the bed, and the other guard put on the ankle shackles.

"You need a shower, dude," the first guard said as he caught a whiff of me. That was true. I had been in here for a long time with no access to water beyond the brown stuff in my sink. I simply replied, "I would like a shower."

The guard said nothing as he hauled me to my feet and cuffed my hands in front of me. Then, without speaking to each other or to me, the guards marched me from my cell and down the hall in the opposite direction we had gone when I visited Agent Weiss. We went through a set of steel doors, just like I had done with Weiss, but suddenly the fluorescent lighting and steel gave way to a warm wood-paneled corridor lit by tall brass standing lamps. It was like we'd walked out of a secret prison and into an airport VIP lounge.

The guards opened a frosted glass door and pushed me into a room that looked like a boardroom. Sitting in a leather chair was a Black woman, about my age, wearing a purple Chanel suit and purple pumps. Pretty, with young eyes, short hair, an intelligent smile, she displayed a strong upright posture. She exuded something I had little of at this point—confidence.

She looked at me, and looked at the guards, and shook her head. "It's going to cost you even more now," she said to them, shaking her head. Her voice was a strong alto, and her accent had a familiar Indiana twang to it. "Take those chains off him before I add three more zeroes to the lawsuit." She didn't punctuate it with "motherfuckers," but that was her tone.

The guards looked at each other as if this was some kind of trick, so she said, "Where's he going to go?"

They considered that, then the one who woke me up—blonde, lean, with angry brown eyes—unlocked my chains.

"Thank you," she said. "I'll press the little button when I need you."

They stared at her, unblinking, and she stared back. Then they turned, crisply, and left.

She turned to me and smiled, a warm smile. "Michael Housen?" she asked.

"Yes," I replied.

My scent and appearance didn't seem to trouble her as she offered her hand. "Nicole Wilkerson," she said with a smile. Her teeth were bright white and straight as arrows.

"Are you FBI?" I asked.

She laughed. "I am not," she said. "I am your lawyer. And I'm going to get you the fuck out of here."

CHAPTER 21

SATURDAY, JUNE 25, LATER.

"How did . . . ?" I started to ask Nicole Wilkerson, but she put a finger to her lips with her right hand and cupped her left hand around her left ear. Then swept her arm around the room. I got the message: The walls have ears.

There were no Armor security cameras that we could see, but Nicole pulled out a chair at a table, and I sat down next to her. Then she produced a yellow legal pad and two black ballpoints and smiled at me. She leaned into me and wrote: "We need to stick close together so they can't look over our shoulders." She wrote in block letters.

I nodded. Then I wrote in block letters: "How did you find me?"

"Zahra."

I looked surprised. "How did Zahra know I was here?"

"Pam texted her just before you were arrested. I made some calls."

I smiled. My brilliant wife had the presence of mind to send a flare as the goons were upon us.

"Where is Pam?" I wrote.

"We don't know. We are still trying to locate her."

My heart sank. "Can you get me out so I can help find her?"

"Yes." She smiled at me. "But a question first: Did you work with Iran to hack into Armor and the US government?"

My expression gave her the answer, but to make certain, I wrote: "No. I clicked on a phishing link by accident. Like everybody else on the planet has done. That's all!"

She nodded.

"Okay. They don't have enough to hold you in here for two minutes, let alone days. And you've already been in here for five."

"I thought the law didn't matter since we're at war, that civil liberties have been suspended?"

She shook her head and slowly wrote back to me. "Davis has suspended habeas corpus and is trying to eliminate all protections for people with ties to Iran, like you. Some judges are going along with it. Some aren't. You got lucky—your judge granted the emergency motion to have you released. And for reasons we don't fully understand yet, the government agreed to follow the order. Some prisoners haven't been so lucky."

"Okay," I said out loud, confused but thankful. She put her finger to her lips again.

"The government is not done with you though," she wrote. "They are going to try and get sufficient evidence showing you colluded with Iran in cyberspace to lock you up permanently. They just don't have it yet."

I grimaced and shook my head. "What do I do?"

"You're going to disappear for a while. Do you have somewhere to go away from Bloomington?"

I nodded. "Yes."

"Good. They should have the paperwork done any minute. Anything else?" she wrote.

"I want my life back."

She nodded and gave me a thumbs-up. Then she ripped out the three sheets of legal pad we had filled with our "conversation." She reached into her briefcase and produced a silver Mylar bag, the kind that X-rays can't see through. She unzipped it and pulled out a gold Zippo lighter. Then she took the three pages over to the potted palm in the corner of the room, arranged them around the base of the palm's trunk, and set them on fire.

I looked around for a smoke alarm, but there wasn't one. When the papers were burned to ash, she used the lighter to mix them with the soil at the base of the palm.

Then she returned to the table and sat next to me, calm as could be, as if setting fire to documents in a secret prison was a daily occurrence.

She held up two fingers with her left hand and started to beat time in the air with her right. She was telling me we had two minutes before she pressed the button.

And after she pressed it, the guards took another two minutes to arrive. One of them held a black garbage bag. Was he going to scoop up the ash and send it to one of Davis's high-tech labs to extract what they could from the ashes of our conversation? Agent Weiss followed them in. She sniffed the air and glanced at the potted palm.

"Don't think," she said, looking at me, her voice cool and soft, "that just because you're leaving, we won't see each other again."

I looked into her green eyes and smiled. "I look forward to that," I said.

"Ha," she said. "You can change into your clothes in the bathroom across the hall."

I was about to say I'd need my clothes first, but one of the guards held up the black garbage bag, and I realized that they were inside it. I took the bag and went across the hall to change. When I came back, Nicole and I started walking, the two guards in front of us. No one spoke. They opened a steel door, and instead of being back in gray steel land, we were outside in a parking lot that looked like one for a suburban law office. The sun had never been brighter and the glare stung my eyes. The fresh air felt wonderful. When I turned to look at the prison that had just held me, the sign above the glass door said: "The Law."

Nicole Wilkerson saw the sign and smiled. Then she put her finger to her lips again and whispered to me. "We need to get you out of those clothes. Just normal conversation, okay?"

Had Agent Weiss and her team put microchip listeners in my clothes? I instinctively felt my forehead, just in case they planted something inside my head, and Nicole Wilkerson laughed. "They're not that smart," she said, extra loud, so anyone could hear.

Then we got into her SUV and drove away. We headed south. Back to Bloomington. After a few minutes Nicole handed me my phone.

"Fully charged," she said. "The judge ordered the feds to give it back. The battery was empty but I charged it this morning."

"Thank you," I said.

I opened my texts first, looking for something from Pam. There was nothing. Same with missed calls: nothing from Pam. It's what I expected but my heart still sank.

Then I looked at my texts. Cliff had texted a few times:

"You okay Housey?"

. . .

"I heard Davis call out your company, without saying its name. You okay?"

. . .

"Dude, can you answer? You okay?"

Steve had also texted me:

"Sorry about that meeting yesterday with the FBI. Not fair to you."

. . .

"Checking in Mike. All okay?"

. . .

"Checking in again, you doing okay? Caleb said all work can be remote till things calm down, so no need to come in. We can learn from all this and be better because of it. Please call when you can."

And the GNC reporter Janine Wood also texted a few times:

"Sorry we got cut off yesterday, Michael. Would still love to talk whenever you can. Please call this number. Thank you. Janine Wood."

. . .

"Hi Michael, any chance we can connect? Would love to hear more about what happened with the phishing email?"

Then I checked my Armor email.

Caleb wrote an email to the whole company the day after the hack went public and Davis started bombing Iran:

"My fellow Armorites," it began, "like all great companies, Armor has been dealt some adversity with this cyber incident. And like all great companies, we will overcome this moment and we will succeed. Please continue to do what you always do and stay focused on your day-to-day jobs. I will handle the hard challenges we face. The key right now, for each of you, is for everything to be business as usual."

I scanned the rest of my email to see if there was anything that might in any way help me find Pam. There wasn't. I exhaled and set my phone down and looked outside the window as Nicole drove down the long freeway toward Bloomington.

CHAPTER 22

SATURDAY, JUNE 25, LATER.

As we pulled up to our white stucco house, with the lilac hydrangeas blooming with life, I felt tears well in my eyes. The door was unlocked as Nicole and I opened it, and Cecil ran up to greet me before I even entered, jumping up and down and wagging his tail as if I had been away in a secret prison for nearly a week.

"He must be starving," I said.

"Nope, he just had his second breakfast." The voice startled me. It came from Grant Woollard, the retired Indiana state trooper who lived across the street and who Pam and I thought hated us. He had silently appeared in our front yard, a few feet to my left. "I hope you don't mind," he said. "I thought this guy needed his grub until you got home. Glad you made it back."

He extended his hand, and I shook it. His hands were large and puffy, and his grip was firm. His thick goatee wrapped around a kind smile.

I was astonished. "Thank you, Grant," I said.

"You'd do the same for me," he replied.

"I'm Nicole Wilkerson, Michael's lawyer," Nicole said.

He extended his hand to her. "Grant Woollard. I used to patrol the highways for the state police."

Nicole smiled. "Did you notice anything unusual while Michael was away?"

He shook his head. "Nope. Just a hungry dog. But he's fine now."

"Thank you, Grant. How much do I owe you?"

"Nothing at all. You had a good supply of food for the guy in the garage." Grant reached down and gave Cecil a pat on the head. The dog flicked out its tongue and licked his hand.

"Your wife okay?" he asked.

"Uh, well . . ." I began, but Nicole stepped in.

"His wife will be fine," she said.

He nodded. "Tell her to take good care," he said, with an earnest smile. "Bad things are happening to her people."

"I will," I said.

"I'll be pushing off," Grant said. "Let me know if you need anything else."

He slowly walked across the street to his house.

"What did he mean by bad things are happening to her people?" I asked Nicole as we walked inside.

She smiled. "You go get cleaned up and change those clothes." She winked. Ah, yes: the possibly bugged clothing. I nodded.

I went upstairs and showered. Then I put on new clothes and came downstairs with the clothes I was arrested in, again in a garbage bag. The living room blinds were drawn even though it was the middle of the afternoon. Nicole was sitting on the couch, with the TV on loud. Next to her was Zahra.

Nicole put a finger to her lips, telling me to be quiet, and then took the bag of clothes from my hands and walked outside to put the bag in the trash.

Then Zahra rose and after several swift steps reached out and held me in her arms. She is in her late sixties and as beautiful and regal as an empress, her thick black hair sprinkled with gray. Her sparkling black eyes were moist with tears. Short and petite, she hugged me tight, the top of her head just below my chin, and I wrapped my arms around her thin body.

"Zahra," I said. "Thank you, for getting Nicole involved. She got me out of prison. Thank you, thank you."

She stepped back and looked at me as if I was her own son. Her eyes were intense, nervous. "Michael, I would do anything for you and Pam."

"I know you would. I know."

"I can't believe she got arrested too," she said, looking terrified.

Cecil jumped up and put two paws on her stomach. Staring at me, she looked as if she didn't notice.

Nicole came back inside. "I just spoke to the lawyer who's representing Pam. The government confirmed she's in a prison but wouldn't say which one. We will find her. But right now, we need to get you both out of here. Michael says he has a safe place you can go."

My mind was racing. Pam was in prison? Which one? How bad was it?

"How will we find her?" I asked.

"Don't know yet. But we will."

I sighed hard and rubbed my eyes with my hands.

"Davis is rounding up Iranian Americans and putting them in his prisons." Nicole said. "It's like the internment camps for Japanese Americans during World War II."

That's what Grant must've meant when he said bad things were happening to her people. "He's locking up Iranian Americans?" I replied, as if I had misheard.

Zahra nodded. "Anyone who has come from Iran and naturalized, as well as any Iranian on a green card or tourist visa."

I looked at Nicole. "How can that be legal?"

She shook her head. "The Supreme Court heard an emergency case on the program yesterday and ruled that Davis had to shut it down. But he ignored them. He said in a Truth: 'Judges have gavels and presidents have guns: the program will remain.' And he's rounding up anyone whom he considers an 'enemy of the state.' While you were inside, shortly after the explosions in LA and Chicago, he declared martial law."

She angled her head toward the TV, and I could see a protest in New York City in Union Square. The GNC report said maybe three thousand people had jammed into the Square to protest Davis's destruction of democracy, and then we saw his response. The army had corralled the protesters and squeezed them all in together bone-crushingly tight. The cameras showed people in terror, unable to breathe, and then being tear-gassed. Of course, the impulse is to flee tear gas, but if there's no room to run, then you panic even more. That's what happened and as the crawl across the bottom of the screen explained, 150 people had been trampled to death.

"I came here from LA as soon as Pam texted me," Zahra said. "And thank goodness Nicole said yes to helping you."

Zahra explained that Nicole worked on human rights as a lawyer and that she had done legal work on three of her films, helping her get sensitive clearances from difficult places including the US government and state news agencies in Russia and Iran.

Nicole shook her head and looked right at me. "The government is going to be watching you. They're looking for more evidence that you and Pam were working with Iran and that you clicked the link on purpose to let the hackers in. They think you did it, so they might even manufacture evidence if they have to. They need to gather enough evidence to show the judge they can keep you locked up. They could be listening in somehow right now. That's why the television is so loud."

"So what am I going to do?"

"You're going to take Zahra and go hide for a bit. Disappear. Or at least try to. Don't do anything to give them any more evidence against you. And keep Zahra safe. Until I can find Pam."

"Then what?"

"Then we need to get her out."

"How do we do that? How do simple people like us—nobodies—get the US government to let Pam out, to do what we want, in the middle of a war, when they think we're in cahoots with the enemy?"

"By forcing their hand and making them let her out. Kindness will get us nowhere. We need coercion."

"Do we know what that might look like?" I asked.

Nicole smiled. "Not yet. But we will. But first we need to find her."

Despite Nicole's confidence, I was distressed. What would it take to make this government see anything like reason? Zahra was watching me process this, and she squeezed my hand.

"Don't worry, Michael. We will find something. We will get Pam home."

Suddenly I understood. If I was ever to see my wife again and sit on the couch with her, drinking a beer, watching baseball, and talking about the world, I was going to have to find something myself. I couldn't rely on Nicole or anyone else. I was going to have to find something that would bring the most powerful organization in human history—the United States government—to its knees.

But how on earth could someone like me find something like that?

CHAPTER 23

SUNDAY, JUNE 26.

Nicole loaned us her SUV and took my Prius. "That way if they're looking for you, they're going to find me, and we win round one."

"Round two," I said. "Getting me out was winning round one."

"Be careful of the checkpoints," Nicole added. "They don't show up on the GPS."

The checkpoints were part of martial law. The army, National Guard, and renegade militias all had them, according to GNC. If you met one, Nicole said, you wanted it to be official and not some pack of freelance lunatics with guns looking for revenge.

We were heading a few hours northeast, to Hoosier Hill, the highest point in Indiana, where Pam had stayed in a cabin belonging to Indiana University during Reading Week. Made of thick, dark wood logs, the two-story cabin has high ceilings and spacious rooms filled with old, comfortable furniture. Framed paintings of the outdoors (mountains, forests, lakes) line the walls. The cabin is big. A dozen students could stay there at the same time. It sits on five tree-filled acres overlooking the modest but beautiful Beane Lake, where Pam and I would go kayaking. But ever since the university constructed another cabin on Lake Wawasee, this cabin had been abandoned, pretty much.

Pam had kept her key, and we had come up three times since she graduated, with no one else in sight. You needed your own lanterns and a supply of water, but the woodstove still worked, and all the bedding had been left by the university. It was almost as if whoever was responsible for it decided to just leave it to its fate.

And now, that fate was as shelter to me, Zahra, and Cecil. I had to bring the dog because I didn't trust what the feds would do to him if they found him home alone. The SUV was rugged, and Nicole said it would go just about anywhere we wanted to go. So if we needed to dodge a checkpoint, we could just use its all-wheel drive to search for back roads.

I didn't want to run into any checkpoints. I had done as much as I could to take myself off the grid, and so had Zahra. We had taken the batteries out of our phones and bought cheap burners at a Target south of Indianapolis, a couple of prepaid Samsungs for sixty dollars each. Nicole had given us $2,000 in cash, so I wouldn't have to access a bank, and the full tank in the SUV meant we'd only have to fill it up on the way back. Whenever that would be.

We didn't see any cars following us on the road, thankfully. We listened to the radio and the news was not good. The US air strikes on Iran had not gone as smoothly as the Davis brain trust expected. The Iranians had a sophisticated air-defense system, and after the first round of US jets had made it through, some in the next waves were getting shot down. As for Davis's missiles, they were about fifty percent successful. The collateral damage was enormous.

"President Davis is making us all suffer because of his own ignorance," Zahra said as we listened to the report. "Even I know how tough Iran's military is, and I have been away for nearly half a century. They won't roll over. Why can't he see this?"

"I don't think he cares," I replied. "The attack was the point. He'll just lie about the casualties and keep increasing the military force. As for America, only like twenty-eight percent of adults can accurately place Iran on a map."

Zahra gave me a wide-eyed look.

I nodded. "Pam told me that."

Zahra smiled. "Pam would know that," she said, nodding.

The radio host explained that NATO condemned Davis's campaign, and various European allies had publicly articulated the various international laws Davis had breached by attacking Iran with bombs and missiles in response to a computer hack. So far, the US military had killed an estimated twenty thousand Iranian civilians. At home, the army and police had killed more than one thousand Americans amidst the social unrest.

"The United States will make Iran pay for their crimes, for first hacking into Armor Security in Bloomington and for then hacking into our Treasury Department and wreaking havoc," President Davis said, his voice thick and inflected with his New Jersey boyhood, making him sound more like a mob boss than a president. "We are increasing our attacks, and we will win. The criminal Iranian regime's days are numbered."

I felt sick to my stomach. Hearing Davis say Armor Security sent waves of shock and nausea throughout my body. Zahra saw the look on my face.

"He didn't say it was you, Michael. At least be grateful for that."

I took a breath and kept my eyes on the road. "I don't get it, though," I said. "Caleb Wagner is one of his biggest supporters. Why would he do that to Caleb?"

Zahra sighed. "Who knows why Davis does anything?" She looked sad.

I gave her a grim smile. There was nothing I could say about any of this to make it better. I kept the SUV on the back roads as we drove toward Hoosier Hill. It took longer than normal, and I thought we'd avoid the checkpoints out on the interstates. I was right for a while. Then we came across a tank unit doing maneuvers in a field outside of Hagerstown. There were three M1 Abrams tanks in the field to our right, and a fourth, a Bradley fighting vehicle, crossing the road toward the others. There were two soldiers in the middle of the road. One held his hand up for us to stop.

"What are these guys doing here?" I muttered to Zahra.

"Target practice," she said, putting on a red Indiana University baseball cap (courtesy of Nicole) to hide her dark hair.

The two soldiers, in green-and-brown battle dress with AR-15s slung across their chests, stared at us through their field goggles as the Bradley humped its way across the road. The one with the two Vs on his sleeve approached us while the other stood guard, his rifle now off his chest and in his hands.

A week before, the most suspenseful part of my life typically involved a close A's game in the later innings. Now I was trying to keep Zahra from being detained by the military while the nation was under martial law for a war I started.

I could feel my heartbeat throbbing in my fingertip as I pressed the button and powered down the window.

The soldier couldn't have been more than twenty-five. He peered in with his light-blue eyes and saw me, Zahra, and Cecil. Then he said, "You and your mother live around here?" He had a southern accent. Maybe Texas.

I smiled. "Yes, sir. Just over there in Fountain City."

He nodded. I was smiling in a way that suggested I was glad the army was doing tank practice in a field and that I was happy to see him. Inside, my heart was pumping fast.

"Glad you guys are here," I said, giving him a head nod. I wanted to get on our way before he asked Zahra any questions and heard her Iranian accent.

He nodded again and looked around, as if for lurking danger. "Keep your eyes open. Lots of scum around here."

I wasn't exactly sure what he meant. Scum?

He saw the puzzlement on my face. "Floaters. Aliens."

I smiled. Right. Immigrants.

"They're trying to escape. Get to Canuckistan. They'll skin you alive and rob you blind. Make sure you got extra ammo."

"Thanks," I replied. "Will do."

Machine gun fire suddenly burst from the Bradley and tore through a wall in the barn. Zahra's body gyrated and she grabbed my right knee with her left hand.

"Shit," the soldier said. "They was supposed to wait until civvies were clear. You better git."

I powered up the window and we drove on.

Zahra looked at me, a soft teardrop dancing down each cheek, and shook her head. She took a deep breath and exhaled loudly. "When did America become Iran?"

CHAPTER 24

SUNDAY, JUNE 26, LATER.

The cabin was cool this midsummer evening. It had been five days since I had seen Pam. I thought of the last time I saw her, in handcuffs, her eyes filled with fear as the hulking solider threw her into the back of a car. Then I thought about the last time we were here at the cabin, about a year ago. We had left our bed as we had risen from it, scented with love, and so it remained. No one had been here since us.

I brushed the cobwebs from the windowpanes and swept the floor, then fed Cecil his dinner. After he ate, I fired up the woodstove and washed out a couple of pans in the little stream that ran past the cabin.

We had brought a few cases of water and some pasta, rice, and canned goods, along with bread, coffee, and milk. We also had a cooler of fresh vegetables, butter, and cheese. I boiled some spaghetti and used the cooking oil in the cabin to fry up some tomatoes, peppers, and mushrooms. Zahra and I ate vegetable spaghetti and sparkling water. The sting of our reality softened a little while we enjoyed the food.

After we were done, it came roaring back with a vengeance.

"I wonder which prison Pam is in and what they're doing to her," I said, staring at my empty plate.

Zahra looked up from the other side of the table and said: "I know it's impossible not to, but worrying about her like that won't help."

"I know. You're right. But I feel so guilty. She had nothing to do with any of this. She doesn't deserve any of this. All she ever does is make my life better and look what I've done to her."

Zahra put her left hand atop mine softly. "It's not your fault, Michael."

I shook my head and wiped away the tears welling up in my eyes.

"When do you think we'll hear from Nicole?" I asked.

"I texted our new numbers to her," Zahra said. "She's careful. She'll get in touch when she needs to."

A silence hung over us for a bit as we reconciled where we were and why we were here. All I could think about was Pam, still, and what she was doing right now, as the sun set over northeastern Indiana.

I knew she would be worried about me, too. More than about herself. I wanted to let her know that I was out. And that I was going to get her out.

"Nicole will somehow let her know you're okay, I'm sure," Zahra said, to console me. I felt a little better, but then I was struck by my own selfishness. Here I was with a woman who the Davis government wanted to lock up, too. They were focused on arresting prominent Iranian Americans, like Zahra, first and foremost. The ones who could cause the most trouble. "I need to get moving soon," Zahra said. "I can't stay with you much longer."

I knew that was true. I was a target, and she was a target, and together we doubled our chances of being hit.

"What are you going to do?" I asked.

"Nicole said she knew a guy who could get me a new passport. Canadian. I'll become a French-Canadian. Once I have that passport, I'll head to Montreal. I know a cinematographer there who will help me out. Until I can get my film going again."

I admired Zahra's calm and her belief that her art would survive the carnage. Or maybe it was her art that would allow her to survive the carnage.

It was dark now, and Cecil bounded up to me, wagging his tail. The bark had been bred out of the Rhodesian ridgeback to make it a silent stalker during the hunt, but the breed could still bark sometimes. I had only heard Cecil bark once, when he was asleep at our feet as Pam and I sat on the couch and watched the A's. He barked while he was dreaming. It had startled us both into laughter, and he woke up, wagging his tail, licking our hands, wanting a treat. Now, his wagging tail and shaking haunches told me something else: he needed to pee.

I took him outside the cabin, and he sniffed around and found the perfect peeing spot, just between two small trees. He let loose.

Just about then, I heard a baby crying, which was quickly muffled. I saw a small dark shape move between two trees, just to my right.

"Hello?" I said. Cecil wanted to go back inside for his treat, so I opened the door and let him in. Maybe the dog was scaring them off. "Hello? It's okay. I am a friend." It's all I could think to say, but I knew that if someone was out there in the dark with a baby, then yes, I was their friend.

I walked toward the trees. Nothing moved. I wanted whoever was there to know I wasn't a danger to them. "I have food, water," I said. "Are you okay?" Then I realized that if they could see it, they might reveal themselves.

So I went into the cabin to get some bottles of water and some bread. Zahra was reading a poetry book on a big leather chair. She looked calm and comfortable under the soft spotlight of a lantern. "Everything okay?" she asked.

"I think we have scum in the bushes," I said. "Going to see if I can help them."

I grabbed a lantern and went back outside. I put the bottles of water and a loaf of bread on a plastic bag on the ground and then placed the lantern next to it, so they could see.

Then I went back inside.

I had just turned around to look out the window when a girl, about ten years old, darted out of the shadows and scooped up the bread and water. Then she darted back into the darkness. She moved quickly, running with springy, athletic strides in a beige T-shirt and worn-out brown sweatpants. Her long black hair was in two ponytails. They bounced on her back as she ran.

I went back outside. I had another lantern and held it up to my face. "Amiga," I said. And then I said the only other thing that popped into my head. "Mi casa es su casa." This was not the right time or place for a little girl and a baby to be outside without shelter. I walked back and held open the door.

It was about a minute until I heard a rustling in the trees, and then the girl emerged. She was followed by a woman, in perhaps her late twenties, holding a baby, and another woman, maybe in her fifties. They looked like a family.

The lantern shone on the little girl's strong, sad face as she neared me. She had big, piercing black eyes, and she surprised me when she smiled and said in Spanish-accented English, "Thank you, sir, for the help."

I smiled at her and said, "Of course. Please come in. There is lots of room."

I knew this was dangerous. Like me and Zahra, these poor people were also enemies of the state. But it was the right thing to do. I realized that one part of my normal life I wasn't proud of was that I didn't do much to help people in need. In the heat of all this drama, now I could. And I was thankful for that.

The girl translated my message to her mother and grandmother, and they conferred in Spanish. Then they walked toward me, slowly, as if I might make a sudden move that would put them in danger. Their eyes were a mixture of vulnerability, fear, and hope. I held open the door, and as the mother with the baby passed by me, she smiled shyly and said, "Gracias señor, nos salvó la vida."

She was telling me I had saved their lives.

CHAPTER 25

SUNDAY, JUNE 26, LATER.

As the family all ate bread and cheese, they told us their story, and Zahra (who speaks Spanish) translated.

The family—grandmother Elena, mother Alejandra, daughter Sofia (who was fourteen but looked younger), and son Rafael (who was a year old)—was from Guatemala. Elena was a little younger than Zahra and a bit taller, but they looked like they could be sisters or cousins. Alejandra was slender and dark haired, like her daughter, with a chiseled and muscular frame. She had fragile and nervous mannerisms and somber eyes that had undoubtedly witnessed the full continuum of human behavior. Rafael had a thatch of black hair and the bluest eyes I had ever seen besides Pam's. They had paid all their savings for smugglers to get them into the US to join Alejandra's husband, Pedro, in Houston, but they had been abandoned in Juárez, Mexico. Pedro had found a smuggler to get them out of Juárez and into Texas, and for a short time they were all together.

Given President Davis's hostility to immigrants, the family decided that their lives would be safer, better, in Canada. So, two months ago, Pedro made his way to Canada. He found a job as a carpenter in Hamilton, Ontario, and told his family he would get them to Canada as soon as he could. He had made arrangements for them to be admitted as his family. He had a sponsor.

Then President Davis attacked Iran, and the family lost communication with Pedro in the tumult that followed. They knew they were not safe in the US and so decided they would make their way to Canada themselves. They had a car, but it broke down south of Bloomington, so they began the journey on foot. They were trying to get to Detroit, as there was someone there who knew Pedro and could help them cross into Canada.

"But now," Sofia explained, "it was too dangerous to move during the day, because of the cazadoras." The hunters.

"The what?" I had not heard this term in either language.

"They are the men with guns who hunt us," Sofia said.

"The immigration police?"

She shook her head. "No. The men with the red helmets. Los caballeros de la Libertad."

"The Knights of Liberty," Zahra said.

I had heard of this group. They were a southern branch descended from the Roaring Boys, who were a very dangerous alt-right organization of white supremacists out of LA. Pam had worked on a film about some of them wanting to come out of the organization and back to civilization, but the television network canceled it because too many of the Boys blamed President Davis for leading them into the darkness. It was too risky to broadcast that kind of claim under this kind of government. I didn't know some of them were here. I thought they were all from Tennessee and Missouri.

"They're here, in Indiana?"

Everyone nodded.

My goodness, I thought. We couldn't leave these people outside on their own.

"You can stay here tonight," I said. "There is enough room."

Zahra didn't have to translate. The grandmother, Elena, started to cry and grasped my hand. Her hand was tender and warm, with thick calluses that revealed a lifetime of working with her hands. I felt like I was going to cry, too, with the weight of all that had landed upon me in the past few days. But I did not.

The family took a room upstairs and settled in.

Zahra took the room next to them, and I decided to sleep on the futon in the living room. Just in case.

Of course, deciding to sleep and actually doing it were two very different things. I just lay on that futon, staring at the cabin's high wooden ceiling, listening for sounds in the woods that might signal danger.

And I thought of Pam. Her sweet smell. Her kind turquoise eyes. Her radiant little dimples. I needed something to bring back to the FBI that I could use as leverage to get her out. But what on earth could some nobody like me find here in nowheresville Indiana? How could we free Pam and get Zahra her passport for Canada? Maybe Zahra could help the Guatemalans get to Canada. They said Pedro had worked things out for them there. Maybe it could all work out.

Maybe.

I rolled over on the futon and tried to get comfortable but that wasn't happening, so I got up and walked to the window. The night sky was bursting with stars and a near-full moon. It was stunning. You could almost forget the terrors of the world by looking at the night sky on Hoosier Hill.

And then they came roaring back with the sound of a gunshot. It was close, and it was followed by laughter, the coarse laughter of drunken men. Then the laughter started to get louder. They were getting closer.

Then the moonlight landed on a flash of red. I saw them, three guys, white and pale, in red helmets and black vests, stumbling toward the cabin. They had AR-15 rifles slung over their shoulders. They were passing a hip flask between them as they walked.

I stepped out the door of the cabin. I couldn't let them get any closer.

The tallest guy, who was maybe six-two, saw me and stopped. His arms and legs were thin but he had a huge midsection bursting from his waist. He had reddish blonde hair and a long sloppy beard. He hadn't shaved in eons, maybe ever. Rasing his right hand, he gave the signal to his team to stop. Then he aimed his gun at me. "Who the fuck're you?" he snarled, his eyes glossy and wet, his voice slurring, thick with booze.

I knew I had to be very careful with what I said next. These guys could kill us all if I said something they didn't want to hear.

"Good evening, gentlemen," I said. "I'm just some guy up here keeping my family safe, that's who I am."

I hit upon the family idea in case baby Rafael started to cry.

My answer caused the leader to lower his assault rifle. "You think this place is safe?"

I smiled. "Aren't you guys making it so?" I asked.

They moved closer and took in the SUV and me. I could see them doing the math. New SUV, probably an expensive one at that, and a white guy talking about keeping his family safe. They didn't respond. "From whom?" was what they were thinking.

"Things were getting hot down in Bloomington," I said. "Too many people opposing our great president's defense of our country." The tallest guy scratched his beard and then muttered something to the shorter, fatter guy to his left. They both looked to be in their mid-fifties, while the third guy, to their right, was probably in his twenties. Maybe a son, learning the family trade. All three wobbled as they tried to stand up straight.

"You from Bloomington?"

"Yes," I said. "Third generation in fact. Terrible what's happening there. With all the scum coming in."

On that word, they seemed to relax. They moved close enough to shake my hand and then the tallest one offered me his hand. "I'm Zeke," he said, as we shook hands. "And this is Travis." His friend, who was carrying an extra fifty pounds and had a shorter, chinstrap beard, shook my hand. "And this is Pablo, my number one son."

My reaction to hearing a Spanish name made them laugh.

"His name's really Paul," Zeke said, and I faked a smile, as Pablo shook my hand. He was about six feet tall with a slim build, a lazy eye, a few missing teeth, and a limp handshake.

"That's a relief," I said, almost in a whisper. "Baby's sleeping inside with his mother."

They all nodded, and Travis put his finger to his lips, harder than he meant to do thanks to the whisky, so it looked like he'd smacked himself in the face. He laughed.

"So what are you guys doing in these parts?" I asked.

Travis sucked in his gut and said, "We're on top-secret business."

"Really?" I asked. "What kind of top-secret business?"

He looked around solemnly and then produced his smartphone. He opened an app and read a post in a loud slurring voice: "For each adult male illegal alien he will pay a bounty of $100, for each adult female $75, and for each child $50."

"Who's he?"

They all looked at me as if I was suddenly an impostor, and so I quickly caught the message. "You mean our president will pay you for catching them?"

Zeke chuckled. "Yep. Too bad it's not for killing 'em."

He grinned at me. He wasn't joking, and was proud of the thought.

"It's good money, anyway," Pablo said.

"'Specially since those fuckers took all our jobs," Travis added.

"Wow," I said. My heart was pounding, and my stomach was twisting into knots. According to messages on this app, President Davis was getting Americans to go out and catch immigrants and turn them into the government for a bounty. The rule of law had weakened since the hostilities with Iran began, but this was intense. Was it true? Or was it just social-media misinformation?

"Pretty cool, huh?" Zeke said.

"Did he send this message to you directly?"

Zeke laughed and spat. "He's way too smart for that. It came from HQ."

"HQ?"

"The Boys. Out in LA."

He showed me his smartphone. He had an app open called Pure. "See?"

I could see the message. The sender was RB Long Beach. Beneath the ID tag was an image of two AR-15 rifles, crossed. I nodded. Were the Roaring Boys really the conduit for a Davis bounty hunt? "So how many have you got?"

"Just three so far," Travis said, snorting out a little laugh. "All kids. Don't pay as much."

"They look like maybe they's sixteen, but of course the fuckers don't have ID. So the feds call them kids." Zeke spat in the dirt. He had a huge pack of chewing tobacco in his mouth.

"How do you turn them in for bounties?" I asked.

"Walk them through the doors at ICE and they take it from there," Zeke said.

"What does ICE do then?"

"What do you think? Ship them back where they come from."

"We heard this place is crawling with scum," Pablo said. "Supposed to be like catching fish in a barrel. It's a direct route to that communist country up north."

So that's why they were here. They thought they could catch immigrants on some kind of underground railroad for Canada.

"You seen any?"

I shook my head. "I think there might have been some around here, but when the army turned up, they moved on. Haven't seen a thing."

"The army's here?" Zeke asked.

"Yeah," I said casually, "they moved in a couple of days ago with tanks. Haven't seen any scum at all since then."

The Knights looked disappointed, as if the army was out to spoil their free enterprise.

"Hey," I said, with as much cheer as I could muster. "Can I get a photo of us together? My wife will be so happy to see some real patriots when she wakes up."

"Sure," Zeke said with a proud smile.

"Hang on and I'll get my phone," I said. I rushed back into the cabin, snatched my phone from the table beside the futon, and made it back outside before Zeke could make it to the door to have a look inside.

"Let's do a selfie," I said.

I got in the middle of the guys and raised the phone toward us, then paused. "Hey Zeke," I said, "can you put your phone with that message in the picture so my wife can see that, too? She's going to be so happy."

Zeke thought about it, then Travis said, "Go on, he's on our side," and so Zeke held his phone with its Pure app open toward the camera, and I snapped the photo, once, twice, three times. I looked at the photos and smiled. "She's going to love this."

"Hey," Zeke said. "You got a john I can use?"

I shook my head. "Installing plumbing is my next order of business. The woods are your outhouse, Zeke."

He nodded, and then I yawned. "Lucky I was awake to meet you guys," I said, giving them the hint that we were done. "But I better get back to sleep. Thank you for keeping us safe."

Zeke saluted me, and then so did Travis and Pablo. "Good to meet you . . ." Zeke said, tilting his head to the right and looking puzzled. I had not told them my name. So I told them now. "Weiss," I said. "Joe Weiss."

Then Zeke offered me a swig from their flask. There was no way I was going to sip from their river of poison. I shook my head. "Doctor says I can't drink for a while until my blood pressure comes down. Thanks to the work you're doing, I'm sure it will sometime soon."

They accepted that, and then they all shook my hand again. "God bless America," Zeke said.

I nodded. "God bless America."

CHAPTER 26

MONDAY, JUNE 27.

"It's something, but it's not enough," I said to Zahra, as dawn broke over Hoosier Hill and the late June sunlight filtered through the window onto our breakfast of bacon and toast. I was feeling optimistic after my encounter with the Knights and thought that maybe what I learned about the bounty program could help me free Pam, but I also knew I needed a lot more information. The Guatemalans were still asleep. I knew that this must be the first safe sleep they'd had since their car died on them.

Zahra looked at the photo of the three Knights of Liberty with their bounty commission on my burner phone and shook her head. "There are far too many people in this country who would approve of what they're doing, Michael. And if it's already on social media, then lots of people already know about it, so there's no leverage with Weiss in threatening to make it public. Assuming Davis really is behind the bounties, of course. Could just be typical social-media misinformation."

I nodded.

"But it's something that we can show Nicole," she said. "Maybe she can help find evidence that Davis really is behind this."

I knew she was right. I needed proof that Davis was actually behind the bounties. Maybe, just maybe, threatening Weiss to take that to the press would coerce her to free Pam. But how could I ever find that evidence? A wave of despondency tore through my body: my wife's freedom depended on me tying these three haggard racists to the President of the United States.

I also knew that the Knights could come back to the cabin at any time and find Zahra and the Guatemalans. So we had to get out of here soon.

"What are you thinking, Michael?" Zahra asked me.

"I'm thinking of going for a walk." I smiled as reassuringly at her as I could. I needed to go back to the Knights and see what more they knew about this bounty program. "If I'm not back by noon, then I want you to take the family to my place. And call Nicole." I handed her the key to the SUV.

"Where are you going, Michael? It's dangerous out there."

I nodded. "I know. But so is having my wife still in prison. Or me going back there. I need to learn more about the immigrant bounty program supposedly sanctioned by Davis." I was sounding braver than I felt, but I knew that if I hadn't clicked that link then none of this would have happened.

She smiled at me. "Send me a text when you know when you'll be back."

"Will do," I said, walking out the door. And as I followed the path that the Knights had taken away from the cabin the night before, I thought up a plan.

I had to find Zeke, Travis, and Pablo and ask them how I could help them. I knew they were connected to the Roaring Boys, who were some very bad dudes with more than a few of their members in prison for murder and sedition. But I had seen in the drunken midnight ramblings of these Knights of Liberty a gap. They were not an organized militia marching in disciplined order to the commands of a military genius. They were drunk rural guys getting orders from an app, and they were doing it for reasons involving both race and money. In that gap, I could see a role for me. I just didn't know yet what it was.

I walked in the sun-dappled woods for about half a mile, along a trail full of rocks and sticks. And then I heard shouting ahead of me. Violent, angry, profane shouting: "You pieces of scum!"

"Hey," someone said from behind me, and I spun around. It was Pablo, Zeke's son and the youngest Knight. He looked sheepish in his red helmet and black vest, as if busted while sleeping on guard duty.

"Hey," I said with the friendliest smile I could muster. "It's me, Joe. I am glad I found you again."

"Why's that?" he said, his glazed eyes suddenly suspicious.

"Because I want to help you guys."

Pablo led the way as we approached the angry shouting man, who was standing in a clearing in front of three Latino boys, who were each tied to a separate tree with thick brown rope. Their stomachs were pressed against the trees, and their arms wrapped around, as if hugging the trees' thick brown trunks. The boys were roughly the same age, early to mid-teens. Two of them were about the same height, fairly short. Both were sturdy and stout. The third was tall and lean. All of them had black hair, dark skin, and wore old T-shirts and shorts laden with dirt and blood. None of them were wearing shoes. They looked tired, scared, and hungry. Pablo moved close to them, his fist raised, as if he was going to strike them. The terrified kids cowered under his fist.

My first thought was to get back to the cabin as fast as possible and call the cops. But then I remembered the cops under Davis's martial law might actually make everything worse.

The man who was shouting wasn't with the other Knights the night before. He looked to be about fifty, roughly the same age as Zeke and Travis. He was short, squat, and muscular, with blonde hair and pale skin. His beard was a thick mix of blonde and gray. Like the others, his eyes were wet and bloodshot. Unlike the others, his red helmet had a gold-colored bar running down the front of it. Nearby, there were two tents. T-4 hub tents: big, rugged things that I recognized from my boss Steve's fly-fishing trip photos. Steve loved the T-4 and told me that they could sleep four, easily.

As he was shouting, the man turned toward us and flinched when he saw Pablo's helmet flash in the sunlight. He pointed a black boxy handgun right at me. I held up my hands.

"It's okay, sir," Pablo said. "We met him last night. He lives around here. He wants to help."

The man thought about this as he looked me over. His head tilted to the left and then the right. Then he holstered the gun and approached, extending his beefy hand. "Can't be too careful these days. Knights Commander Robert Montrose," he said proudly.

"Joe Weiss," I replied, shaking his hand. His grip was hard, and it lasted too long. But I just held my smile and he finally relaxed. I had passed his crude test. "So you want to help, do you?"

Zeke and Travis emerged from their tent, shaking off drunken sleep. I could smell their booze-ridden breath from ten feet away.

We sat in folding chairs around the smoldering remnants of their campfire, dozens of crushed beer cans and three empty 1.75 liter bottles of Jim Beam scattered about beside the fire. I hoped that this was not merely last night's consumption, but from the look of this group, ragged and florid, I suspected it was.

I wanted to help those poor kids tied to the trees—or let them know I would help them soon—but there was no way to do so now without getting myself tied to a tree too. What I needed to do now was something I was no good at doing, because my face always gave me away. Pam said she knew I loved her before I told her because my face had told her a thousand times already. I knew now that if I ever wanted to see my wife's face again, free and happy, watching a baseball game on our couch, then I had to be someone different in these next moments.

So I took a deep breath and lied through my teeth.

CHAPTER 27

MONDAY, JUNE 27, LATER.

The sun was almost overhead, and the Knights were now all pretty drunk. I had to get to Zahra and the family and get everyone out of there before the Knights started stumbling back toward the cabin. But I also needed to learn more about the bounty program and President Davis's involvement.

The three kids that they had kidnapped were asleep on their knees, tied to the trees. I wondered what kind of sleep they would have. And if they would dream. I hoped not. I wouldn't want to wake from a dream to this nightmare of reality. I knew that feeling well, having experienced it in Davis's secret prison. And I didn't know what was going to happen to me then. Or now. The safe, quiet pond near the tree at my childhood park was a million miles away. Even a minute into the future could not be predicted. At any moment everything could go sideways.

As Montrose opened another bottle of Jim Beam, I reviewed the lies I had told them and the blanks that they had filled in.

I was an executive at Armor Security, a company that specialized in security. Of all types.

They took security to mean "weapons."

As soon as I saw that, I knew what I could offer them.

"Armor Security," Montrose mused. "The guy who runs that is rich, isn't he?"

I nodded. "My friend Caleb Wagner is very rich. And a great supporter of the president."

They were all impressed by this. "What do you do there?" Zeke asked.

"I'm Caleb's right-hand man," I said. "I make what he wants to happen, happen."

They grinned at me as if I could deliver them whatever they wanted.

"Well, we got guns," Zeke said, twisting his dirty beard with his fingers and thinking about what they might need. "We could always use more ammo, I guess."

I had to think fast. What kind of weapons could they use that they didn't have?

"You can get us land mines?" Travis asked.

"That's tough," I replied. There was no way I could get land mines. But Zeke saved me.

"What the fuck would we do with land mines?" Zeke asked. "They can't spot scum walking on trails. We'd end up killing good Americans."

This gave Montrose his genius idea while sucking on the Jim Beam bottle. "What if we could make better use of these captured immigrant kids? What if we brought the war to Indiana and helped generate more patriotic support for the president?"

"What do you mean?" I asked, a cold wave rushing through my body.

"Well, we get a bounty for them, but it doesn't say we gotta bring 'em in alive. Just gotta capture them."

"So you're thinking of using them," I said. "In our war."

He nodded at me. "You're pretty sharp. I am thinking just that thing. It would help the mission. And you can help us. If you can get me the ingredients for suicide-bomber vests." He looked over at the sleeping kids and grinned. Then he looked back at me. "I need three of them. And some Iranian-looking clothing. People need to think it was the enemy when they sift through the wreckage."

I understood. The Knights of Liberty wanted to turn these three teenage boys into Iranian suicide bombers in order to fire up support for Davis's fledgling war. If Davis's supporters thought Iranian bombers attacked innocent Americans on our homeland, it would galvanize public opinion for the war.

"Yeah, I can do that," I said, trying to keep my heart under control. "Where are you going to attack?"

Montrose took another sip of bourbon. "Hmmmm. How can we stir up the most good-ole-fashioned patriotism? Hmmmm. Well, where will we find the most libtards?"

He grinned at me again, as if I was taking a test, which I realized that I still was. A dribble of whisky was oozing out of his grimy teeth and down his chin.

"Well, that would be Bloomington. Where the university is," I said.

He grinned and closed his eyes, imagining blowing up not-so-good Americans into a bloody mist.

The Knights believed that I was part of the management team at Armor Security, and that in my top-secret work, I could get them the explosives that they would need to create havoc with these terrified teenagers. They were so happy with my offer that they even agreed to my request that the tied-up boys receive water and some food, as it would be no use to have a dead suicide bomber before they had a chance to press the button on the bomb.

Travis took some bread and bottled water to the kids, and even he realized it was hard to eat and drink if you were asleep with your hands wrapped around a tree and tied up. As he untied the boys, they awoke, barely, their heads low, their eyes fixed on the ground. I walked over to the trees to do a visual inspection on the size of bomb vests that they would need. When the oldest boy, maybe sixteen, handsome, with black eyes and a strong face, dared to look up at me, I winked at him. Three times. My back was to the Knights. I was letting him know I wasn't bad like the other men were.

They all looked more alike up close. Young. Scared. Three brothers, I surmised, trying to make their way to safety. He responded with a look of relief that said "finally, a human being," and I gave him a very subtle nod.

"How much is this all gonna cost?" Zeke asked, and Montrose looked as if he had just asked the stupidest question in the world.

"It isn't going to cost anything, you dumb fuck. Joe Weiss here is doing this as a patriot, as a great supporter of our war against Iran, for freedom, aren't you, Joe?"

I smiled. They had bought my lie completely, and now all I had to do was say yes.

"Indeed, I consider it my duty, and that of Armor Security, to help restore this country to what it was. To what we know it can be. Let's consider this mission our collaboration. I will provide the ordinance, and you will deliver the blow."

Montrose popped open a couple of watery beers and shoved one toward me.

I shook my head. I repeated what I had told the others last night. "I would love to, but I really can't until my blood pressure comes down. But thanks anyway."

I told them it might take a couple of weeks to get everything that they needed. That wasn't a problem. "We got everything we need to survive out here for a while," Montrose told me.

"Just make sure that you keep those guys in shape," I said. "No use getting all this gear if you can't complete the mission."

Montrose saluted me. "You got it, Joe Weiss. In fact, that's what we'll call our first bomb. Mean Joe Weiss, in honor of you."

I felt like I was going to throw up. "I need a photo of the bombers," I said. "So we get their vest sizes right. Can you go stand with them, Robert? You're what, five ten, eleven?"

He smiled at me with the pleasure of a guy who'd just had three inches added to his height. Then he heaved himself up and walked over to the boys, who cowered as if they were going to be beaten again. Montrose held his hands up to indicate not this time.

I walked over and took photos of each boy next to the Knight Commander in his red helmet slashed with its gold bar, and his black vest, and his big black handgun holstered to his right hip.

Then I gave Montrose the number for my burner phone, and he gave me his. I told him I would text soon with an update.

Then I texted Zahra. "On my way back. Time to go."

CHAPTER 28

TUESDAY, JUNE 28.

The good thing about Nicole Wilkerson's SUV windows is that they were tinted black. Hard to see in.

Even though the sun was bright, it was hard to see me, Zahra, Cecil, and the Guatemalan family all crammed in and taking the back roads to Bloomington.

I knew that if we hit a checkpoint now, we were all doomed. No red Indiana hat could camouflage this crew. Thankfully the roads were mostly empty. Martial law prohibited travel on the roads after 10:00 p.m. But the government allowed it from dawn to dusk, so we drove out as the sun beamed down on the Hoosier Hills.

Zahra texted Nicole. "Where should we meet?"

Nicole texted back. "So soon?"

Zahra replied: "We need to get out of here. Ran into some loonies. Not safe."

Nicole texted back. "Go to Michael and Pam's. I will meet you there."

CHAPTER 29

TUESDAY, JUNE 28, LATER.

Driving up to our house a few hours later with a carload of fugitives was different than the last time I arrived home, to put it mildly.

I half expected Agent Jo Weiss to be staked out, waiting to pounce on me for some manufactured breach of my release. But there was only my Prius parked in the driveway and our white stucco bungalow gleaming in the June sunshine.

I edged the SUV past the Prius in the driveway and drove into our garage, where Pam and I stored boxes of our things from college and her dad's physics notebooks. There was still enough room to park the SUV. Barely.

"Follow me," Zahra said, and she took the Guatemalans inside.

I exited the garage and surveyed the street. Grant Woollard was out watering his begonias. He gave me a wave that was part salute, and I waved back. If he was working for the feds, they'd soon know that I was back. Or maybe they already did.

Inside my house, Nicole Wilkerson was waiting for us. Along with another woman, who looked like she could be related to Zahra or Elena, the Guatemalan grandmother, with her curly black hair and her tawny complexion.

"Welcome home!" Nicole said, smiling. She was wearing a gray sports suit and dangly earrings. Her white teeth shone like jewels.

Once behind my locked front door, with Cecil jumping up and down in glee to be home, Nicole turned the TV on loud to GNC. And I introduced the Guatemalans to her. Elena, Alejandra, Sofia, and baby Rafael. We did not ask their surname. It was as if knowing this detail would give the law one more weapon to use against us if we were caught.

Nicole introduced Hannah Gottlieb to us. "Hannah's my law partner. She's representing Pam."

"And Pam is doing okay, all things considered," Hannah said. She had a confident New York accent, pretty face, and an easy smile. She was a little older than Nicole, or maybe her New York life had just been a little more stressful.

She told us all about Pam. My wife was in a Public Protection Center in Whiteland, which was a suburb of Indianapolis in Pleasant Township. I felt a wave of relief flood over me just hearing where she was. But I was also sick at heart that I had put her there.

"Does she know about me?" I asked.

"She knows you're safe and now out of prison. She's happy about that."

"Do you think they'll let her go soon?"

"We don't know. With her Iranian background it's harder to get her out than it was with you. And our judge, appointed by Davis, denied our emergency motion."

"Is there any way I can visit her? Or talk to her on the phone?"

Hannah shook her head. "I'm sorry, Michael."

I shook my head. The room fell silent. "Be right back," I said, and walked upstairs.

Dear Pam, my baby, I wrote onto a blank piece of paper, sitting at my desk in our shared office next to the bedroom.

I am so sorry I did this to us, to you. I never should have clicked on that damn link. And I should have realized they would come after us the moment Davis launched his first bomb. We should have escaped then, not waited. We'd be together if I had thought of that, somewhere far away from Bloomington, from America, from this madness. We'd be free, safe, and together.

But I will never, ever stop until we are together and free again. Never. We will be together, hand in hand, very soon. I promise you. I will not stop until this is so.

I love you,
Mikey

I folded the letter and put it into an envelope and wrote *Pamela Housen* on the envelope. Then I walked downstairs and handed it to Hannah. "Please give this to Pam the first chance you get."

She looked at me and nodded.

The Guatemalan family and Zahra had gone out into our back garden to enjoy the sunshine of this late June afternoon. They seemed happy.

I started showing the two lawyers the photos on my burner phone.

"Interesting," Nicole said. "The Knights of Liberty are connected to the Roaring Boys. Their leader got twenty years for trying to kidnap the governor of California."

"The Roaring Boys are also seriously connected to Davis," Hannah added. "They did unofficial security at his rallies out west before he was elected."

I told them about my first encounter with the Knights. About the immigrant bounty program circulating on social media they said was authorized by Davis.

"It wouldn't surprise me if he signed off on this bounty for immigrants," Nicole said, as she looked at the pictures of the Knights. "I mean, Davis is criminal, but this is . . ." She looked at Hannah, who nodded. "This is just obscene."

We were all silent for a moment. It was shocking, but she was right. Hunting humans for money.

I told them about my trip to find the Knights' encampment the next morning, and when I did, what I found there. Then I showed them the photos of the three teenage boys.

"These are the kids that the Knights had tied to trees when I arrived," I said. "They captured them in their bounty hunt." I paused, to let the images sink in. "But they don't plan to turn them into the feds. They plan to dress them in Iranian clothes and turn them into Iranian suicide bombers and blow up people here, in Bloomington, to help rally public support for Davis's war in Iran. They think I'm helping them. What they don't know is that I will be giving them fake vests."

The two lawyers were silent. Thinking about that.

"Why are you doing this, Michael?" Hannah asked.

"To buy some time and save the kids. We can't count on the cops right now."

She nodded.

"And maybe this can help get Pam out of prison too," I said.

"How so?" Nicole asked skeptically.

"If we tie the attempted murders to Davis and his bounty program, maybe it will give us leverage with Weiss?"

"Maybe," she said. "Do you have proof this plan is real?" Nicole asked.

I smiled. "I have proof. This is what they asked me to get them." I opened the voice recorder app on the burner and played them the conversation of the Knights telling me about their plan to turn their captives into weapons. I had my phone record the whole thing, and for a sixty-dollar burner, the sound quality was very good.

Nicole nodded. "So these guys think that you are going to help them?"

I nodded. "When they learned I worked at Armor Security, the game was on."

Nicole smiled. "Nice. That's a way forward."

I needed it to be more than that. "Is it enough to get Pam out? Can we take this to Agent Weiss?"

Nicole shook her head gently. "Right now, it's just criminal reporting, Michael. There's no leverage for us with Weiss. But like you said, if we connect the bounty program to Davis with real evidence—not just drunken ramblings and statements on social media, but actual evidence—then maybe we have enough." My heart was pounding as she continued. "If we get that evidence, then we could threaten Weiss to go public with Davis's involvement in the bounty program unless she releases Pam."

I understood. But I also knew that even if we found enough evidence to get Pam out of prison, the government wasn't done with us. They thought we had been working with Iranian hackers and wouldn't stop until they proved it. As long as Davis and his loyalists were in power, they wouldn't be done with us until we were in prison for good. Or worse.

"We have breaking news," the GNC anchor said, the group of us uniformly turning to the television. Images of rioting across the US and the police responding with live ammunition while the army looked on gave way to Janine Wood, standing outside the White House. Tall and tan, with short brown hair, she stared into the camera intensely with her dark brown eyes. "Our political correspondent Janine Wood is here with breaking news from Washington."

We all moved closer to the television.

"Thank you, Terrence," she said. "GNC is receiving unconfirmed reports from sources close to President Davis that the US has killed Iran's Supreme Leader Ali Rhouhani in a Special Operations mission earlier today. GNC has not been able to independently verify that report and Iranian State Television is denying it, and they released this footage about half an hour ago."

On-screen was the Iranian Supreme Leader, Ali Rhouhani, his black turban matching his large black horn-rimmed glasses and his black robe as he gesticulated to a table of Revolutionary Guard officers seated before him. The translation on the screen said "We are defeating the infidel America! Keep strong people of Iran, and do not believe their infidel lies!"

The time stamp on the video indicated that it was from today, at 16:35 p.m. Iran was eight hours ahead of Bloomington's eastern time zone. So either the Special Ops had killed Rhouhani this morning, their time, or Iran was lying.

I turned to the lawyers. "Who do you believe?"

"So Davis is now lying about something easily provable," Nicole said.

"So long as his robots believe it, that's all that matters," Hannah added. "But it must mean that we—sorry—*he* is losing pretty badly to have to toss out pointless fucking whoppers like that."

Then President Davis himself appeared on-screen from the Rose Garden at the White House. He was forty-seven years old, but today looked a decade older, his slicked black hair streaked with gray and his face bloated and red.

"My Americans," he began, as if we were his property. "As your commander in chief, I am here to inform you that we have the Iranians on the run. They are scared, and they are in retreat." He paused, as if listening to the applause in millions of American living rooms. "We took out their leader this morning. They say we did not, but as a technology executive, I can tell you how easy it is to fake videos like this. And that's what they did." He paused again. "We have delivered an ultimatum to the Iranians. Surrender. Or be bombed deep into the desert—"

On that, the screen went black. The lights were still on in our living room, so it wasn't a local electrical issue this time. Someone had taken Davis off the air. The TV flickered to life and GNC came back on and Terrence, the anchor, apologized. "We're sorry, folks, we just lost the feed from the White House. We'll get the president back as soon as we can."

"Wow," Hannah said. "The Iranians are good."

"You think they hacked into the White House?" I asked.

"You tell me," she said, and winked.

I knew that if the Iranians were hacking into President Davis's performances that things were not going well for the commander in chief. And I knew that the worse things got for him, the worse things would get for everyone else.

I stepped outside into our backyard to breathe the fresh air. Looking up into the sky I thought about Pam, about what she was doing. Where was she sleeping? What was she eating? Who was interrogating her?

I wondered if I would ever see her again.

Then it hit me like a lightning bolt—what I had just seen on the television—the person who might actually help get Pam out of jail. Janine Wood. Yes, Janine Wood wanted to talk to me about the Armor cybersecurity breach. She had called me the day I found out about the hack, just a week ago, while I was driving home. I ran upstairs into our room and put the batteries back in my phone and turned it on. Then I tapped on "recent calls" and there was her number from her call on June 20, eight days earlier, at 6:46 p.m.: 202-245-9561. A famous Washington, D.C. political reporter wanted me to be her source. Maybe—just maybe—this was a pathway to Davis, to connect him to the bounty program and the Knights of Liberty and get the leverage we needed with Weiss. I could help Janine Wood and she could help me. A light at the end of the tunnel began to flicker, ever so faintly.

CHAPTER 30

TUESDAY, JUNE 28, LATER.

Janine Wood was glad that I had called her back. I probably should have made sure Nicole and Hannah were okay with me calling her, but I needed to call her back even if the lawyers said not to. In addition to her texts, Janine had left me several voicemails while I was in jail. Ever distrustful of Davis, she smelled something wasn't right about the Armor hack and thought I could be a key source for her reporting. "Michael, thank you for getting back to me," she said. Her voice was friendly, open.

Then she paused, waiting for me to spill the beans.

I took a breath. I loved her work. But I had no experience talking to national news reporters and yet I had to convince her she needed me enough to help me, so I could get my wife, and my life, back. "I'm sorry I didn't speak to you the other night, a week or so ago, when you called. I have more now." It was clumsy, but I was nervous. "I mean, I have information that could help you."

She paused again, for too long, and I thought I had lost her. Then she said, "Sorry, just getting out of traffic. Hang on."

It didn't sound like she was driving so maybe traffic meant ears listening in.

"Okay," she said. "First of all, how are you?"

"I'm better than I was. Thanks for asking."

"How are you better, Michael? It seems pretty, well, you know."

"It's even worse than you think, Janine." And I told her all about my recent stay inside the secret Davis prison.

She paused for a couple of seconds. "That's terrible. Terrible."

I could hear an angry edge in her voice.

"Did they charge you with anything?"

"No. They did not. In fact, they seemed to make a point of that."

"How?"

"By saying it out loud. No charges yet."

"But they let you out? I mean, I heard that you were involved in the hack into Armor. The guy that let Iran into the house and gave Davis what he needed to start this war."

"That's what they tell me."

She paused again. "So you're saying that you didn't do it?"

"I don't remember, Janine. I mean, who remembers every link they click on, especially from like six months ago?"

She laughed. "Good point. So what are you going to do?"

"I need to prove that I had nothing to do with this. But first I need to get my wife out of prison."

This was news to her. "Why is your wife in prison?"

"Because her parents came from Iran, and so . . ."

"Fuck 'em," she said. Angry. This was good.

"Yeah, the FBI thinks I clicked the link on purpose, to let the hackers in, because my wife happens to have Iranian parents."

"So what are you going to do to get your wife out?"

"You know the Knights of Liberty?"

"Yeah," she said. "White supremacist goons connected to the Roaring Boys." She exhaled with disgust. "Christ, Michael, as a guy, can you tell me why they think these names are cool?"

I had an idea after seeing them in action. "They're cool to a certain type of guy who is still a ten-year-old in his head and a failure in adult life. But these guys are adults, and they have guns, and the ones I met are going to cause trouble."

She paused again. "How do you know that?"

"They're camped out near a cabin my wife and I use. I went there after I got out of prison to lay low, on the advice of my lawyer."

She paused, thinking.

"Who is your lawyer?"

"Nicole Wilkerson."

She let out another laugh. "I swear, this world gets smaller every day."

"You know her?"

"Yeah, you could say I know her. Haven't seen her for a while."

"Well, if you come to Bloomington, you can see her. And I can tell you everything I know about Armor and the Knights."

She paused again.

"Tell me more. Why are you working with the Knights?" There was an edge of caution in her voice.

I told her everything, about the captured kids, and the bounty program, and the fake suicide bomber vests, and how these drunken violent Knights wanted to dress these kids in Iranian clothing and blow them up in Bloomington. To galvanize support for the war.

"They said that Davis had sent word on the DL about the bounty program to the Roaring Boys, who had put out the message on social media and elsewhere."

Another pause. Then she spoke very quietly.

"You say these guys got word from the Roaring Boys to do this?"

"And they apparently got it from the White House."

Then, almost in a whisper, she said: "That lines up with some other things I've been hearing lately. They could be connected. Or not at all. Not sure."

I smiled and pumped my fist. "I can tell you more about that. And more, lots more, about Armor Security and the cyber hack that started everything. We can help each other." My heart was pounding.

"Looks like I'm coming to Bloomington," she said.

I was surprised. "You are?" I whispered back.

"Yes," she said, louder now. "I've been there plenty, actually. You'll be around all week?"

There were a hundred different ways I could answer that, given my recent life, but I just said, "Yes. I will be."

I just hoped that this was true.

CHAPTER 31

THURSDAY, JUNE 29.

Janine Wood was at my door about thirty hours later. She's in her mid-thirties, with short, dark brown hair and triple piercings in her ears, the silver studs an act of defiance to Washington's establishment media. Her face is intense but pretty, with tan skin and symmetrical features. She wore light-blue jeans and a black blazer with a white button-down shirt. She's even taller than she seemed on television.

She had come to my house because, as Hannah said, "If they're watching you, and they probably are, they may as well see how many cards you're playing."

Nicole had said nothing, but when Janine arrived and they shook hands, I saw a professional formality in Nicole that I had not seen before. One that suggested a history with emotion attached.

"Nice to see you again," Nicole said.

"And you, Nick. Who'd have thought?" Janine said, smiling, as if to warm up Nicole. But Nicole stayed cool, and I didn't think this was the time to ask questions about their past. I had my own future to focus on.

The Guatemalan family were camped out in our den, eating pizza and watching a telenovela on Univision. They were relaxed, even laughing. They looked less tired than when we met. Zahra and the two lawyers and I met with Janine in the kitchen.

Nicole and Hannah sat opposite Janine at the table, both of them drinking Pam's peppermint herbal tea. Zahra sat at the head of the table with a glass of red wine. I sat next to Janine. She sipped on the IPA I had offered her, and I sipped on mine as I told her my story.

She frowned as she listened. "So you don't remember clicking on this link, but they think you helped Iran hack into Armor and threw you and your wife into prison?"

"That's right. And Nicole got me out. Hannah is trying to get Pam out."

Janine smiled at Nicole as if she was going to say something, but Nicole moved the conversation along:

"That's right. Hannah's working on that now."

Janine nodded and looked at me. "And your wife is not only Iranian but works with Iranians?"

I took a sip of beer and nodded. "She's an archival producer for documentary films. She's working on one at the moment about how Iranians who fled the revolution in 1979 punched way above their weight out in the world beyond Iran. Proof in point is the director, Zahra Nasseri."

Janine smiled. "Zahra Nasseri? I love her work. It's so cool that your wife gets to work with someone like her."

"And to be sitting at a table having a drink with her as well," I said, looking at Zahra.

Janine sputtered into her beer. "You're Zahra Nasseri?" she said to Zahra, who beamed in delight at being recognized. I had not used any surnames when I made the introductions. It was nice to see how much this meeting meant to Janine, who was looking at Zahra like a goggle-eyed groupie.

"I am," Zahra said. "I came from my home in LA to help get Pam out of prison."

I winced every time I heard the words "Pam" and "prison."

Janine leaned thoughtfully on an elbow. "This whole thing smells bad. I mean, Davis and his cronies, especially Christopher Clay, have had Iran in their sights ever since Davis first thought about running for the White House."

"Who's Christopher Clay?" Nicole asked.

"Wasn't he one of those neocon nutjobs in one of the Bush administrations?" Hannah said.

Janine smiled in appreciation. "You're spot on. He was a security adviser—behind the scenes—to baby Bush."

"Behind the scenes?" Nicole was puzzled, but there was a touch of aggression in her question.

"Yeah, he was one of those shadowy guys that Bush liked to have around to bolster his gut feelings about geopolitics," Janine said, smiling at her. "It was Clay, so I'm told, who came up with the weapons of mass destruction scam. You know, the one that brought American democracy to the people of Iraq."

Janine's smile remained, but her blue eyes glittered with the contempt she felt for Christopher Clay, who, I had to admit, I knew little about. He really was in the deep shadows. "But Clay always wanted to take out Iran," she continued, "and when Davis got elected, he saw he had a fellow traveler. They both wanted the glory. And they found their hook to do that when Iran hacked into Armor and then the Treasury Department."

She looked around the table and then continued: "Or do we think that was a setup, a manufactured excuse to attack Iran? I don't have proof yet, but it all seems too convenient to me."

We all let that thought hang in the air for a moment. My heart started pounding and I took a gulp of IPA. Maybe it was a setup? But why would I be at the center of it? I had no power or influence. And neither did Pam. We were just some married couple in Indiana.

Janine held up her beer, as if to sip, but instead said, "So you said you have some photos to show me?"

"Pictures and sound," I replied.

"Too bad we don't have popcorn," Hannah said. Janine laughed. Nicole frowned.

I put my Samsung burner phone on the table in front of Janine, and she scrolled through the pictures. Then I played her the voice recording of me and Montrose, the Knight Commander, putting together the suicide bomber plan.

"So this looks legit," Janine said and handed me back my phone. "I have met these Roaring Boys in D.C.—what a fucking stupid name—and know that they have more than a few friends in the Davis"—and she said Davis like it was a word that would get your mouth washed out with soap—"so-called government."

Janine took another sip of beer and grinned. "So it's no surprise that the Roaring Boys have franchised out their evil to these rubes from Flyover. And a bunch of other clans, too, I'm sure. I wonder how Davis pays them these bounties. Venmo? Zelle? PayPal?"

Even Nicole laughed at that. It was a classic Davis kind of trick. Sure, go catch immigrants and we'll pay you for them, but good luck collecting from us.

"It will be an issue when these guys want to turn their catches into suicide bombers," Nicole said. "A very messy one."

Janine nodded at Nicole and smiled. "Yeah, and that's where I come in."

I cleared my throat, prepared to tell her we needed her help, but Hannah beat me to it. "Here's the thing, Janine. We need more. We need evidence connecting the bounty program to Davis. Threatening to out Davis is what will coerce the government to release Pam."

Janine stopped to think as she drained her beer. "Yes, I agree. I think what Michael has is great, but what I might be able to get will push us across the line."

Her eyes glittered with the story she saw in her head. "I have someone on the inside."

"What do you mean?" Nicole said, again with heat in her voice.

Janine smiled at her. "You remember. That source I had in Davisland?"

Nicole looked down and gave a quick nod. So they did have a history.

"So apparently, they have a tape. Of Davis and Clay 'saying bad things.'"

"Do you know what they're saying?" Zahra asked.

Janine shook her head. "Not specifically, they won't be too specific. But they say it's something about rounding up and deporting immigrants. Perhaps even about the bounty program. They have stopped drinking the Davis Kool-Aid because they finally got sick to their stomach, shall we say."

"Can we hear this tape?" Nicole asked.

Janine put her beer down on the table. "I don't have it yet. I've just heard about it. The source is nervous about what Davis and Clay will do if the tape gets out. He might never leak it to me or anyone else. But we might be able to get it if we combine it into a bigger story that is sure to take Davis down. I think that's the only way the source will give up the goods."

"How would we do that?" Nicole asked.

"With what Michael just told us. We just need more footage of the Knights and of what they're planning to do. We need to capture the drama for the screen. If we combine my source's tape with the on-the-ground imagery of the scheme in action—the bombs about to detonate in the crowd—then we just might have enough to get Davis. I can make this happen. I just need to embed myself with the Knights."

I realized then that Janine wanted to film the Knights in action, sending the kids into the crowd with the vests on.

"You don't want to do that. What if the Knights sniff this out and catch you? These guys are dangerous," Nicole said, not as my lawyer, but with the tone of someone who was still in love.

And that's how Janine heard it. "I know, babe, but this is the only way. How else can we free Pam and take down Davis? It has to be big."

They exchanged a look, one which said they had been down this kind of road before together. Maybe that's why they weren't together anymore.

Nicole nodded slowly, seeing that Janine was right. "And so with this recording of the president and the guys that Michael met on Hoosier Hill, you can tie them together to a great crime."

Janine smiled. "And get Davis into that orange jumpsuit that he so richly deserves."

I nodded. I wanted to get Pam out. Janine wanted to take down Davis. Maybe we could kill two birds with one stone.

"But will it even matter?" Zahra asked. "Has America backslid so far into dysfunction and rage that even if we out Davis for his bounty program and get it all on film, the people, the Congress, the courts won't even care enough to do anything about it?"

"Good question," said Janine. "We don't know. But we have to try. What else can we do?"

Zahra nodded. "This will be a test of America's conscience."

"I will give you the address and a key to the cabin," I said. "But Janine," I repeated my warning, "these guys are willing to kill."

Janine nodded. "I know that. But if we don't try, then we won't ever know if we can get back our country, will we? Or get you back your wife."

"You're right. I just want you to know how dangerous they are."

"I understand. I've covered a lot of nutsos in my time as a journalist. Been to a lot of dangerous places. Mean streets. War zones. It's part of the job and I know how to handle these people. I will be fine. This could be huge if we play it the right way. It's worth it."

I felt a rush of heat in my stomach. She was going into danger to get her story. Was it love of country? Or raw ambition as a journalist? It didn't matter. She was motivated to help, to take down Davis. I had to do everything I could to help her, because if she got what she needed from the Knights, we might get her source's tape of Davis and Clay.

Hannah leaned forward, her face serious but a little wary. "The thought occurred to me," she said. "Can we use what you told us to try to get Pam out of prison now?"

Janine leaned back. "Well, good question. I suppose you can say the tape exists, and you have heard some of it. Just don't say my name. Whatever you do, don't say my name, okay?"

"Understood," Hannah said.

This got me excited. Maybe I would see Pam soon.

"So you told the Knights that you were going to get them suicide-bomb vests?" Janine asked.

I nodded.

"And so why do I show up to the cabin? How do I introduce myself to them? What's our story?"

"You can be my sister or something. Keeping an eye on the property while I do my work in town."

Janine grinned. "I like that, bro. Okay, what did you tell them your name was?"

I smiled at Nicole and Hannah. "Weiss. Joe Weiss."

They both laughed and Janine leaned forward to catch the joke.

"It's the name of the FBI agent who's after me and Pam," I said. "But she's a J-O."

"Ah, got it. Okay, I can be Janine Weiss. These guys won't know who I am. They don't watch GNC."

Our laughter was punctuated by the doorbell. I looked to Nicole, and she looked at her watch. And nodded.

"That should be the medication delivery," she said and went to the door.

She returned with a polyethylene bubble mailer. She ripped it open and pulled out a dark blue passport. She opened it and looked at Zahra. "Here you go, Ann-Marie Mathieu. Citizen of Canada."

Zahra took the passport and looked at her new self. "Je me souviens," she said. It was the motto of Quebec and the motto of Iranians of her generation. "I remember."

Nicole then turned to me. "Do you have any of that two grand I fronted for your trip?"

I felt like an idiot. It was still in my wallet. I had forgotten all about it because I hadn't touched it.

"It's all here," I said.

Nicole took the money and handed it to Zahra. "This should be enough to get you and the family to Canada," she said. Then she handed Zahra the keys to her SUV. "I'll pick it up in Montreal. Love that city."

CHAPTER 32

THURSDAY, JUNE 30.

Zahra and the Guatemalans left before sunrise the next day. Our street was empty. Some of my neighbors had left town and boarded up their windows on their houses beforehand, as if we were expecting a hurricane. And we were, a kind of human hurricane: the windows were boarded to stop looting.

The electricity was still glitchy thanks to the grid attacks by the Iranians. It was hard to believe that initial attack on the grid was only nine days earlier. It would be fine if they just stuck to the White House, though I realized that maybe it was Davis who was knocking out the grid. To gin up support for his offensive. It was normal to be paranoid in this country, and now, for me, after everything that had happened, it was essential.

So it was an early-morning farewell to Zahra and the Guatemalans. They all hugged me. They were nervous; I could see that in their eyes.

"Give Pam my love when you see her," Zahra said.

"You can count on that," I replied.

Then Zahra gave me a kiss on the cheek and squeezed my hand. "You are a good man, Michael. The world needs men like you."

And then they drove off.

The sun was just up when I started the Prius and aimed it toward Indianapolis. Or its suburb, Whiteland, in Pleasant Township. It was finally time: I was going to try to get Pam out of prison.

I met Hannah in a coffee shop in a strip mall about a mile from Public Protection Center #8.

"You know what you're doing?" Hannah asked me, practically inhaling the foam on her cappuccino.

I nodded. "I'm going to convince Agent Weiss that I am dangerous. So dangerous that she cannot destroy me and Pam without consequences. Bad ones, for her."

Hannah smiled, her dark eyes beaming with pride that Michael Housen, a marketing guy who likes baseball and IPAs, was going to play hardball with the FBI.

Special Agent Weiss was waiting for us in the parking lot of the Public Protection Center, along with her trio of cybercrime agents, McGarvey, Ortiz, and Cole. Hannah told her that we couldn't meet inside, as we had something electronic to show her, and outsiders' electronic devices weren't allowed in the Davis prisons unless they were flat-screens bolted onto the recreation room wall, tuned to Davis News, broadcasting Davis Truths.

"Mr. Housen," Agent Weiss said, standing with her arms crossed. "Nice to see you again."

I nodded.

"Mr. Housen has acquired something we think you'd like to see," Hannah said. Her New York accent made it sound like an offer Weiss couldn't refuse.

"Show and tell," Agent Weiss said. Agent Ortiz had an iPad and was taking notes.

I showed Weiss the photo of the Knights with their bounty app. And then I showed her the photo of the three immigrant kids, tied to trees, with the Knight Commander, Robert Montrose.

"So we have some militia guys allegedly snatching illegal aliens for the government based on social media statements," Weiss said. "A lot of voters would vote for that."

She was unimpressed, as we had expected. Then I told her what the militia guys planned to do with the kids and where they planned to do it.

"How do I know that's true?" she asked, but she was paying attention now. So were her agents, who exchanged worried looks. Agent Ortiz stopped typing.

"Because they told me." I pushed play and she listened to the plot unfold.

"You told them you'd help them get the vests so you could buy time to tell all this to me," Weiss said, as if she was the smartest kid in the class.

"I told them that to get my wife out of this place, right here."

Weiss folded her arms, unconvinced. "I'm confused, Mr. Housen. What you're describing is really bad, if it happens to be true. And we can let the right folks in law enforcement know and try to stop them from harming those kids any more. But why would I release Pam because of that?"

That's when Hannah said, "We also have a recording of President Davis and Christopher Clay authorizing the very program that led to these kids being captured."

Weiss's eyes flickered with fear and suspicion. She looked at her team. Then back at us. "How do I know that's true?"

Hannah smiled, like someone holding all the face cards of the same suit. "Because, as an officer of the court, I could get in serious trouble for lying to a law enforcement officer."

For the first time since I met her, Weiss looked vulnerable. As if what she had just heard had knocked her off her perch, and now she needed another one.

"And you also," Hannah continued with a smile, "might already know a thing or two about this bounty program, Agent Weiss."

"Blackmailing a law enforcement officer is not a good idea," Weiss said, trying to sound tough, but I knew what to say to that.

"We're not blackmailing anyone. We have come to you with information. I want my wife released from prison."

Weiss looked at me with new regard, as if she had underestimated how far I would go to protect myself and Pam. "I hear an 'or else' in your offer, Mr. Housen."

"That's because there is one," I said. "If you don't let her out, then we will let the media know about all of this—the Knights, the kids, the bounty program, the tape of Davis and Clay."

My heart was thudding.

"You can go back to the office," Weiss said abruptly to her team of agents. I saw Ortiz exchange a glance with Cole, which suggested they knew how Weiss rolled when she was off the books. Only McGarvey didn't seem to get it.

"Do you want backup, ma'am?"

"No," she said.

The trio walked quickly away. Weiss watched until they were out of earshot, then turned back to us.

"You can't go to the media with any of this," Weiss said, now calm, cool. I could tell by the look on her face that she knew about Davis's bounty scheme and thought it was plausible the tape existed. Maybe she was even involved in the program, as Hannah had suggested. Either way, she didn't want the tape to get out.

"Then let my wife out."

Weiss thought about this. Then she looked at Hannah. "You're not going to be so foolish as to ask for anything in writing now, are you?"

Hannah paused, as if weighing the merits. "You haven't charged my client, so no, there's nothing in writing." She smiled. Point made.

"How do I know you won't just go to the press after I let her out?" Weiss asked me.

"Because you'd just throw us both back in jail if we did."

She looked straight into my eyes: "I will let her out but don't think we're done with either of you. You and your wife helped Iran start this war, and your time will come."

I waited in the parking lot alone until the sun was over my head, at high noon. It was maybe an hour, but it felt like a year. I had never been more excited or nervous in my life. Then Hannah emerged from the Public Protection Center, holding Pam's arm. Her long silky black hair sparkled in the bright light.

I ran to Pam and hugged her. We both started sobbing. She clung to me like I was the lifeline in a hurricane. We hugged for a long time, and then she leaned back and looked at me as if seeing me anew. She gently grabbed my wet cheeks with her soft hands and kissed me on the mouth. I could feel my entire body relax for the first time in more than a week.

We drove home and showered off the debris of the week behind us then we fell into bed and extended our kiss late into the afternoon.

And then we slept. For the first time in more than a week, I didn't have nightmares. I had my wife beside me. Again. And tomorrow, we would come up with a plan to go forward. To reclaim our quiet life together.

CHAPTER 33

FRIDAY, JULY 1.

"Here you go, baby," I said, handing Pam a piping-hot cup of coffee as she was lying in bed trying to wake up for the day. Her turquoise eyes and silky black hair made me feel like I was home for the first time in years.

"Thanks, hun."

"How'd you sleep?" I asked, settling back in next to her.

"I slept okay . . . under the circumstances. You?"

"A lot better than I have the last several days."

"So," she said, sitting up and holding her coffee in both hands, "were they okay to you in there?"

"It was fine," I said, not wanting to worry her. "It wasn't fun, but it wasn't too bad. Agent Weiss is pretty nasty. She's playing a game we need to figure out. She thinks I clicked that link on purpose to let Iranian hackers into Armor. That, or she's part of some big effort to frame us and there really was no phishing email at all. She wants blood either way."

"Yeah," she replied. "She's insane." Then she thought about what I had said. "Do you really think they're trying to frame us?"

I smiled at her. I didn't know. "It's crossed my mind, but now I think it's worth checking out. To put it mildly."

She smiled. Thinking.

"How about you," I asked hesitantly, "did they treat you okay?"

The look on her face told me the answer was no. But she forced a smile and said, "I will be fine. And it could have been a lot worse."

I wanted to know more, but I knew now was not the time to press.

"Where do we go from here?" she asked.

I took a big swig of coffee. "I don't know for sure. But I do know we need to prove one of two things: either that I did not click on that link on purpose in cahoots with Iran or that something bigger is going on and I never clicked on it at all. The answer resides at Armor Security."

"Do you really think something bigger could be going on?"

"I'm not sure, but it's possible. Janine Wood called me after the hack to try and get information and now she's helping us."

"Really?" Pam asked. "Janine Wood?"

"Yes, really. And she said this Davis adviser, some guy named Christopher Clay, hates Iran, just like Davis, and they found their reason to invade because of Armor. Because of the hack. She asked if I thought it was a setup."

"But why would they pick Armor? And why would they be out to get us? Me and you? Who are we?"

"I don't know. We need to find out if they are."

"And what do we do if the email was a fake and you didn't let the hackers into Armor and there's something more going on?"

"I guess it would depend on who was behind it all, how far up the chain this all goes." I spoke in a low voice, exuding calm, but inside I felt terror. What if we did expose a setup? I thought. What would happen to us then? Could make the wrong people our enemies. It might even make things worse.

Pam felt it, too, as she looked at me with fear in her eyes. She took another sip of coffee. "When Weiss was questioning me a few days ago she said some things that made me think she's working with people at the highest levels."

"Yeah, me too. She's ambitious. And that can be very dangerous."

We sat quietly, staring out the window, contemplating. Neither of us spoke for several minutes. The sun's glare was growing stronger as the morning took hold.

"Could she be working with Davis?" she asked.

"Could be," I replied. "We need to escape to Mexico now and hope we make it. Or we need to find out."

Seeing the scared look on my face, she smiled at me and grabbed my hand. "As nice as it would be to have a few days on a Mexican beach before they found us, I plan on living a long time here and taking our grandkids there for vacation. So, after you, Michael Housen. Lead us on our quest."

I smiled back at her. "No, Pam Farahmand . . ." I paused as she stared at me wide-eyed. "We're going to solve this one together."

CHAPTER 34

FRIDAY, JULY 1, LATER.

Nicole Wilkerson and Hannah Gottlieb showed up early with a bag of pastries and a carton of coffee from Crumble's bakery, one of the best in Bloomington.

I turned up WFIU, NPR's classical music station out of Indiana University, and we all sat at the kitchen table and munched the cinnamon pastries and drank coffee as Camille Saint-Saën's "The Youth of Hercules" blasted out for the benefit of whoever was listening in.

"You look good," Hannah said to Pam, who smiled tightly.

"For someone who has spent a week in a Davis prison," Pam said.

Hannah laughed. "Well, we'll do our damnedest to keep you out of that hotel."

"Thanks. It's not a points program I want to have," Pam said.

I asked Nicole if Zahra had made it to Canada.

"Yes, she and the Guatemalans got safely across last evening. She sent me this photo . . ."

She pulled up the photo of Zahra and the Guatemalans standing on the Canadian side of the border at the Ambassador Bridge, with the Canadian maple leaf in the foreground and the Stars and Stripes in the distance. The look on their faces was one of relief, joy, and possibility.

I felt tears welling in my eyes at their success and how it could so easily have turned out the opposite. If the Knights of Liberty had found them before Cecil and I heard baby Rafael cry out in the night, then they'd be tied to trees. Or worse.

I am not superstitious but took their safe passage as an omen. Things would turn out alright.

"So what are you guys going to do now?" Nicole asked.

"We need to prove we aren't working with Iran," I said. "That I didn't click that link on purpose. Or that this whole damn thing is a scam, and we were set up."

"We need to prove Michael is innocent," Pam said quietly.

We all looked at her as if she had a plan. It turned out that she did.

"Michael has to go back to work."

Nicole leaned back from the table. "They could do more damage to him there," she said. "Maybe Armor is best avoided."

Hannah nodded. She clearly agreed.

"No, Pam's right," I said. "I need to confirm that the truth at Armor is what they say it is. And we have Janine on our side now. They will know that if they mess with me, they are messing with her."

"Assuming Janine survives those . . ." Nicole trailed off. Then she looked up at us. "She and I were together. In D.C." She paused. "Together as a couple. But it didn't work out."

Pam reached across the table and squeezed Nicole's hand. "I'm sorry," she said, and Nicole squeezed back.

"It's no one's fault," Nicole said. "Just one of those things. So I came back to Bloomington. I just didn't expect to see Janine here, too, but hey, she's on our side. And we'll do everything to help her get the goods."

"Have we heard anything from her yet?" I asked.

Nicole nodded. "Yeah she texted me this morning. She got to the cabin yesterday afternoon, camera in hand. Said the Knights have fully overtaken the cabin. They believed her story, that she's Joe's sister, just checking up on the place. There were a few dicey moments in the beginning, but things are on track now. She even has a few clips already. Still needs a lot more footage."

"Good to hear."

"Yeah."

"Though with those guys things can change really quickly. She needs to stay on her toes and abort right away if necessary."

"Agreed," Nicole said, and exhaled. "That's what I texted her back." And then she changed the subject: "So, what's our next move here?"

"Michael has to find out what really happened at Armor," Pam said quietly. "There's only one way to do that, and that's inside Armor."

Nicole thought about this, her hands folded before her like she was a judge. "Okay, but at the first sign of trouble, you bail, okay?"

I nodded. I wondered if I would even see the trouble coming. I certainly had missed it the last time.

"We need to work on a plan of what you're going to get on Monday and how you're going to get it," Nicole said.

"He can't go in on Monday," Pam said.

"Of course, it's the Fourth of July," Hannah said.

I felt my heart speed up and a smile splash across my face.

"What is it, Mikey?" Pam asked.

"Every Fourth of July, Caleb hosts a party at his house. I've been keeping an eye on my email and his are still getting thorough, even with the spotty grid. So the party is still on. He's trying to keep things business as usual at Armor even though that whole place is falling apart."

Now Pam smiled. "And every year we've found a reason not to go. But now we have a reason—to gather information from people at Armor, to see if we get any clues."

"What do you mean clues?" Hannah asked.

"We need to talk to people," I said. "And preferably after they've had a few drinks, to see if they can shed any light on what happened to us and what's happening now. Maybe we will learn something; maybe we won't. But it's a good place to start."

I squeezed Pam's hand. "Want to go celebrate the Fourth with me at the home of Armor's founding genius?"

She squeezed back. "I wouldn't dream of being anywhere else."

CHAPTER 35

MONDAY, JULY 4.

This being the Fourth of July under martial law meant that there were checkpoints in places where just days ago there were only traffic lights. The parade that ran through downtown was over by the time we set out, but tanks and armored carriers on the road produced their own kind of parade as we made our way to Caleb's place.

Normally we'd drive right up Rogers Street through the center of the city, but the army had that route blocked off with Humvees parked diagonally. We thought about going up I-69 but suspected that the army or National Guard would have checkpoints in and out of the city, so with Pam navigating the GPS, we took side streets southeast and then swung back up toward Caleb's house. What would under normal circumstances be a twenty-minute drive today took forty minutes.

Caleb Wagner lived just outside the city, in Gramercy Park, a little northeast of Griffy Lake and the university. He lived on a six-acre lot with a majestic pool and professional-grade tennis court. The house was a one-and-a-half-story brick-and-wood architectural juggernaut. It had six bedrooms, five bathrooms, a bowling alley, and a movie theater. The six-car garage was about the size of our house. And, of course, an Armor camera was mounted to the wall in most rooms.

Caleb lived alone.

We did a drive-by in the Prius to check out the number of vehicles in the large open driveway and adjacent street. There weren't many, perhaps a dozen, but Bo's bright white vintage Mustang (blue stripe down the middle blazing) was there. And so was Kerry's red Indian Scout Bobber motorcycle.

There was no sign of any cop cars, marked or otherwise. If the FBI were watching this house today, they were probably doing it from the sky. I made a mental note to look up and smile at any drones.

We parked on the street, for a quick escape if we needed one. The sky was thick with heavy gray clouds. And with the hot, humid air that hit us when we stepped out of the car, a storm was likely to show up as another guest.

"You okay?" I asked Pam, squeezing her hand as we walked up. She looked dazzling in her orange-and-white summer dress. Her long black hair bounced a little with each step.

"I am," she said. "I feel a sense that justice is coming, you know?"

I knew. I just didn't have a clear idea of how we'd achieve it. But the way Pam smiled at me before she kissed me suggested that she just might know.

There was a note on the front door: "Party is out back! Happy 4th!" in red and black. Armor Security colors.

Pam and I walked around the side of the house. We could hear a vibrant mix of conversation and music. It was that southern heavy metal, extolling the virtues of some swamp somewhere. The same kind President Davis used during his campaigns. By hearing it, you could imagine the revival of the culture that inspired it: redneck, angry, gunning for revenge.

Pam and I rounded the corner into the patio by the pool and I saw Caleb conferring with Steve. Bo was hanging out with some people from IT, and Kerry was sipping a beer alone, their bare feet dangling into the deep end of the pool.

When Caleb clocked me and Pam, he looked surprised. The look on his whisker-stubbled face was at first one of shock, then of suspicion. What might he suspect? That I knew something he didn't? That the slippery Agent Weiss was now using us as a trap to get him? And if that was the case, what was he hiding? I squeezed Pam's hand as we walked toward him, smiling as if everything was normal as could be. Finally, he smiled back.

"Michael! Pam! What a pleasure to see you!" He was smiling, but his voice, usually so deep and confident, was high and tight. Short and thick as always, his blonde hair was shining with gel. He was wearing a white Hawaiian shirt with light blue shorts and annoying beige sandals that exposed far too much of his coarse feet. He extended his thick, hairy right arm and offered us his hand to shake, and we shook it.

"Michael!" Steve now joined in with the handshakes. "So happy to see you, my friend." He hugged me—squeezing tight for a few seconds—and then, his hands on my shoulders, looked me square in the eye. "So glad you're here. Then he turned to Pam, his long nose extending out toward her. "Great to see you again Pam."

He seemed both happy and nervous, his eyes darting over to Caleb, then back to us. His outfit was the same as Caleb's, but the colors were reversed: light-blue Hawaiian shirt and white shirts. His sandals were ever-so-slightly less annoying than Caleb's because Steve got pedicures.

"Glad we could make it this time," I said, and Caleb and Steve laughed.

"Yes, I heard you were, how shall I put it, helping the FBI with their inquiries," Caleb said.

A waiter, in a white shirt and red vest and blue trousers, sailed past us with a tray of white wine. Pam grabbed a glass and took a sip. She was more nervous than she looked.

"Yes, we were both doing that," I said quickly. "When we had helped them enough, they let us go."

Steve nodded. "Glad you got out of there. Was worried about you."

Then Caleb asked, "What did they want to know, Michael?"

"They wanted to know about life inside Armor. Corporate culture, that kind of thing."

Caleb stared at me, as if he now thought I was working for the FBI. It's what I wanted him to think.

"So they weren't investigating your Ad Supply adventure?" Caleb asked, as if my click on an Iranian phishing email that had launched an awful war was some kind of lark and not the thing that had killed thousands and landed me and Pam in Davis prisons.

"I think they're looking into everything. Right, Pam?"

Pam took a sip of wine. "Yes, I think so. They asked me a lot about Armor, too."

Caleb smiled at Pam. "What would you know about Armor?"

"What Michael tells me. He's a good watcher. I'm a good listener."

Caleb smiled at her as if she had just said that she knew sensitive things going on inside the company. We wanted to plant that thought.

"What's new with you guys?" I asked. "Armor hanging in there?"

"Well, we're—" Steve started to respond. Caleb cut him off: "Couldn't be better. This is an opportunity for Armor to learn and grow into something even better."

I nodded without responding. We all exchanged awkward looks.

"I'm thirsty," I said after a few seconds. "I need a beer." I took Pam's hand and wandered over toward a bar set up by a cabana. We could feel their eyes on our backs. There was an ice bucket full of Indiana IPAs: Westy, and Deal With the Devil, and Permanent Funeral were all there, as if Caleb was telling me something. I snatched a DFG and cracked it open just as Bo sidled up, looking surprised.

"Hey Mike, Pam," he said. He was drinking from a can of White Claw, and the flush on his chubby cheeks suggested he had already had a few. He was wearing a way-too-tight fluorescent-green tank top and red-white-and-blue American-flag shorts that fell well below his knees. His dark, curly hair was protruding out from an Oakland A's hat. His clothes didn't just not match—they were in violent conflict. "How are you both?"

"We're good man. How are you?"

"Couldn't be better," he said, holding up his White Claw. "I didn't think I'd see you guys here."

I took a sip of beer. "Why not, Bo?"

His face reddened. "I mean, you guys never come to these parties."

That was true. But his surprise suggested something else. Did Bo know we were in jail?

"Well, here we are," Pam said, smiling. "What's new, Bo?"

He blinked, still taking in the fact we were both standing in front of him. "Not much. Happy to see you both. I thought we'd lost our boy Mike, here."

"How's that?" I asked.

"Well, when you didn't come into the office . . ."

"What were people saying?"

Bo shook his head and looked around, checking out what Steve and Caleb were doing, but they were at opposite ends of the patio now, talking to small groups of Armor staff, and not paying attention to us. "People weren't saying much," Bo said. "Just Steve talked to me."

I didn't say anything. I just held my gaze, unblinking on him.

"Steve said you'd left town. Because of, well . . ." He turned to Pam and smiled.

"Because my family is from Iran?"

Bo nodded and finished off his White Claw. "Yeah. I guess the government has some concerns, from what I heard."

I took this in. What exactly had Steve told Bo? "Where did he say we went?"

Bo shook his head again, as if to clear it of White Claw. "He didn't know. He was very concerned about you both. Me too."

"Interesting. And good to see you, man," I said, and nodded toward the pool and took Pam's hand. We walked along the pool until we reached the deep end.

"Hey Kerry," I said.

"Hey Michael," they replied with a smile. "Hey Pam." Looking nice in a light-blue sleeveless summer dress that went just past their knees and was a nice compliment to their green eyes and red hair. They seemed very relieved to see us, and their smile was broad and happy.

Then looking up at the sky they said, "I think we're gonna get wet soon."

Pam nodded her head. "How are things in customer service these days? I bet 'interesting' doesn't begin to cover it."

Kerry smiled again. They had an open, hopeful smile, one that seemed so at odds with the world around us. "Yeah, these days, some of our customers need a lot of service. Everyone thinks our products are tainted 'cause of the hack. Not good for a security company."

A rumble of thunder punctuated the moment.

"How is your film going?" Kerry asked.

"Well, it's about Iran, so it has kind of stopped for a bit."

Kerry blushed. "Right. Of course. Can't wait to see it though. I love documentaries. I took a film class at Ivy Tech. Video technology."

"Did you learn how to edit film?" Pam asked.

Kerry shook their head. "No, it was more introductory stuff. How to read a film, mainly. And I guess there are a lot of ways to do that. I would have loved to learn how to edit."

Pam smiled. "I'm happy to show you some basic stuff. I mean, I know how to edit on DaVinci Resolve. It's freeware. Very user-friendly. Great stuff."

Kerry smiled. "Offer accepted with major props," Kerry said. "I'm a techie at heart."

"Do you get much tech stuff in customer service?" Pam asked, being polite.

The thunder rumbled again, louder and closer now. Rain was moments away.

Kerry smiled. "Not really. It's pretty minor tech. I keep our website portal updated, which isn't hard. And we keep a record of all the calls. We record them all and save them as MP3s, so we can have them transcribed if we need them."

This was news to me. "How long do you keep them for?" I asked.

Kerry shrugged. "I'm actually not allowed to delete any. Those are my orders."

The sky opened up and the rain pounded down hard, bouncing off the patio. We all made our way for the cabana, which was an idea that everyone else had, so I grabbed Pam's hand and we ran instead toward the house. We weren't going to go inside. We just wanted to get under the sloping roof that hung over the patio.

The kitchen led out onto the patio, and I glanced at the kitchen window, which looked expensive, a double-glazed job that kept things quiet inside. Steve and Caleb were in the kitchen, and I pressed my face against the glass to catch their attention, to wave goodbye. Steve glanced toward me, then quickly turned away. Then Steve said something to Caleb, and Caleb's face went red with fury. Steve then put his hands up, as if trying to summon reason from some magical place, but Caleb wasn't having it. And then he decked Steve with a sudden punch that landed squarely on his massive nose. Steve's head snapped back, and he grabbed his face with both hands. I could see bright red blood gushing through his fingers and down his arms.

It was time for us to leave.

CHAPTER 36

MONDAY, JULY 4, LATER.

By the time Pam and I made it home, the downpour had calmed to a drizzle. But inside, I was anything but calm. My head was pounding.

"Happy Fourth!" Grant Woollard said, appearing as we got out of the car. "Good to see you back home."

Pam looked at me with a little surprise in her turquoise eyes, then smiled at Woollard. "It's good to be home."

He moved in close, his smile still there but his blue eyes wary. "There were people poking around here," he said, barely above a whisper. "This afternoon, just after you left."

I thought about that. Why did he know when we had left? Was he watching us? But for whom? The FBI?

"What did they look like?" Pam asked.

"Three guys, wearing overalls and baseball caps. Maybe one was a lady."

I looked to Pam and she said, "What did they do? They didn't go inside . . ."

He shook his head. "All I know is that they went out back, in your garden, for about fifteen minutes. Seemed like maybe they got into the garage too. Couldn't quite tell. Then they came out and drove away."

We had nothing of interest in our garden except our tomato plants, our little portable charcoal grill, and a picnic table. And the garage was just a storage area.

"Did they have any gear with them?"

He nodded at me. "One of them had a tool kit."

"What did they drive?" Pam asked.

"Panel van. White. No markings."

I looked Grant Woollard in the eye. "Who do you think they were?"

He patted his beer gut. "Three people in overalls and ball caps, unmarked van, nosing around on the Fourth of July. I'd say law enforcement. I'd say they planted something out back."

Pam and I entered the house, and I turned on the TV, loud.

"What the hell would they plant out back?" I asked Pam.

"We'll look when it's fully dark," she said. "We don't know who is watching."

"Grant Woollard is watching," I said.

She gave me one of her Pam looks, head tilted down, eyes unblinking straight at me. As if to say "give me the complete book on him." I didn't have that. I just said, "He's been helpful. Fed Cecil while I was in prison."

She nodded. "Okay. So he's an ex-cop who could be working with them. But I don't get that vibe."

Neither did I. But I couldn't wait until it was dark. "Let's just go sit at the picnic table," I said. "Bring Cecil out for an airing. And see what we can see."

Cecil was happy to sniff around the garden, and of course, it was Cecil's nose that told us where to look. He stopped by the fence between us and our neighbor's house and was sniffing the ground as if something had been buried.

We walked over to where he rutted, offering Cecil a treat of dried chicken strips, his favorite, in exchange for his detective work. He took the bait and loped off to chomp, and we looked at where he had been exploring.

Protruding from the earth was a small viewfinder. The viewfinder for a buried camera aimed at our picnic table.

I looked at Pam and smiled and said, "Cecil needs his dinner!" as cheerfully as I could.

She smiled back, and we went inside.

GNC was blaring something about rioting in San Francisco as I turned to Pam. She was shaking. I put my arms around her. We were whispering face-to-face, like a couple about to kiss in some twisted movie love scene set in a time of utter chaos.

"They buried a camera in our backyard?"

I told her about the Guatemalans who had been out there with Zahra. "They must have had eyes on the house and saw we had guests. So now they want a more constant view of who we have in the garden."

She took that in. "Do you think Grant is involved with this?"

I didn't think Weiss would use a former state trooper. It was beneath her lofty sense of self.

"It's Weiss," I said.

"How do you know?"

"She has a team of three agents in her cybercrime unit. Two guys and a woman. They were there with Weiss when I was first interrogated at Armor. Woollard clocked a woman. It was them."

Pam was still shaking. "Do you think they put them inside the house?"

I nodded. "Let's assume that they did. So all we have to do is pretend we don't know that."

She went and plopped down on the couch, in a state of exhaustion and despair. I sat next to her.

"We're okay," I said, squeezing her hand. "We just have to keep them off guard. All of them. And keep going."

She turned to me with that gentle Pam smile and squeezed my hand back. "I love you, Michael Housen," she said.

I replied to that with a kiss.

Then GNC started announcing news that interrupted the kiss and that was sure to ruin President Davis's Fourth of July hot-dog-eating contest at the White House.

"We have breaking news from Iran," the anchor said, a woman I didn't recognize, doing holiday duty. "The Supreme Leader of Iran, Ali Rhouhani, has announced that Iran is preparing to launch a tactical nuclear missile at the United Arab Emirates if President Davis does not cease what Rhouhani called 'this criminal act on the people of Iran' within twenty-four hours. Experts say such a strike would cause fallout in neighboring Saudi Arabia."

Pam and I looked at each other. For one thing, Ali Rhouhani was not dead, like Davis said he was. For another, if they hit the UAE, then Israel (UAE's staunch ally) might react. But how would the Iranians have nuclear missiles to launch?

Pam folded her arms. "My uncle told me this was going to happen. You know, in my role as a spy for Iran."

We laughed and then GNC went to the Pentagon, and up on-screen was the chairman of the Joint Chiefs of Staff, General Randall McCluskey. Short and rotund, he was in his early sixties, with a crisp graying buzz cut. His face was a map of Ireland, his voice seasoned with his Boston boyhood. Standing behind him were the other eight chiefs, looking very serious.

"We want the American people to know that we will defend the United States of America against all enemies, at home and abroad."

"Does that mean you support President Davis?" a reporter called out.

"He is our commander in chief," McCluskey answered. "We have a war to fight," he said, and then he and the Chiefs left the room.

I looked at Pam. "That wasn't exactly a ringing endorsement of Davis, was it?"

She nodded. "These army guys never say much," she said. She knew from her work in documentary land that the military in the US stayed out of politics. "It's what they don't say that matters."

I thought about what McCluskey had said. "Defend the United States of America against all enemies, at home and abroad." That could be taken a couple of ways. I hoped that he meant he would defend us from the treasonous Davis. But hope wasn't going to win me anything.

GNC then told us how Iran got the missiles. "Sources at the State Department confirm that Iran accepted the missiles as payment for the drones it provided to Russia in the war that Russia lost to Ukraine earlier in this decade. We are told that Russian scientists work with the Iranians to arm and aim the missiles."

A Davis Truth now crawled across the bottom of the screen: "If Iran uses tactical nukes, we'll show them what full force nukes look like."

Pam and I sank into the couch, numbed by the news. Davis was now openly threatening to launch nuclear war. Iran had just given him that low door in the wall.

"I'm calling my family in Iran," Pam said and held out her hand for my burner phone.

"The Signal app is already on it," I said.

Then I turned the TV up even louder as Pam made her call.

First, she called her uncle Behzad in Shiraz. I listened as Pam made contact, a smile of relief crossing her pale, lovely face. Then, in rapid Farsi, she asked him questions. She looked over at me and raised her eyes, then nodded. "Okay, *mersi*," she said, which the Persians had borrowed from the French and which even I knew was "thank you." Then she signed off.

"He's fine, and my cousins are in hiding, to avoid the call-up that Rhouhani has imposed on all males between eighteen and thirty. He says if anyone thinks that Iran has nukes, they may as well think Davis can build electric cars on Mars."

I laughed, imagining Davis on one of his Davis-ship rockets, floating around the red planet, trying to find an electric power station for his overpriced and fragile Davismobile.

"I'm calling Foad," Pam said. She smiled again with relief when she made contact and nodded as she listened. I heard Zahra's name a couple of times. Pam was frowning and thinking. Then she signed off and turned to me.

"He's okay?" I asked.

"He has no electricity or internet, but he had a connection to a BBC crew, so he put all of the footage on a hard drive, and the Brits sent it by UPS to Zahra's house in LA."

I sighed. "And Zahra is not in LA."

"But she needs that footage for her film. Foad got gold, not only of back then during the revolution but of now, with the US bombing him and his country."

"Is there someone in LA you can call to get it for her?"

"Only her ex-husband. And he wouldn't lift a finger." Pam ran a hand through her hair nervously. "I will call Zahra."

"It's so good to hear you," Pam said. "How's Canada? You're in

Montreal? Great city . . . Yes, yes, I'm fine. Michael and I just came back from a Fourth of July party . . . Yes, surreal begins to describe it . . . Look, Zahra, I have some great news and some challenging news. Foad got the footage we needed, and some more. Bonus stuff from now . . . Yeah, I knew you'd be happy. But Foad has no electricity, no internet. So he took advantage of a BBC crew he knew who took the footage he had compiled on a hard drive. And they sent it to you via UPS . . . Yeah, they sent it to you in LA."

Pam paused. I could hear Zahra's voice through the phone across the room. She wasn't angry; she was excited. "I don't think that's a good idea, Zahra," Pam said.

Then Pam listened and surrendered. She looked at me and grimaced. "Okay, you know best. And I know how incredibly important this footage is to you. But things are getting more hostile to Iranian Americans every day. Be careful. If you need a place to hide out, you know where we are."

Pam handed the phone back to me. "She's going to go back to LA herself and get the hard drive. This film is everything to her. She says it's too dangerous for me, and I'm the only person she would trust besides herself."

"Well, she has that Canadian passport giving her another identity. That helps."

Pam nodded. "She escaped the mad mullahs in 1979. She'll be okay." The way she said it was more to convince herself than to convince me. Then she grinned.

"I think it's okay to have another glass of wine right about now," she said. "Want a beer?"

"Sure," I replied. "It is, after all, the Fourth of July."

CHAPTER 37

TUESDAY, JULY 5.

Pam was sleeping like a baby hours later, in the wee hours of the night. But I was wide awake. I was sitting at the little desk in our bedroom scrolling online on my laptop, trying to figure out if the feds were playing a game with Armor and me. I had allegedly clicked on an Iranian phishing email and now after bombing Iran for more than two weeks, the US was threatening nuclear warfare against the country.

I found the death toll so far. We had killed more than fifteen thousand Iranians. The Davis government called every Iranian a soldier in the service of the Islamic republic. The UN and the civilized world called them civilians. Our own security services had killed six hundred US civilians in their application of martial law.

I knew that if Agent Weiss had a tap on my laptop, then I was leaving a trail, so I decided to make that trail interesting. I typed "Christopher Clay" into the search box. Surprisingly, for a guy who had been so involved in shaping American foreign policy, there wasn't much out there. Not even his own Wikipedia page. It was as if Christopher Clay had his own team of internet washers to keep him in the shadows. None of the articles I found had any pictures of him.

There were references to him in articles from the *Washington Post* and the *New York Times*, and they were not flattering. The *Post*, in an op-ed by a former intelligence agent, called him "the most dangerous man in America." The *Times* said that he had been brought in to advise the Boris Johnson government on how to punish all the Russian oligarchs they had allowed into Britain after the Russians invaded Ukraine. It was Clay who had come up with the sanctions plan that was so swift and effective that it left oligarchs' yachts stranded in ports around the world and the oligarchs stranded, too, when commercial airlines eliminated Russia as a destination. And no one would let them use their private jets to escape.

I knew there must be more than this. Janine Wood thought he might be involved in the Armor hack.

I wanted to check in with Janine but didn't want to put her in any danger. I sent her a text. "How are you sis?" I asked.

I had barely hit send when my phone rang. I jumped up and hustled out of the bedroom so as not to wake Pam. I didn't recognize the number but thought it might be Janine, being careful.

"Weiss? Where's my fucken bombs?"

It was the Knight Commander, Robert Montrose, and he sounded pretty drunk.

"I'm working on it," I said. He had told me that two weeks would not be a problem for me to get him the goods, and here, after only a week, he was cussing at me in the middle of the night.

I could hear him take a sip and swish the booze in his mouth. "I don't believe you," he said. He was angry, and he had hostages, and I could hear the threat between the lines. I don't have a lot of experience dealing with homicidal drunks who want to kill teenage boys, but I knew I had to keep those kids alive.

"You'll believe me when you see what I have lined up," I said.

"Then show me. I want to see evidence."

I shook my head. "Okay," I said. "It's at the office. I'll send it to you tomorrow."

He paused again and sipped. "You mean later today."

It was after midnight. "Yes, later today."

"And when can I get my hands on the goods?" he said, a little more curious than angry now.

"I think by the end of the week," I replied. "I'm just waiting on the detonators."

I knew that if I was going to succeed in my lie, I had to pay attention to the details. So I hustled back to my laptop and searched "best detonators for suicide bombs." The UN had a very helpful site and I scrolled down until I found what I needed. "I am going to get you electronic signal detonators," I said. "You operate them via remote control. In case your bombers get a case of the nerves or try to turn themselves in, you can finish the job on your phone. Armor uses them. I'm just getting them shipped from the plant that makes them in Kentucky."

"It's what we call a dead man switch," said Montrose, in a happier voice. "That's a good plan, Weiss. A good plan. These fuckers are costing a fortune to keep alive."

I closed my eyes in relief.

"I met your sister," he said. "She's been hanging around us. Taking videos. She looks like a dyke." He was angry again.

I paused now, wanting to keep everything moving forward. "It's her sense of style. Kind of like you guys wear red helmets and black vests, you know?"

He was silent.

"I'm joking, Robert. She's a scientist, and she can help you set up the gear when it comes."

"You better be bringing it," he said.

"Yeah, I'll be bringing it."

There was another pause. "'Cause if I don't have my bomb stuff by the end of the week, I'm going to kill these fuckers." He took another swig. "And get to know your sister a lot better."

Then he hung up.

CHAPTER 38

TUESDAY, JULY 5, LATER.

"Hey Mike!" Bo said a few hours later at the office. He was surprised to see me walk past his cubicle, back at work, after the holiday weekend. Like normal.

The tone of his voice was anything but normal. He sounded worried.

"Hey Bo," I said with a smile. "You stay late at the party?"

Bo rose to greet me with a handshake. He was wearing a white shirt and a plaid suit. No tie today, and no socks with his espadrille slip-ons. He was dressed, of all things, like a normal person. But why? Was he being interviewed by Weiss? He looked around. Steve's door was shut, and Caleb's office was empty, and those were the two places that his eyes landed.

"No, I left a little after you guys did." He lowered his voice to a whisper. "It got kind of weird."

If Caleb was punching out Steve in the kitchen, I could only imagine.

"Oh, really? What happened? Did Steve go skinny-dipping?"

Bo's eyes bugged out at that thought, and he seemed to relax a bit. "No public nudity, no. But Steve had a bloody nose." His voice dropped again. "I think Caleb punched him out."

I jerked my head back. "Why would he do that?"

Bo grabbed my arm and steered me toward the kitchen. "You need a coffee, right, Mike?"

"I do."

Bo fired up the Keurig K-Duo 12-brew, then opened the fridge and grabbed the half-and-half. "I know you like a little coffee with your cream," he said, handing me the carton.

"What's up, Bo?" I asked. "I mean, why would Caleb punch Steve?"

Bo shook his head. "I know things have been very strained between them. Since the FBI thing."

"Caleb must have taken a beating on the stock."

"We all did."

Changing the subject, I said: "Bo, can you get me an Armor invoice?"

He nodded. "Sure." Then he thought about it. "Why?"

I had to make it seem like the most reasonable request ever. So I took a risk and went the other way. "I need a blank one. I need to create a fake invoice for explosives and such for a guy who's making some suicide bombs."

Bo's eyes bugged out again and he laughed. "That's funny, Mike."

I grinned at him. "Seriously, Bo, can you send me the Armor invoice template?"

I needed the company letterhead on an invoice to convince the Knights that things were in motion and that I had the power they believed I had.

"Sure, no problem," he said, satisfied. "I'll email you the template."

That was something I did not want on an email chain. "Can you give me a hard copy instead? I will make some copies."

Bo nodded. "I'll drop one at your desk."

"Thank you," I said. And then drifted over to the customer service department to find Kerry.

They were happy to see me. "Hello, Michael. You and Pam left before all the fun started yesterday."

"So I heard. Bo told me Caleb punched Steve?"

Kerry shrugged. "And I think Steve punched Caleb. They were both a little battered when they came out of the house."

"I know tensions are high around here," I said.

"That was terrible what they did to you and Pam."

What did Kerry know? "What did you hear?"

"I heard everything from Bo. Just terrible."

What exactly did Bo know? What did he tell Kerry?

I wasn't sure what to say, so just kept quiet. I could see that Kerry was sympathetic and maybe even wanted to help me. And suddenly, I had an idea. "Yesterday you told me and Pam that you kept a record of all the calls that come into customer service."

Kerry nodded. "Yeah, we do."

"Could you do me a favor?" I said, lowering my voice. "I was supposed to have clicked on an email from a company named Ad Supply on January 25. This was the phishing email from Iranian hackers that apparently let them into Armor and led to this war we're now in with Iran."

Kerry arched their eyebrows. This was news to them, apparently.

"So I'm wondering if you could see if any unusual calls came in on that date. And maybe on the day this all went down. On June 21?"

Kerry went quiet, their auburn head bowed, and I thought that maybe I had gone too far in telling them about the email and what I wanted. It could make them my accomplice, should things get worse.

Then Kerry looked at me and smiled. "Happy to help. Just don't say a word to anybody, obviously."

"Yes, of course. Thank you."

I entered my office a few minutes later and saw a blank Armor invoice on my desk, as promised.

I made a few copies of it, then shut the door and got to work. I was going to create an invoice for three suicide bombs.

I wrote the C-4 plastic explosives and ball bearings and screws and bolts and electronic detonators in by hand, along with three suicide bomber training vests. I didn't put any dollar figures into the invoice, as I had promised this would be on the house. And frankly, I had no idea how much explosives cost.

Then I took a picture of the invoice and sent it to Montrose. A few minutes later he replied: "Very good."

CHAPTER 39

TUESDAY, JULY 5, LATER.

Cecil bounded up to greet me when I arrived home. Digging my fingertips into his thick brown fur soothed my fraying nerves, at least momentarily. The sun was setting, and he jumped up and down to let me know that he either needed to pee really badly or he had not been fed.

The street was quieter than usual. It looked like more of our neighbors had left, and the number of boarded-up windows had increased. So had the number of American flags flying from front porches of those who had stayed. Grant Woollard had a flag flying since we moved in two years ago, and it was still there. It was the ones that hadn't been there before, and I counted six of them, that made me wonder. Was it a gesture of support for the rule of law? Or for what President Davis was doing to destroy the rule of law? I suppose everyone had their own definition of patriotism.

I went into the house with Cecil jumping alongside me, licking my hand. He wanted dinner. Or maybe his second dinner. He had been known to try for seconds if one of us hadn't been present for the first feeding.

"Pam? Has Cecil been fed?" I called out as I walked into the kitchen. "Pam?"

No answer. My heart speeded up. Then I saw her sitting in our back garden under the glow of the receding sun, scrolling through her burner phone. She knew the camera would be watching her. So what was she doing?

"Hey Mikey," she said when I walked outside, IPA in hand.

I gave her a kiss before I sat down and pointed to the bouncing hound.

"Yes, I fed him," Pam said. "He's just trying to convince you that he gets no love or food unless you're around. Clever little pup."

I saw that she had moved the old wooden lawn chairs we had out back so that the camera couldn't see them. Clever. She saw me see that and said, "Yeah, I moved them because I wanted today's last blast of the sun on me. Feels great."

I knew that the FBI was probably listening to us inside and outside, no matter where we were. So I sat down in the chair next to Pam and was careful with what I said.

"What's up, babycakes?"

"I got a new phone," she said. "Do you like it?"

It was an older iPhone.

"Refurbished iPhone 7," Pam said. "All the bells and whistles."

"That's great. You can do online research and stuff."

"That was why I got it, Mikey." Then she Googled WFIU, the classical music station NPR ran out of Indiana U, and Mozart's Requiem blasted from the phone with the volume turned up full.

Then her face turned serious. She looked afraid.

"I did some investigating into Armor and its leaders."

"What's up hun. You okay? What did you find?" I said, putting my hand on her knee.

"Something is going on at Armor, Mikey. It's scary."

My midsection tightened.

She held up the phone. "This is what I found in a few hours, on the Wayback Machine. I expect that there's more."

I could see what she had been looking at. It was a photo of two guys. One of them was a much younger Steve Velarde. He was in some tropical place, by the ocean, with palm trees. And a flag flying in the background. I knew that flag. A white star on a red triangle, the sharp end leading into rows of blue and white stripes.

"They're in Puerto Rico," I said.

Pam shook her head. "They're in Cuba. The two flags are almost the same, but the colors are inverted. That's Cuba."

I looked at it more closely, and, suddenly, seeing the other guy in the photo made my heart speed up. He was wearing a pale yellow straw fedora. And had this weird smile. In the photo, he fixed that smile on Steve.

"Who's that with Steve?" I had seen him before, but couldn't place it.

Pam squeezed my hand. "That guy in the picture with Steve," she said, squeezing my hand again, "is . . . is none other than Christopher Clay."

"The shadowy guy Janine told me about—the Iran hawk working with the Davis government."

"That's right."

"How do you know?"

"I ran this picture through FaceFind, the app that has online search results for faces. It goes straight to Clay. Check out this article from the *Guardian*."

She showed me her phone and there was an article about Clay, along with a picture of him. It was unmistakably the same guy. The same crooked smile.

Where had I seen this guy before? Then it hit me. "I think he was the guy with Agent Weiss, the guy who came into the room when she was interrogating me."

Pam squinted at me.

"When I was first put in prison, Weiss tried to make me confess to clicking the phishing link on purpose. A guy came into the room we were in. Didn't speak. Sat behind me, but I saw him give Weiss the same smile he's giving Steve. Crooked. He looks way older now but Christopher Clay was there with Weiss during my interrogation."

Pam shook her head, nervous and concerned. She nodded toward the house. We got up and went inside.

"Christopher Clay was at your interrogation?" She sounded as if she didn't believe it.

"It's the same smile."

She thought about that, then looked at me with fire in her eyes.

"So what's he doing with Steve? How on earth does Steve know Christopher Clay?"

"I don't know, but I do know this isn't just some coincidence. My boss at Armor, the place where I supposedly clicked on a phishing link, which supposedly let Iranian hackers into Armor and the US government, knows Davis's close confidant Clay? And Clay, the Iran hawk, is part of the government's investigation into the hack, into us?"

Pam was nodding. She understood. Her eyes were wide, as the frenzied thoughts connected in her brain.

"Something's really, really wrong about all this," I said.

"Can you confront Steve? Can you ask him? He's always been good to you, right? He's your friend, right?

I knew now it was dangerous to think anyone at Armor was my friend. And I couldn't trust Steve anymore. If I was to find out what really happened, I would have to become an archivist myself. And go back into my own past at Armor.

CHAPTER 40

WEDNESDAY, JULY 6.

I hit the road an hour earlier than usual the next morning. The roads were mostly empty, and I had found a new route that was not only faster but kept me away from the checkpoints. I listened to the news on the radio. Defying the Supreme Court, the army had rounded up more than five thousand Iranian Americans and put them in camps in Nebraska and Iowa. I knew that they could come for Pam at any minute.

So here I was, early to work, hoping to poke around Steve's lair to see if I could find any more information that would explain Steve's connection to Clay and what had happened to me and Pam.

Pam had found the photo on the Wayback Machine online, which preserves old websites. It was from a trip taken by fraternity brothers from Alpha Kappa Sigma at Indiana University, here in Bloomington, to Cuba in 1998. The photo was on the fraternity's old website, which was taken down years ago. Steve must have just graduated, and Clay looked about the age Steve is now. To get to Cuba in 1998, you'd have to go through Canada. So it wasn't a casual kind of trip.

The fraternity was no longer active, but Pam had found her way in by going after Steve. She knew he had gone to IU, and like any good archivist, she had gone as far back in time as she could, and she had found gold.

Pam had prepared a set of notes and sent them to me through the Signal app, which is encrypted, so that if Agent Weiss had somehow found a way into our burners, she at least couldn't read our mail.

Steve majored in computer science and volunteered as a sophomore for the congressional candidacy of a former Special Ops guy who hated Iran with a passion. This guy had also been in Alpha Kappa Sigma, and he knew Clay, as they were of the same vintage. Steve may have met Clay on the Cuban trip.

But why would they go to Cuba, a Communist country with no direct way to get there from the US? Pam thought maybe it was because they were doing something dark and secret and didn't want to be found.

But what?

Maybe this was the beginning of the Game Changer, the secret project Steve was always alluding to without really explaining.

"Hey Mike," Steve said, emerging from his office and spotting me scrolling through Pam's notes on my burner phone in my office. "You're here early. How are you, my friend?"

I gave him a weary smile. "It's kind of hard to sleep these days, Steve," I said.

He put a hand on my shoulder and squeezed, like he was my best pal. His eyes flickered. He nodded at me awkwardly. "I'm just going to get a coffee . . ."

It was an invitation to follow him, so I did. He loaded up the Keurig K-Duo with coffee and pushed START. Then he looked at me as if he wanted to say something that his mind was still working out.

So, I just stayed silent, even though inside my head I was yelling "What the fuck were you doing with the guy who was with Agent Weiss when I was in jail? With the guy who helps President Davis do bad things to the world? What were you doing in Cuba with him? Why, Steve? What, Steve? Who are you, Steve?"

Steve poured me a cup of coffee and left about a quarter of the cup unfilled. "I know you like your dairy, Mike," he said, then punctuated that with his warm smile. Too warm, today.

I walked over to the fridge and pulled out a carton of half-and-half. I sniffed it, and it smelled like it was well on its way to becoming sour cream. I dumped it into the sink and threw the carton into the trash.

Steve winced in sympathy. "This martial law situation has created issues in the supply chain," he said.

"Sorry about that," I said.

"No, I didn't mean this was your . . . it's not, I mean, I'm on your side, Mike. I might be the only person in this place who is."

I didn't know what that was supposed to mean, but now I had an opening. "Why do you think President Davis would have mentioned in his speech that the breach came from Armor? I mean, Caleb was a big donor to his campaign."

Steve looked up at the security camera above us in the kitchen. Then he jerked his head toward his office. I followed him. And I left my uncreamed coffee behind.

I had not been in his office since the day he told me about my click on the phishing email from Iran hackers. Seeing it now made me view it differently, not so much as an office but as a set. Those fishing and surfing photos and the political flag of Davis-O'Neil ("Keep America Great!") were there to send a message that Steve was an all-American kind of guy. I knew that he was a certain type of all-American. One who apparently walked on the dark side. I needed to find out who he really was.

"I went to bat for you, Mike, I really did. I told Caleb, and the FBI, that there was no need to blame you for what was probably an honest mistake. Anyway, I have a plan going forward."

The way he said it also surprised me. He had a plan? For me?

"Pam works in films, you said, yeah?"

I nodded.

"She was working with an Iranian director, right?"

I had not said that, but I nodded again. How did he know about Zahra?

"Okay, so let's say it was this Iranian director who was the connection to Iran and served you up to them on a platter. You and Pam were victims."

I almost laughed. "But she didn't, Steve. She left Iran in 1979. She hates the mullahs."

"Then why did she flee to Canada?" he asked.

I could feel my pale Scottish cheeks firing up. How the hell did he know that? I could tell him that she fled because of the fascist policies of his president, who was locking up Iranians and hunting down immigrants.

"She's not in Canada," I said. "Who told you that?"

Steve smiled. "You must know that the FBI is watching you, Mike. I have a very good relationship with them. I am only trying to help you. And they'll play ball with me."

I took a breath and thought about how to respond. Then my phone rang, and I could see it was Montrose.

"Excuse me, Steve," I said. "I have to take this. It's my lawyer."

He shrugged sympathetically, and I stepped quickly out into the corridor and strode down the hallway.

"Hello," I said.

"Where are the bombs?!" Robert Montrose howled.

"I sent you the list," I said, with a touch of anger in my voice. "You were happy with it."

"You sent me a fucken photo of the list," Montrose said. He sounded hungover, twitchy, more dangerous than ever. "I want the goods today."

"I don't know if I can have them all today," I said.

There was a pause, then I heard a gunshot and screams. "Okay, now we only have two suicide bombers. You get it, Weiss? The clock is ticking, and if you don't get me what I want, I'm gonna kill everyone. Your dyke of a sister included."

After a few minutes to gather my composure, I headed back to Steve's office to finish our conversation. I needed to see what his plan was and if I could get anything from him that would explain his role in everything that had happened. His door was closed and the blinds drawn. I knocked. A few seconds later I knocked again. Then I opened his door, but he was gone.

CHAPTER 41

WEDNESDAY, JULY 6, LATER.

"I'm coming with you," Pam said, not long after I got home that evening. And she said it in that way I had come to know and love.

"You shouldn't come, it's not safe."

"But I need to be with you. We have been separated enough. And we are safer together, even amidst lunatics in the woods. I shouldn't be alone."

"Okay," I said. "You're right. But we need to get Grant to feed Cecil."

She gave me a funny look, her turquoise eyes bright with purpose. "How long do you plan to stay up there?"

I had no plan to stay there a specific amount of time. I just needed to get Montrose his bombs.

"I'll go let him know," Pam said. "You can check out my bomb-making talents in the living room."

I walked into the living room. It looked like three suicide bomber vests were lying on the couch where, in more gracious days, Pam and I would sit and talk and drink IPA and watch A's games.

Now it looked like I was planning Armageddon.

When I told Pam what I needed, she got right on it. She'd managed to get three military vests from some army surplus store in Indianapolis, the kind with the pockets for ammo on the front. She'd taken white modeling clay and wrapped it in plastic, then stuck on black lettering indicating this was C4. She loaded ball bearings, nails, and bolts into cloth jackets and wrapped them around the fake C4 explosives. Black wires led into the "explosive," and they were connected to cheap cell phones duct-taped to the C4. And the bricks of explosives were stuck into the ammo pockets on the vests. I had never seen a suicide vest up close, but it looked real to me.

And next to the vests were three sets of Iranian clothes for the boys to wear, long robes and keffiyeh headdress. These were the costumes that people would see them wearing, with the vests on top, right before detonation.

"Grant says he's happy to feed Cecil," Pam said, as she walked into the living room.

I turned to her and gave her a kiss. "I don't want to know how you did it, but I believe it," I said, looking at the vests and costumes.

She kissed me back. "The internet is a pretty useful place sometimes," she said, and we laughed.

Then she handed me a cheap cell phone and, giving me a wink, said, "And this is the master switch. You call those phones with this one, and kaboom."

On that, GNC issued their breaking news music, a snappy trumpet fanfare, and up on the television screen was President Brian Davis, standing in front of a podium inside the White House. Behind him was the American flag with Davis's face imprinted on it.

"My people," he said, the weary tone not as confident in its implication that we all belonged to him. "This is a momentous time for our country. We have been attacked by Iran, who have killed our fellow citizens and wreaked havoc upon our infrastructure. Who have sent sleeper agents into our cities to kill and destroy. We have responded to them with bombs and sanctions, but still they do not seem to understand that they can never defeat us. So we need to make them understand."

He paused and blinked a few times. His eyes were wet and glazed. Pam and I stood there, wondering if he was going to say he had leveled Tehran with a nuclear bomb.

"We have sent our brave Special Forces into some dangerous places. They have, as usual, done brilliantly. We now have something those mad mullahs cannot ignore."

On-screen, the president gave way to footage of a room full of people, maybe two dozen. Some were kids, some looked like college students, their parents, and their grandparents. It looked like an extended family. Except that they had their arms behind their backs, as if they were cuffed. Their faces were pale, their faces expressionless.

The president came back to share the screen with the images of the captured people. "These Iranians you see on your television screens are relatives of Iran's so-called Supreme Leader, Ali Rhouhani. Our Special Forces found some of them inside Iran and some of them in Europe.

"So this is my message to the so-called Supreme Leader Rhouhani. You couldn't protect your own family members. How are you going to protect the people of Iran? There's only one way, and that's by ending your tenure. By resigning from office and surrendering to the might of America."

He paused, and his pathological eyes lit up with pleasure. "I will give you seventy-two hours. Or else."

The camera lingered on one of the captured kids, a little girl, maybe eight years old. With black hair and pale skin and blue-green eyes. She looked like Pam.

The screen went black for about three seconds, as if the Iranians had once again canceled the president, and then the GNC anchor came back to tell us what we had all seen.

"That was President Brian Davis threatening members of Iranian leader Ali Rhouhani's family with . . . something undetermined . . . if Rhouhani does not surrender and resign within the next seventy-two hours."

The anchor shook her head. "We'll take a short break and be right back."

Pam looked at me with total disbelief. I returned the look. "He's a monster," I said. "I mean, 'or else'?"

She nodded. "And it's unfair to monsters."

Yes, I thought, it is. But what mattered to me most was to save the most wonderful person on the planet, standing in front of me, willing to go to war with me. If everything worked out, Davis would be finished, and the government would be off our backs. I didn't know if I was as insane as Davis was in thinking that. Could some schmuck like me really take down the president of the United States? But I only had one way to get the government off our backs and truly secure our freedom—and that was it.

CHAPTER 42

WEDNESDAY, JULY 6, LATER.

I had been very worried about Janine. Being embedded with the Knights was a dangerous place to be. So I texted her and asked her if she could talk.

Yes was her reply.

"How are you," I asked.

"Okay," she said. She sounded tired and nervous.

"Are you?"

She paused and then whispered, "I have some great footage. But it's getting scary. These guys are nuts. You and Nicole were right. I mean, I want to bring down Davis, but I want to be alive to do it."

"We can abort everything and get you out," I said.

"No, no," she whispered. "This is the kind of story that's going to change everything, if we can tie it all together. I'm staying with them until I have it all. We need to stick to the plan." Then her whisper got softer. "We need to get the Knights forcing the boys at gunpoint into the crowd in their fake vests and Iranian costumes, trying to blow every thing up. Get it all on film. That's the drama we need. I think we can get it. And that should be enough for my source to give me the tape connecting the bounty program to Davis."

"Okay," I said. I was impressed with Janine's bravery—and her ambition. All reporters who make history have both, and I knew Janine wanted to make history.

"What are you doing?" she asked.

"On my way. We'll be there in three hours."

She ended the call. Or I sure hoped it was Janine who ended it.

Pam and I loaded the suicide bomber vests and Iranian clothes into a purple suitcase and wheeled it out to the Prius. The afternoon sun was starting to soften in Bloomington, so we'd be arriving at Hoosier Hill just before dusk. Our timing was perfect for the mission ahead.

Grant Woollard was out watering his lawn when we loaded the suitcase into the trunk.

"Have a great vacation. You guys going for a long time?" he called across the street.

"Not too long," I said. "But there's a couple of crates of food for Cecil in the pantry."

Grant gave me a thumbs-up. "Have a good trip!"

If only he knew we were enemies of the state. Then again, maybe he did. Maybe he was the FBI's watcher, who knew our every move and now would be calling Agent Weiss to let her know we were leaving. If Weiss and her team showed up at Hoosier Hill, a shoot-out between the Knights and Weiss's team seemed likely.

"Does Janine know we're coming?" Pam said.

"Yes," I said. "Just spoke with her."

Pam stared at the abandoned cars littered on the sides of I-69. People had been pulled out of their vehicles by the Guard or the army after curfew. And locked up. The cars were a reminder of what would happen if you defied the state.

"Okay. So what are we going to do once we deliver everything to Montrose?" Pam asked. "What if he wants to kill us?"

It was a good question. It was a risk that Montrose might want to take any witnesses out of the picture as soon as he had the bomber vests, but on the other hand, the witnesses were the point. He wanted everyone see what a patriot he was. He wanted Janine to capture his heroism on film. He wanted to stir up as much rage as possible. And he wanted people like me to supply him for his next round of terror.

But there wouldn't be any terror if things went according to plan. Once he had unleashed the kids in the vests, I was going to have Agent Weiss lock up him and his Knights. As for the kids, I had a plan for them, too.

We drove along with the music of Bach playing on Sirius XM's Symphony Hall. When I was an undergraduate, I had listened to the sublime orderliness of Bach during times of chaos within. How he could create the most beautiful melody out of the strictest musical rigor. I wasn't feeling chaos within now, just a raging sense that Pam and I had to save these kids and expose Montrose and Davis if we were to have a chance to save ourselves.

"What's that?" Pam asked, wearing the red Indiana hat that Zahra had worn, looking at red flashing lights up ahead.

"It's a checkpoint," I said. I could see the blue berets under the wash of the arc lights that had been rigged to a metal frame, the kind that forms an inverted U-shape like you see on concert stages. The sun had started to set, and we were at the exit from IN-109 to US-36E, which was the last stretch of the road into Hoosier Hill. They had stepped up their checkpoint architecture since I last was here. Like they were planning on staying.

"Who wears blue berets?" I asked Pam.

She asked Siri on her iPhone.

"Blue berets are worn by US Air Force Security Services," Siri said.

So we had real cops and not just teenage soldiers about to check us out.

"Just relax," I said to Pam.

"Couldn't be more relaxed," she said and touched me on the arm. "I mean, we're about to go through a security checkpoint with three suicide bomber vests on us."

I smiled. "Good thing we thought of plan B."

There was one car ahead of us, an older model green Beamer, maybe from the early aughts. A blue beret asked the driver a few questions, and then one of them waved to a hut at the side of the road, and a guy with a bomb dog emerged. A Belgian Shepherd.

The military police made the man get out of his car. He looked like he was Latino or Middle Eastern and I felt a wave of pity for him. This wasn't going to end well.

The dog sniffed inside his car and then in the car's trunk. It didn't find anything, but that didn't satisfy the cops. They directed the guy to drive his car over to the side of the road so they could interrogate him further.

That's when things got a lot worse. The guy gunned his engine and made a break for it. The blue berets shouted after him, and then the one who had questioned him aimed his M16 at the fleeing BMW. He fired in burst mode, three rounds. It was enough.

The green BMW veered sharply to the right and then crashed into a light pole at the side of the road.

Pam squeezed my hand, and I squeezed back. We watched as two blue berets, their rifles aimed, ran up to the green BMW. We saw the car's door open and the driver try to get out. He managed to put one leg onto the pavement and then the blue berets opened fire. The bullets tore into the man's flesh, and blood shot out of his leg and his head. He was dead.

We were breathing hard now, having witnessed a murder. A murder by the state. I shuddered. Now we had a bunch of ramped-up killer cops to deal with.

I looked in the rearview mirror. There were a half dozen cars behind us, all trying to beat the curfew. I didn't think the building lineup would have any effect on these guys.

"Where you going?" said the blue beret, approaching our car. He had three chevrons on his sleeve. A sergeant. His accent was local, his tone flat and emotionless.

"On vacation," I said. My mouth felt like it had been in a sandstorm, dry and gritty. "To our cabin on Hoosier Hill."

He shone a flashlight on Pam, and she gave him a slight polite smile.

"Open your trunk," he said to me.

I got out of the car slowly, aware of the M16s following me as I walked to the rear of the Prius. The sergeant was shorter than me, and his muscles—shoulders, traps, delts, biceps—bulged underneath his camouflage uniform. He was speeding with adrenaline from the recent kill.

"Hurry the fuck up," he snarled.

I reached under the rim at the back of the car and popped the button that released the trunk.

The sergeant shone his light on our purple suitcase. "Open the case," he said.

With my heart racing and sweat trickling down my back, I had no choice but to open the suitcase. I turned it on its side and unzipped it. The light from his beam hit our clothes and toiletry bags and hiking boots. The sergeant used his truncheon to poke around to see if there were any secret compartments.

"How long are you at the cabin for?"

"A few days," I said.

"You have weapons?" he asked.

I knew there was only one right way to answer to this. "Yes," I said. "At the cabin. Hidden so no trespassers can find them."

He thought about that, then he nodded. "You can go now. Have a good vacation." He said the word "vacation" as if it was an obscenity, that only Prius-driving city folk like Pam and I would go on vacation in the middle of a war.

"Thank you," I said. I walked slowly back to the car and got in.

The sergeant leaned in the window. "You be careful, ma'am," he said. "Lots of bad guys around. Keep an eye out when you're having a glass of chardonnay at sunset."

Pam smiled like this was the best advice she had ever received, and I drove forward like a centenarian in a church parking lot on a Sunday at dawn.

Once we were clear of the checkpoint, Pam started to sob.

"Oh, Mikey, what have we become?" she said, her body heaving, tears flowing down her soft cheeks. I pulled the car off to the side of the highway, took her in my arms, and just held her.

I knew how we had become what we had become. He was sitting in the White House. He had attacked Iran and was now going to kill relatives of the Supreme Leader because of me. Or maybe not because of me. It was something I had to find out. If we survived the next twenty-four hours.

"I thought . . . he was going . . . to find them," Pam said about the suicide vests, sucking in air between sobs. "I thought . . . we were going . . . back to prison."

I squeezed her tight. "Thanks to you, we are not," I said.

Pam had insisted that we pack for a vacation, and so we did. We had stashed the vests in the spare wheel compartment under the floor of the trunk.

We sat like that, hugging each other tight for about five minutes. My right shoulder was drenched from her tears. Pam's sobs subsided, and then her breathing slowed, and she released me and smiled. "I'm okay now, Mikey," she said. "Are you?"

I smiled back at her and nodded slightly. I was not okay. But it didn't matter. I pushed the button to start the engine and swung the Prius back onto the highway. There were only a few other cars on the road.

The sun had just gone down when we pulled up to the cabin, and we could see Janine's SUV parked in front. She had a white Jeep Cherokee, but I had never seen one quite at this angle. Someone had removed the rear tires and placed the wheels on wooden blocks.

Then we saw Janine coming out the front door, smiling tightly at us. And behind her, the Knight Commander, Robert Montrose, his rifle in his hand, his fingers resting over the trigger. He was smiling at us too. In charge of everything and drunk out of his mind.

"How I've missed this place, Pam," I said.

She took a deep breath. "We're going to be fine, Mikey," she said, watching the Knight Commander heading toward us.

Yes, I thought, we will be fine. I just had to trust that what we were helping him to do would not end with these kids and a bunch of other people—including Pam and me—dead. The plan had to work. Failure was not an option.

CHAPTER 43

THURSDAY, JULY 7.

It was dark now, and we were all sitting around the Knights' fire in the pit they had dug, staring at the flames. Montrose had examined the suicide vests, and Janine had filmed him doing that, and he was happy with what we delivered to him.

We hadn't seen the kids yet. Pablo, Zeke's son, had taken the remaining captive teenagers down to the lake for their evening ablutions.

"What did you do with the kid you shot?" I asked Montrose.

He just took a pull of Beam and grinned at me. Then he spat in the fire, and the alcohol flared up in the flames.

We drank in silence, or Montrose drank, and we faked it. Janine sat next to Pam on a log, the flames' light flickering off their faces. She looked tired, like she had been running on adrenaline the whole time she'd been with the Knights. She was wearing the same clothes she was in the last time I saw her.

We heard the rustle of feet on the path and Travis was on his feet, AR-15 at the ready. "Halt and state the password!" he shouted into the dark.

"Scum" came lazily back, from Pablo.

"Proceed!" Travis shouted, and Pablo emerged from the trees with the three captive teenagers. I felt a wave of relief roll over my shock, and I smiled when I saw them.

"You surprised to see three of 'em, aren't you, Weiss?" Montrose said, taking another pull from his bottle.

I was. I thought he had killed one.

"I wouldn't kill one of my weapons now, would I?"

"I thought you were going to kill my sister."

Robert Montrose sputtered out whisky as he laughed. "Now why would I do that, Weiss? She's gonna make us famous. I took her wheels to make sure you'd show up."

I smiled at Janine, and she smiled at me, winked, and nodded, trying to be sisterly. Sending a message. She had some really good footage.

"Well, I delivered what I promised," I said.

"We'll see," Montrose replied. My heart thudded. *We'll see?* Was he going to keep us all hostage until the bombers did their work? I couldn't let that happen. Because the bombs would not work, and then we'd be dead for sure.

"They'll do the job," I said, with a calm I did not feel. "When we get back to Bloomington, just give us a heads-up so we're not in the target zone."

"You planning on going back to Bloomington, huh?"

Travis and Zeke opened another case of beer and took bottles from it. They offered them to Pam and Janine, who took them to avoid conflict, and then Zeke tossed one to Pablo.

"We are, Bob. We can't stay up here without raising suspicion. The checkpoint guy was already suspicious of us. We were lucky he didn't find the vests. And if I don't show up at work tomorrow, well, they'll come looking. Besides, something tells me that this is not going to be your first operation. You'll need me to stay clean to help you."

Montrose thought about this. "Okay. But your sister stays. To do more filming, right?"

"That's fine, Joe. I need to stay with these guys. I've got some really great stuff for the doc."

I knew that she needed to film them all the way to the end of the line. That's what her source would need in order to give her the tape of Davis and Clay authorizing the bounty program. I just worried whether she could continue to do it without Montrose realizing what was up and shooting her in the head.

We drank in silence for a while, then I said, "When's the attack, Bob?"

He belched and then spat. Some spittle stuck to his beard. "In a day or two. I'll let you know."

I nodded. "Do you know where you're going to strike?"

He looked at me with eyes that were hard and cold, not the sleepy eyes of a drunk. "Where's the most people this time of year in Bloomington? Not at the fucken woke college, I bet."

I looked over to Pam. The university started up in August, thank goodness.

"I'd say you want to set them off on Walnut Street, on a Saturday afternoon," Janine said. "Near where it turns into College Avenue. Maximum bang for the buck."

"You would, huh?" Montrose replied. He was curious. It was more than strange to be sitting here with a guy prepared to send three teenagers to blow up a bunch of innocent people and he didn't know where he was going to do it.

"It's laws of physics," Pablo piped up.

"Like you fucken know physics," Montrose replied. He got a sharp look from Zeke who took offense at his own son being demeaned and yet could strap suicide vests on to the sons of other fathers. It made me feel—just a little—sorry for Pablo.

"The vest is like a shotgun blast," Janine continued. "The C4 is going to blast out all the goodies in the fragmentation jacket like one big Benelli M4 Super 90."

The Knights of Liberty all looked at Janine as if she was speaking another language.

"That's the shotgun used by the Navy SEALs," she said.

"How you know that?" Montrose asked, squinting at her in the dark.

"Because Joe and I have worked with the SEALs," she said.

I smiled tightly. "Can't say more than that, sis," I said, and she nodded.

Montrose took another pull of Beam and stroked his beard. He looked over at the teenage suicide bombers, hands tied around the trees, heads bowed. I could only imagine what those poor kids were thinking. That we American adults could sit drinking around a fire, chatting into the night, while they were held captive. I wanted to let them know it would all be okay. But I didn't know if it would. Montrose was so unstable. Our plan so tenuous. The future so hard to predict. I thought of the tree and the pond from my childhood park. It was all so quiet, so easy, so predictable. Things were so different now.

"You know," I said, "because of all the checkpoints, you want to split up. Put the wheels back on Janine's Jeep and let her take the kids."

"No fucken way."

"It will seem a lot less odd than you guys traveling with them. If you get stopped. And you will get stopped."

Montrose thought about that.

"I think it's a good idea," Zeke said.

"I do the thinking, you do the fucken following," Montrose barked at him. Zeke looked down at the ground, but his eyes were angry.

I could see that their time together here holding these kids captive, waiting for my suicide vests, had created a strain between them.

"How many vehicles do you guys have?" I asked.

"Just one. My Dodge Caravan."

The Knights of Liberty rode around in a minivan.

"Okay, so what happens if you guys roll up to a checkpoint with those three in back? What are you going to tell them?"

Montrose snuffled. "That we are bringing them in for bounty."

"Not everyone knows about the bounty," Janine said. "Or approves of the program. The army guys especially. It could create an awkward situation."

Montrose was mad that a woman was speaking with confidence.

"Okay, so if you take the bombers," he said, looking at Janine, "you're taking Pablo, too. So if you try anything funny, he can kill you all."

Janine held up her hands like this was going way too far and smiled. "I'm on your side, remember? I don't want them to get caught in some checkpoint."

"What if you do get caught?"

"I'll say I'm a social worker. Taking them to a shelter for processing. Something very neutral. Pablo is my assistant."

Montrose closed his eyes tight, like he was imagining how wrong it could all go. Then he popped his bloodshot eyes wide open, like a mad scientist, and grinned at Janine.

"Okay, you take the kids, and we follow you. With the vests."

Relief flooded over me. It was a kind of victory.

"Bury the vests in the spare tire wheel well, and put luggage on top," Pam said.

Montrose smiled again. "I'll let you do that. You're coming with me."

My heart started to pound. This killer was going to keep Pam with him. I looked at Pam, who gave me a reassuring smile. First, I had gotten her into prison, and now I had gotten her captive to a group of homicidal racist maniacs. A wave of horror cascaded throughout my body. I was going to be separated from Pam *again*. I just got her back. If she was still speaking to me after this, I would promise her the world all over again. A better world than the one we knew now.

Montrose spat again. "You'll have to be a bachelor until we're done, Weiss. You okay with that?"

"Yeah," I said, my stomach aching. "But if you lay a hand on my wife, just know that you will have a lot of time to think about that mistake in the afterlife."

The words came out of my mouth with a cold fury that I did not feel. I felt terrified. But the words landed with a bullseye on Montrose.

"It's all gonna be okay, Weiss. Relax." He gave me a creepy smile, showing his decrepit teeth. "We're going to be in business for a long time."

CHAPTER 44

THURSDAY, JULY 7, LATER.

Pam and I sat up late, listening to Montrose and the Knights snore in drunken slumber. The kids were asleep, tied to trees. And Janine was conked out next to the fire in a green sleeping bag.

"What happens if it goes wrong?" Pam asked in a whisper.

"It won't," I whispered back. "I'm going to bring in law enforcement."

She tilted her head to the left and arched her eyebrows. "As if law enforcement can be counted on."

"I know," I said. But we're going to have to risk it."

"It just seems like so much could go wrong Mikey. I mean, we're trying to capture a fake bomber attack on film, in the middle of martial law? To bring down the president? These Knights are trigger-happy—and lunatics. What if they sniff this out?"

"I know, but we have to use the cards we've been dealt. This is all we have."

"I'm scared, Mikey," she said, fear and uncertainty welling up in her tired eyes. Her face exuded beauty and vulnerability in the glow of the fire.

"Me too, baby. But it will all work out. The feds are all over us for something we didn't do. Weiss told me she wouldn't stop until we were both behind bars again. This is what we need to do to get our life back. Half measures won't work. We have to go big."

"Why can't we just run away? Just get in the car and start driving. Leave the country. Escape. Me and you. Together."

"They would find us. And everything would get worse. We will be public enemies as long as this president gets to define right from wrong from the Oval Office. No, we have to act. We have to force the government to bend to our will, or it will destroy us. I know it sounds nuts, but it's where we are."

"Okay," she said, looking me in the eye with feverish intensity. "Okay," she said again, both of us aware of how much our life had changed in so short a time. And that this plan, in all its horror, was our best—our only—shot to get it back.

We managed to doze off into a shallow and dreamless sleep. I wasn't surprised when my phone buzzed in my pocket with the sunrise alarm. Pam woke when I stood, and I leaned down and gave her a kiss.

"See you soon."

She smiled.

"Be careful baby," I said.

She smiled again. "You, too."

I did not run into a single checkpoint on my way back to Bloomington. A trip that normally took nearly three hours took me just over two. It was 8:30 when I rolled into the city and saw the boarded-up shops, some of them scorched by flames. There were army Humvees parked on Third Street when I exited I-69, so I did not stop at the Taco Bell for a breakfast burrito. I kept going east toward my morning date.

I rolled into the Hopscotch Coffee Roaster on North Madison and got myself a half-caff cappuccino and a Rainbow Bakery donut.

I parked myself on a chair near the front window and sent Pam a text. The kind of text that could not be misread by anyone looking at her phone. "Morning, sweetheart."

Whoever said watching a pot while water is on the boil is a slow process has not known the slow-motion drip of time when waiting for a text from your wife when she's the captive of gunned-up lunatics.

After about a minute, her reply landed. "Love you."

"Love you, too. See you soon."

She sent me back two emojis. ♥ 🙏. Yeah, me too.

Nicole Wilkerson and Hannah Gottlieb entered the café about ten minutes later. They skipped the office attire today and had gone for jeans, with Nicole in a tan blazer and Hannah in a button-down blue cotton shirt, untucked. They were in a good mood, smiling like old friends. The smiles soon vanished.

"You left Pam with those Nazis?" Hannah asked me, her dark brown eyes fixed hard on me. She ripped open a Stevia packet as if she was ripping off my head.

"I wasn't given a choice. It was part of their deal to keep me from talking to anyone."

"But you brought them the vests. Why would you talk?"

I shook my head and slugged back a big mouthful of coffee. "It's not how they think. Everyone is an enemy. Even me. Potentially."

"You have to tell Agent Weiss," Nicole said, raising her hands in an "I know, but you gotta" manner. "She can stop this. She'll want to stop this."

"I'm going to tell Weiss," I replied. "Once I know the strike time and location. I need those two things to . . ."

Nicole took a sip of her sparkling water. "If those kids walk down College Avenue in Bloomington wearing suicide vests, fake or not, in Iranian clothing, they could get shot to pieces. The army is everywhere now. We don't want that."

No, we didn't want that. "I know, I know. We have to do it the right way."

Hannah took out her phone and composed a text. She then turned the phone to me. "This okay?"

The text read "Hi Pam, looking forward to our drink tomorrow. What time should we meet?"

It was a clever plan. To get Pam to give us the time and date she would arrive back and make it seem like business as usual.

"Okay," I said, and Hannah hit SEND.

We sat there with the sun leaping into the café on a lovely July morning, waiting for Pam to reply. My heart was pounding, and I was bouncing my knee up and down a million times a minute.

After about a minute of staring at her phone, Hannah put it faceup on the table. She exhaled loudly.

"So," Nicole said, "I heard from Zahra."

I brightened. "Did she make it to LA? More importantly, did she make it out of LA?"

Nicole shook her head. "She saw an unmarked white van parked near her house when she got a few blocks away. So she turned around before she got home."

"They probably are watching her house. They're still watching mine."

Nicole nodded. "Yeah. But they didn't see Zahra go in."

I blinked. "Zahra's at my house?"

Nicole nodded again. "We put her on the floor of my SUV, in the back, then drove it into your garage. Walked her straight into the house."

I thought about her route. The camera buried in the back would have most likely seen her enter, not to mention any other snooping devices hidden on our premises. So now my wife was with the Knights and a wanted woman was in my house. I thought I had moved forward, closer to safety for me and Pam. But no, I had gotten us further stuck in this dangerous muck. Maybe Pam was right. Maybe we should have just run. Nicole read my face, an open book as usual, and the story was getting dark fast.

"It's okay, Michael. Zahra is going to be gone soon. She's so passionate about her film, I get why she wanted the footage Foad sent to her house. But she never should have left Canada to begin with. We're going to get her back to the Canadian border." I heard an unspoken "but" in her voice.

Nicole smiled. "But getting her there depends on how you do with Agent Weiss. We need the government to back off of her."

I felt that aching hole in my stomach again. Zahra was now part of the deal with me and Pam.

Hannah's phone pinged and she grabbed it and read the message. "Okay, Pam is coming back on Saturday, and we're meeting at Wolfgang's Beer Garden on College Avenue. Two p.m."

Saturday was in two days. And on a Saturday afternoon in the summer, even this summer, Wolfgang's patio was overflowing with people. It would be the kind of target that a whisky-drinking scumbag like Robert Montrose would pick.

"Okay," I said, exhaling. "Forty-eight hours."

The two lawyers looked at me closely. “Do you think you will have enough, Michael, if this all works out the way you want it to?” Nicole asked.

“Enough?” Enough to avoid prison? Enough to take down Davis? Enough to get our quiet life back? I couldn't know for sure. “I'm putting my faith in the Knights of Liberty. And some others. You tell me.”

The two lawyers laughed nervously, but their laughter was cut short when four white guys in dark suits strode into the café and made a beeline for our table.

“Nicole Wilkerson and Hannah Gottlieb?” the tallest one asked in a deep voice. Thin and awkward-looking, he had a blonde comb-over and a weak chin. He didn't take off his aviator sunglasses.

“Who's asking?” Nicole said.

“I'll take that as a yes,” the man said, and with a curt nod, his companions had Nicole and Hannah in cuffs.

“Who are you and why are you handcuffing us?” Hannah snarled at the guys.

“We're federal agents. And you are under arrest for helping the Iranian fugitive Zahra Nasseri to procure false travel documents and to escape our jurisdiction,” the agent said. “Of course, this could all end if you tell us where she is.”

Nicole looked as if she was going to spit in the man's face, but instead she just smiled and said nothing.

Hannah said, “Start sending out your résumés, boys, because by the time I'm done with you, you'll be lucky to get a job sweeping the toilets at a gas station.”

The agent raised his hand as if to strike Hannah, and she flinched.

He grinned at her and then the squad led Nicole and Hannah out of the café, with the baristas pretending that they hadn't seen any of it.

I had seen it, though, and now I knew three things. Pam was in danger, Zahra was on the run, and Hannah and Nicole were on their way to a Davis prison. I knew four things, actually. Now I was all alone.

CHAPTER 45

THURSDAY, JULY 7, LATER.

I drove the Prius into my driveway shortly before 10:00 a.m. An air-raid siren screeched as I got out of my car, and above me a trio of drones zoomed toward the sound of the siren. They were sleek, with flashing green lights on their noses. From the look of them, they were camera drones, not killing drones, which were bigger and boxier. I had learned the difference in the past two weeks. It wasn't something I thought I'd ever know.

I gave myself an hour to shower and get my head together before I went back to Armor.

Grant Woollard was at my side as soon as I exited my car. It was as if he had been waiting for me. Then his eyes cast down our street and I realized he was watching, or waiting, for someone to return.

"Hey, you and the wife have a vacation spat?" he said, chuckling.

I forced a smile. "I had a work issue come up. Pam decided to stay in paradise without me."

He nodded. "Your dog eats like he's twice his size."

"Thanks for feeding him."

Woollard nodded, one hand on his gray mustache, the other resting on his beer gut, as he studied me closely. His double chin was bulging far out in front of the rest of his face. "I know it's not my place to ask but I'm gonna. You in big trouble?"

I felt my stomach lurch. Yes, in massive and utterly epic trouble was the correct answer, but that was not a conversation that we were going to have. So I responded with a question of my own. "Why do you ask?"

He scratched what hair was left on his head. "Well, there were the three people in overalls out back of your place, like we discussed. And since you been away, there have been a lot of official-looking vehicles cruising around here," he said. "And some folks even came inside your house when I was feeding Cecil."

Now I was sweating. If they were coming inside when the neighbor was there, they didn't care who saw them. "Who were they? What were they doing?" I asked.

He shrugged. "Hard to say. A blonde woman with cold eyes. And three youngsters with her, not that she was ancient. Two guys and a lady. Might have been the same folks as before. Looked like feds. Just waved some electronic gear around in the air, like they were chasing flies."

Special Agent Weiss. Along with her team that buried the camera in the backyard. MOC. McGarvey, Ortiz, and Cole.

"They didn't say anything to you?"

"They asked what I was doing. I told them. I'm keeping your dog fed while you're away."

"Did they ask where I was?"

He shook his head. "Besides, I didn't know, did I?"

I thought about this. "And they just waved around devices? What kind of devices?"

He shrugged again. "Looked like those tablets, you know. One guy found something and typed it into his device."

My head reeled. What on earth could they be looking for? They had already tapped into the place, so what did they need? My Wi-Fi? They could get into that from our service provider or just hack into it themselves. I had no idea, but it couldn't be anything good.

"And that was it? He typed something into his device, and then they left?"

Woollard shook his head. "No, they started to search your house. Upstairs, downstairs, everywhere. Even went into the garage."

I knew at least one thing they were looking for. Zahra. They had probably been trying to pick up a cell phone signal and when they did, they had found her.

"Did they find what they were looking for?"

He smiled slyly and rubbed his belly. "I can't say for certain who they were looking for, but if you mean the nice Iranian lady, no, they didn't."

The look of astonishment on my face made him laugh. "Got you there, didn't I?"

"Where is she?" I asked.

"She's safe at my place. They're not gonna look there. I'm an ex-cop, one of the team, right? I wouldn't be harboring no fugitives now, would I?"

I smiled. "No, you wouldn't."

"I'm just doing what any citizen would do in the face of these . . . fascist goons." He paused and looked around. "And that's fighting back. She can stay as long as she needs to."

Grant Woollard was a patriot. I had never expected he'd be the kind of patriot that I would support. But he was; he had saved Zahra.

I needed to talk to Zahra, but doing so on the phone was not possible, not with all those ears listening in. "Can I see her?"

Grant looked around, like he was releasing a crick in his neck. "You want to bring the dog over to my place and leave him there for the day. Right?"

I smiled. "Right. We'll be there in a minute."

Cecil was happy to wander over to Grant's with me, thinking that seeing Grant again meant he was getting fed again. Grant gave him a treat as he ushered me in, paying all of his attention to Cecil until the door was shut. I had never been inside Grant's house, and it was unexpected for a state trooper. Overstuffed furniture and potted palms and little red and white china bears on the mantelpiece.

As soon as the lock clanked on the front door, Zahra stepped out of the shadows to give me a hug. It was more like a desperate plea for help, squeezing me tight as if a solution to this nightmare would come pouring out of me if she squeezed hard enough.

I hugged her back, and we stayed that way for a good half-minute, and then she stepped back. Tears were in her eyes. She looked tired, and thinner than when I last saw her. The features in her face more pronounced.

"I'm so sorry, Michael," she said softly. "I never should have left

Canada. That footage just sounded so important. Anyway, after I left LA, I didn't know where else to go."

I smiled at her. "Zahra, you came to exactly the right place. Thanks to Grant here, you are safe. And now I'm going to work on getting you out of this mess."

She exhaled with relief. "I just need to get to the Canadian border, Michael."

I nodded. "Yes, we can get you there. Once I get Pam safely back home. Again. We'll make it part of the deal."

"Pam is in trouble?" Zahra's deep brown eyes searched mine as if I had somehow misspoken.

"She'll be fine," I said. "She'll be back in a couple of days." I didn't see the need to add that she was in the company of gun-toting, alcohol-crazed, immigrant-hunting maniacs—and not the good kind—as Zahra was already stressed enough.

"How's Nicole? Is she helping?" Zahra asked.

I had to tell her the truth, to protect them both. "She was arrested. This morning. By the feds. For helping you escape. Hannah too."

"You know this for certain?"

"I was with them."

Tears welled in Zahra's eyes. "But they left you alone?"

I nodded. They did. And now I felt cold shock waves travel down my body. Why would they leave me alone and arrest the two lawyers when Pam and I were the ones helping Zahra? They were still watching me, waiting for me to make a mistake. Had they followed me and Pam to the cabin? I didn't think so. There had been no cars in the rearview mirror. But maybe they sent a drone.

Zahra put a hand on my arm. "I know that you are telling me this so that I don't try to get in touch."

I nodded. "That's right. Besides, she and Hannah are lawyers. They'll know what to do."

Zahra looked at me with pity. "But there is no law, Michael. Not now. I hope it will come back, but that madman in the White House is now threatening to kill family members of the Iranian leader. In two days. Where is the law?"

I didn't know.

In two days, Pam would be back in Bloomington. I took a breath. The Knights of Liberty were in play, and I wasn't going to let them harm a soul, especially not Pam. Nicole and Hannah were in jail, but they were lawyers and could hold their own. Zahra was safe and hiding out in an unexpected refuge. And I was still free. I wanted to stay that way. So I got in the Prius and went to work.

CHAPTER 46

THURSDAY, JULY 7, LATER.

"Mike!" Bo leapt up from his desk as I walked in and came over to shake my hand. It was weird.

"Good morning, Bo," I said. His face looked thinner, and he looked anxious, his black eyes shifting back and forth as if he was expecting an ambush. He was wearing a bright white dress shirt, red suspenders, and a blue tie. Bo was the flag.

"Coffee?"

"How about outside? I need a smoke."

He gave me a funny look, as he knew I didn't smoke, but he saw the anxiety in my face. And nodded.

Once we were in the parking lot, I turned to him.

"What's up, Bo?" I asked.

He smiled, like he had a secret. "I know we don't always agree, Mike. On politics and stuff."

"That's true. But we get along." I didn't know where he was going with this, and he was twitchy and nervous.

"But what's happening now is wrong."

I nodded. There was a lot happening now. "Yeah."

"I mean, what happened to you and Pam was wrong." I still didn't know what he knew about what happened to us. "But now . . ." He swallowed hard, as if he was going to confess a sin, a crime, something. "I think he's going to kill the family of the Iranian dude. That's what 'or else' means. I know, the Iranian's a bad dude, but they had no choice in being his family. I mean, one of them is just a little girl."

Bo was upset not that Davis had bombed Iran and killed tens of thousands of Iranians. He was upset because now that crime had a human face. The little girl.

"Yeah, it's bad," I said. I didn't really have time to become Bo's therapist on the crimes of President Davis, but then he surprised me with a gift.

"Yes, this whole thing is really bad."

I nodded.

"Anyway, I got to thinking. About your email. The one they said you clicked on."

Bo the IT guy was now back, his eyes steady, his breathing calm.

"So I went back into the system, to January. To check."

"I thought emails get deleted after thirty days," I said.

Bo ran his hand through his curly black hair slowly, like he was massaging his thoughts. "They get removed from your email application, but they're stored in our backup systems. Every company keeps backups."

Now my heart sped up. "And did you find my email? The phishing one?"

He shook his head. "That's the strange thing, Mike. I found every email you received on that day in January and on the days around it, but the phishing email was not there. There were no emails from Ad Supply or anyone else with a similar name."

"You mean I never received it?"

Bo shook his head. "No, I mean someone deleted it. From the system. A couple of weeks ago."

My head was pounding with the blood racing from my heart. A couple of weeks ago was just after Pam and I had been put in the Davis prisons. "Do you know who?"

He shook his head. "You can find out who deleted emails if you have system privileges, which I do. So did the deleter."

My mouth was dry. "So who was it?"

He shook his head again. "No way to know. They didn't leave any tracks."

"Is there any way to find out anything else?" I asked.

Bo now grinned like it was Christmas and he was five years old. "I haven't been able to find out who deleted the email. But I did figure some things out. The deleter didn't permanently delete it—which takes additional steps—and I found the email in our cloud-based backups."

His smiling face then transformed into an expression of bewilderment and concern. "Here's the thing Mike," he said, "you never clicked on the link."

His words hit me like a gut punch. "You can tell that?"

He nodded his head, and his black curls bounced. "Yes, I can," he said, his face now beaming with pride. "Because I went into your internet browser history, and you never visited that site. You never visited the site linked in the email."

"There is an actual site? It wasn't faked?"

"Yes, the hackers took a real survey from Ad Supply and redirected the URL to a new website.

"I didn't visit it?"

"You didn't. I saw all your traffic on that day. You never visited that site. If you had clicked on the link, your browser would have gone to the site linked in the body of the email. Someone has set you up."

"Why did they create the email with the fake site, if only to delete it?"

"Good question. I don't know for sure. But they probably wanted you to click on it, and when you didn't, they wanted to erase their tracks, make it so you couldn't go back and find the email later."

"I saw a printout of it though, at my meeting with the FBI."

"Whoever deleted the email probably gave them the copy first." His face went pale as he thought all this through. He whispered: "The FBI is probably involved in all this too."

My mind was exploding with a thousand harrowing questions all at once. The basis of the United States military campaign in Iran was a fake email *in my inbox*. Who did this? And why? Out of three-hundred-million-plus Americans, why me?

"Thank you," I said to Bo softly, looking him squarely in the eyes.

"You're welcome, man. Good luck."

I got up and walked back to my office and saw Steve talking to Caleb outside of Caleb's office. He waved to me and beckoned me to come over.

I felt a surge of panic and anger. Those two waving me to come over and into their orbit had not worked out well in the past. But I couldn't turn away.

"Mike! Good to see you," Steve said. Maybe he could read the anger and stress on my face. So I smiled, and he seemed to relax.

"How are you doing?" Caleb asked. He looked older, thinner, weaker, as if he hadn't been sleeping or eating. The focused, driven confidence in his blue eyes, which seemed oddly bigger, was gone, replaced by nervous vulnerability. He was pale.

"I'm okay," I said. "How are you?"

He looked surprised by the question. "I'm surviving," he replied.

"And Pam?" Steve quickly intervened.

"She's okay, too."

Caleb put a hand on my shoulder. "We're so sorry that you got tagged for all the Iran trouble, Mike. But what can we do? Forces beyond our control."

I breathed deep. "What are those forces doing now? I mean, how is the investigation going?"

Steve looked to Caleb, who ushered me inside his office. The shelves had been cleared, and boxes were stacked in the corner.

"I'm stepping down as CEO. For a short time. Until the investigation is over."

"Who is going to be in charge?" I asked.

"Steve is. He's a safe pair of hands, as we know. And with me on the sidelines for a while, maybe things will get better." He said it as if he didn't believe a word of it. His stock was in the tank, he was stepping aside from the company he built, and he was caught up in the same investigation that had snagged me.

"But why are they investigating you? I thought all of this was my fault?"

"We thought so, too, but it seems that Washington is now looking deeper into the company. They want to blame us for our own security in allowing the Iranians in to begin with."

Caleb looked so defeated that I wanted to tell him I never clicked on the link. It was all a lie.

Steve smiled sympathetically at Caleb. "I'm just the steward, boss. I'll keep the lights on until you can come back."

Caleb smiled in a sad way that looked more like a frown than a smile. He looked as if he was never going to recover from this. But I was not going to be a victim. I was going to be that very thing President Brian Davis had always claimed that he was: a winner. I just needed to find out who was trying to frame me. And why.

CHAPTER 47

THURSDAY, JULY 7, LATER.

I went out into the parking lot to get some air. Kerry was out having a smoke.

"Hey Michael," they said. "How are you doing?"

"Better, thanks," I replied.

"How's Pam?"

I wanted to tell Kerry the truth, but I couldn't. "She's great. She's up at our cabin for a couple of days."

Kerry took a drag and smiled. "Sounds wonderful. I wish I had a cabin. I'd love to get out of Dodge for a while, you know?"

"Oh? Are you okay?"

Kerry finished their cigarette and crushed it out on the ground with their Doc Martens heel. "The thing I liked about customer service is that I could help people. But now, we don't have any customers calling in. They've all left us."

"Makes sense."

"Just the bosses, asking us to clean things up, delete recordings and transcripts."

"Who's asking you to delete?"

Kerry looked as if they'd realized they had said too much. "It's just housekeeping, I guess."

I nodded.

"I guess Caleb was just worried," Kerry said.

"So it was Caleb who asked you to delete the records?"

They nodded. "He just came by and said to get it done. Nothing in writing."

Kerry gave me a look that suggested it was suspicious.

"And you haven't done it."

"We've started. But we're slow-walking it. With the way things are these days, the last place a trans person wants to be is in prison." They chuckled, but their eyes were not happy. I figured it was time to give Kerry some rope so they could help me hang the villains.

"Look, Kerry, you know they tried to pin this on me," I said. Kerry nodded. "I have found out that I never clicked on that phishing link."

"Really?"

"Really. I have a friend in IT who did a search and discovered that I never clicked on it."

"Wow. Spooky. What are you going to do?"

I wasn't going to go that far, but I needed to see how far Kerry would go. "I don't know yet. But I am wondering if you could check your customer service records for calls that came in on and around January 25, the day I supposedly clicked on the link. And on and around June 21, the day the feds took Pam and me away."

Kerry tilted their head. "You think there's something connected to you?"

"I don't know. But I'm hoping you can let me know."

Kerry sighed. "Okay. We just handle customer service calls." They didn't think there would be anything there.

"And after you do, what happens?"

"They get logged into the system."

"As in noted down, date and time, that kind of thing?"

"Noted and transcribed."

"Who sees the transcriptions?"

"They go straight to the bosses. For the files."

I smiled. Transcribed was good. "Can you do it?"

Kerry lit up another cigarette, took a drag, and blew out a stream of smoke. "I'll make you a deal."

I stiffened. What would I have to do in return?

"I'll get you those records, if you and Pam will take me to your cabin some time."

I smiled and extended my hand. "We have a deal."

CHAPTER 48

THURSDAY, JULY 7, LATER.

I turned on the TV out of habit, not that there was anyone to talk to in the house except Cecil. I opened an IPA and sat on the couch, just like I had done with Pam a thousand years ago, when we had a quiet life. Now, it was the drink before the war. My war.

GNC told me the other war, the one against Iran, was going badly. The US had lost nearly two dozen F-35s, blown out of the sky by Iran's air defenses. Yet another example of President Davis's technological genius, waging an air war on a country that was ready for it. GNC showed six US pilots taken prisoner by the Iranians. Guys a little younger than me, looking dazed and bruised. Beaten by their captors. Now they would be killed if Davis's "or else" meant that Iranian hostages were killed by US forces.

Then Vice President O'Neil appeared on screen. "My fellow Americans," O'Neil said, his voice sandpapery, tinged with the bayou of Louisiana, where he was from. "We are at a critical time as a nation. We are under existential threat from this criminal regime in Iran. President Davis has entrusted me with supervising our domestic security, which has been breached by enemy agents. From this moment on, any Iranian national, even if a US citizen, will be taken into custody by the United States government, without exception. This program is being put in place for the protection of the country at this time of war."

I shuddered. Did this mean that they would again come after Pam for being born to Iranian parents?

Then Davis himself came on-screen, all gunslinger bluster now, his hair slicked back and dyed, as there was no gray in the black now. His eyes, brown and angry, stared into the camera and his lips barely moved as he told the world what was coming next.

"The so-called Supreme Leader of Iran has twenty-four hours to meet our demands or we will kill his other accomplices. To show him how serious we are, we have already executed two. The United States is not playing games here. Iran attacked us, and if the so-called Supreme Leader does not step down by this time tomorrow, we will execute his accomplices, and then we will end Iran. We know that our captured pilots support us. They will die as patriots." Then he smiled. He was looking forward to the death to come.

The screen shifted back to the GNC news anchor, who stared into the camera speechless for several seconds. "Rioting continues in several cities tonight," the anchor eventually said, sounding nervous and distraught. "Protesters opposed to President Davis and the war with Iran clashed with the civil protection units the president has deployed to, as he declared, 'protect our way of life.' Fifteen people were killed in San Francisco when the civil protection units opened fire on a crowd of protesters, while a civil protection officer was killed by protesters in Brooklyn. Vice President O'Neil has ordered the army to lock down New York City as a search for the 'assassins,' as he put it, 'continues.'"

I turned off the television. I couldn't take any more of this. President Davis had, in his narcissism, expected this war to be a walkover. That's the thing about people, their egos are always tripping them up. Even the smartest, most rational, most competent people get overconfident about their own abilities. Half the problems in the world are because of over-confident smart people.

I exhaled loudly. Even if I did all I planned to do, and it all worked, what would the country look like? Unless Davis was in prison and deprived of all his levers of power, it was only going to get worse.

I walked outside into the front lawn to look at the sky. The night was a beauty, the sky shimmering with stars. I thought of those photos from a few years back, from that telescope, the Webb I think, that photographed the universe. We are a little blue dot orbiting in a vast sea of little blue dots.

"Hey there," Grant Woollard said, strolling up my driveway. He had an envelope in his hand.

"Hi," I said. "How's your guest?"

I had not gone over to see Zahra this evening because I didn't want to trigger anything with whoever was watching me.

"She left you this," Woollard said, handing me the envelope.

"She's gone?"

He touched his thick and tangled mustache, like he was checking for crumbs. "Yep. She left when I was on a grocery run. Ate like a bird she did."

I took the envelope and opened it. It was short and in black capital letters. "Thanks to you both. I have decided it is time. Zahra."

I knew why she had gone like this. To keep us in the dark. To keep us safe.

But we all knew that none of us were safe. Not until this was over. Not until Davis was gone.

"Thanks, Grant," I said.

He patted his beer gut. "It was nice having her around. Ever since the wife died it's been kinda lonely."

I didn't know he had a wife and she had died. I felt sorry for him and was about to invite him in for an IPA when a red Indian Scout Bobber motorcycle came roaring up the street. And into my driveway. It was Kerry. Grant took in Kerry, this tall pretty woman on a hot bike, and then he looked at me. I said, "Grant, this is Kerry. A work colleague."

They shook hands.

"I'll leave you to it," he said. "I'd imagine your security company is pretty busy these days." He saluted me and walked back across the street.

Kerry and I walked inside the house.

"I'm so sorry for just showing up like this, Michael, but I felt it was safest."

Then they pulled a thumb drive out of their pocket. I held up a hand and turned on the radio, loud. "The feds are listening in," I said. Kerry blinked hard and nodded. As if to say, of course they are.

I took the thumb drive from Kerry. I couldn't plug it into my laptop because the FBI had eyes on it. Or I had to believe they did. So I walked over to the TV and plugged it into a USB port. Then I turned on the TV, scrolled to the USB drive, and up came a document.

"It's a log of the calls," Kerry said. "Nothing weird on January 25. But June 21 is a different story."

I scrolled to June 21. The calls started coming in before Armor was open.

"Click on the next document and you'll get the transcripts," Kerry said.

I clicked. The 6:45 a.m. call was short but panicked. "This is The Law. All of our security cameras are down. We need them back up ASAP."

I looked at Kerry. "Do you know who The Law is?"

They nodded. "It's a prison. I don't know the location, but we put cameras in lots of prisons."

It hit me. The Law was what the sign said outside the prison I had been thrown into. The sign that I saw after I was discharged and came out into the world with Nicole.

"The rest of this set are also from The Law, which finally got their cameras turned back on at lunchtime," they explained.

After I was brought in.

"Scroll to the last set of messages," Kerry said.

I did, but I had a feeling that I knew where they'd be from. They came in the same day, the same early morning time frame. "This is PPC #8 in Whiteland. All of our security cameras are down. Need you guys to fix it, and fast, OK?"

Pam's prison.

"They got theirs fixed by lunchtime, too," Kerry said.

I took a breath and thought it through. On the day Pam and I had been hauled into prison, both the prisons we had been parked in had their Armor security cameras malfunction. This was not a coincidence. This was someone who didn't want us to be seen.

"Any idea who turned the cameras back on?"

Kerry smiled sadly. "No. Wish I did. But we can't access that."

Maybe Bo could, I thought.

"You did a brave thing by bringing this here," I said.

"The FBI knows I'm here, I guess," Kerry said.

"Yeah, they probably do. But they don't know why. So let's mess with them."

Kerry's eyes lit up, as if this was a plan they could get behind.

"You stay the night here. We have a spare bedroom. It's all on the up and up. But the FBI will wonder what is going on, that I have a guest sleep over on a night when my wife is away."

"What will that make them think?" Kerry asked, not defensively, but intrigued.

"They know you work for Armor. It will let them know I have allies on the inside."

They ran a manicured hand through their long red hair, for comfort, to think. The conclusion came along with a broad smile. "Sounds like a plan."

I couldn't sleep at all, and I didn't dare to touch any of Pam's lorazepam. I needed to have all my wits about me when day came. So I just stared at the ceiling. I tried to imagine how everything would play out. All I could see was Pam, running to me, and me taking her in my arms, and the two of us escaping into the future. Where we would be safe.

When I rolled onto my side, I saw the space where Pam should be.

Empty.

I thought about the weapons in my arsenal. I had evidence from Bo that I had not clicked on the phishing link, which was supposed to be how Iranian hackers got into Armor and then the Treasury Department. And that someone had deleted that email. I had evidence from Kerry that someone had turned off the security cameras at the two prisons where Pam and I had been taken so there would be no evidence of our arrival. And then there was Davis's adviser Christopher Clay—the Iran hawk—those pictures with him and Steve, and his presence in the room when Weiss interrogated me.

Fury surged through my body at all they had done to me. At all they had done to Pam. To Zahra. To America. To the Iranian people. I thought of those Iranians that Davis was holding hostage. I thought of the little girl with the blue eyes, the one who so reminded me of Pam. I thought of the US pilots captive in Tehran. I thought of the three teenage boys captive to the Knights of Liberty. And I pictured President Brian Davis. He had a sadistic grin on his face, daring me to squeeze the trigger on the gun I was pointing at him.

CHAPTER 49

FRIDAY, JULY 8.

I told Kerry the next morning to stay at our place until the day was done. But I gave them directions to the cabin and my keys to the place, in case I didn't come back.

"Thanks, Michael," Kerry said.

"My thanks to you," I replied, but Kerry had tears in their eyes.

"You and Pam have suffered so much. I am just a small part in what will be your victory."

If victory was to come, what would it look like?

About an hour later I took a deep breath and looked ahead as I entered Armor. The mirrored doors told me I was thinner and looking older by a lot more than three weeks, as if I had seen a lot in a short time. And that time was not yet done with me.

Usually the copiers are humming or an early morning Roomba is giving the last touch-up to the floor, the security cameras are blinking, and people are working. Not now. It was quiet, still, and dark. I didn't see anyone.

I walked into the kitchen. Turned on the light switch, but nothing happened. I tried to turn on the Keurig coffee maker, but nothing happened.

The stock ticker screen was blank as I walked past it to my office. I turned on my computer. It came to life, but I saw it was running on its battery. I flicked on the light switch, but nothing happened. The power to Armor Security had been cut.

I walked down the corridor to see if Bo was there, and I passed by Steve's office. The door was open, and as I glanced in, I noticed that his computer was gone. It was a desktop, so not the kind of thing you'd slip into a briefcase or a backpack.

I poked my head inside. Aside from the missing computer, his office was mostly as it had been when I was last in there. There were his fly-fishing photos. And the red-white-and-blue Davis-O'Neil 2032 flag ("Keep America Great!") was hanging above where his computer used to be.

The power was cut, the computer was gone, and so, apparently, was Steve. He was supposed to be the steward for Caleb, the guy who was going to see Armor Security through the storm.

I sat down in the chair at his desk and surveyed the office. He had left in a hurry, it seemed, given that he had taken his computer and left numerous belongings. Why would Steve bail on Armor?

He surely had something to do with all of this, given his friendship with Christopher Clay, so maybe he fled before he was caught? But how would he know he was about to be caught? And since Davis and Clay were still in power, who would catch him?

"Hey Mike, you in charge now?" Bo was standing in the doorway. He looked pale—and worried.

"Ha ha. Not quite. You okay?" I asked.

"Not as long as Davis has that little Iranian girl, no, I'm not."

He came in and sat down in a chair opposite me.

"I think Steve is gone, Bo," I said.

"Really? But he's supposed to be in charge."

"The power has been cut; his computer is gone . . ."

Bo just shook his head.

"Any way to turn the power back on?" I asked.

"We have backup power, Mike," Bo said. "There's a generator that should give us enough to get through today."

I smiled at him. "Can you turn it on?"

"Yes, was about to."

"Okay great. Then can you do me a favor?"

"What's that?" he asked, wearily.

"Can you get into the customer service logs? And see who fixed the cameras that went out at two prisons on June 21?"

Bo ran a hand through his black curls, massaging out a plan. "I can try."

I walked with Bo to his desk and watched as he started up the generator with a few swift keystrokes. The lights came on. Then he accessed the repair logs.

"Which one?"

"First one of the day."

Bo tapped in some more codes, and the transcript delivery log showed that it had been accessed by one person. Steve Velarde. Who had issued the repair order.

Bo scrolled down to the prison in which Pam had been held, tapped in another code, and up came the result. Steve Velarde.

So it was Steve. I knew he had to have been involved one way or another. Now I knew he was a central player. This was the proof.

"Is there any way to find out if Steve Velarde sold any shares in Armor before all this came down?"

Bo thought about that. "He's a senior executive at Armor, an insider, so it should be public."

"Okay, can we try to find out?"

Bo typed something into his computer and up came EDGAR, the US government's Electronic Data Gathering, Analysis, and Retrieval system. It keeps track of submissions by companies and others who are required by law to file forms with the U.S. Securities and Exchange Commission.

"Armor is a public company, so insiders have to reveal any sales of stock within two business days of selling," Bo said, reading from the site. Then he typed in Steve Velarde's name. Steve sold 205,000 shares of Armor, which were valued at $164 a share, not in June, but in January. On January 25. The same day I didn't click the phishing email.

"Hold on, hold on," said Bo. He kept typing. "He sold another 150,000 shares on June 15."

"Wow," I said, shaking my head.

"Wait, stop, I'm not done yet," said Bo. "Let me see if I can't run this down."

"Okay, okay."

"Dude," he said, typing fast and clicking on his mouse repeatedly. "Dude . . . Dude . . . Steve fucking Velarde sold short 250,000 shares of Armor on June 4, just over two weeks before the hack became public and Armor's stock tanked."

"Are you serious?"

"Yes, he unloaded a ton of shares he had and then later made millions selling Amor shares short. He knew what was coming."

"What are Armor shares trading at today?" I asked Bo.

He didn't have to look it up. "They sank below $10 in Asia last night. When the NASDAQ opens, they'll sink further."

"But wouldn't that have flagged something to Caleb?"

Bo looked troubled, as if there was more here than he wanted to know. "Maybe that's why Caleb punched Steve at the Fourth of July party. Maybe they were on the outs."

I shrugged. "Can you print all this out? Along with my deleted email, which was probably Steve too?"

Bo paused. Thinking about how this could go more wrong.

"It's just us now, Bo. You and me," I said.

He took a breath, a smile on his lips but his eyes dark with worry. "Sure. I don't think we can get into any more trouble, can we?"

I forced myself to smile back at him. I knew that trouble could get a lot worse.

And the only chance I had to stop that from happening was to go back to the one person it could be most dangerous to see. Agent Jo Weiss.

CHAPTER 50

SATURDAY, JULY 9.

Jo Weiss looked like she hadn't slept much since I last saw her. And she didn't touch the coffee sitting in front of her now. I had insisted we meet at a café near her office, as I did not trust that anything good would happen to me if I went into her turf again. She had complained that it was a Saturday, but I told her if she wanted to save her career and maybe her life, then she wanted to hear me out.

Her strong face sagged a little, and a few flecks of gray interfered with her sleek blondness, as she stared at me across the sun-dappled table. She looked as if she had been carrying a burden that she couldn't continue to bear. And now I was going to give her a choice.

"I didn't do it, Agent Weiss. As you know, I didn't click the link and let the Iranians into Armor. That Ad Supply email you showed me when we first met. Remember that? I never clicked on that link like you said I did."

Her facial expression stayed stone cold.

"Do you have proof?"

I dealt the proof out like I was dealing myself a full house in seven-card stud. The email with the link, a record of its deletion, the record of who did it, my browser history, and the call logs and transcripts from customer service. Steve issuing the repair orders at the two Davis prisons where Pam and I were locked up. The stock transactions with Steve Velarde. And Steve's connection to Christopher Clay, the pictures, who was in my interrogation. With Weiss.

"Steve Velarde was behind it all," I said.

She looked at my documents. Her face tightened. Her jaw muscles clenched. She looked angry. I was gambling that the anger would land where I needed it to. And that her instinct for self-preservation would kick in.

"Steve Velarde is second-in-command at Armor," Weiss said. "Why would he want to destroy the company?"

I took a breath. Why would he want to destroy my life? That was the more important question.

"I don't know. To help Davis and Clay by giving them a pretext to invade Iran? To make money with the stock sales? Both?"

She looked at me now with a flash of alarm in her green eyes. This FBI agent, who had always seemed as if the law had been made just for her to enforce at her whim, was in the middle of all this and was now scared. She looked back at the documents, as if to consider what kind of deal she might make, but I wasn't finished.

"At two p.m. this afternoon, the Knights of Liberty are going to launch suicide bombers near Wolfgang's Beer Garden."

Now Weiss's eyes were wide. "How do you know this?"

"Because, as I told you ten days ago, I gave them the bombs." I paused to enjoy her confusion. "Allow me to refresh your memory: They're not real. They just look real. And there's no way to tell unless you try to detonate them. Which the Knights commander Robert Montrose is going to do in a few hours on a busy summer weekend afternoon."

"And why, exactly, are the Knights of Liberty trying to set off suicide bombs?"

I took a breath.

"Because they want to blame it on Iranian terrorists, stir up hatred of immigrants, and galvanize support for Davis's war. And because they think Davis will pay them for their work. They captured three immigrant kids who they have held captive and are going to strap the bombs to them and dress them up as Iranians and then blow them up. Except they're not."

Agent Weiss frowned at me. "You made the bombs? That could be entrapment. But keep going." Her tone had shifted, and her "please" was present but unspoken. I was now in control.

"Janine Wood of GNC has been embedded with the Knights since I told her of this plan. As you know, she also has audio of President Davis authorizing the immigrant bounty program at the center of all this. We will soon have proof of this scheme, on the ground, with human faces as victims. Not even Davis can wriggle out of this one."

I was betting that what I said was all true. Agent Weiss looked as if her entire world was about to tumble, but instead of asking for a lifeline, she tried one last attack. I had expected nothing less.

"Making the bombs for these guys is entrapment."

I paused for maybe fifteen seconds and just smiled at her, like I was amused by her desperation. "I don't think so, Agent Weiss. I think that after I was set up by Armor, by you and Steve Velarde and Christopher Clay and President Davis—and nice touch turning off the Armor security cameras at the prisons you threw me and Pam into, by the way—after you set me up to take the fall for this crime against Iran, no one would blame me for doing whatever I could to save myself and my wife.

"Pam is being held captive by the Knights of Liberty, by the way. Janine has it all on film."

I could see Agent Weiss calculating her future with three rapid eye blinks. Her role in the frame job, in generating the pretext to invade Iran, was exposed. So was Davis's bounty scheme, which she may have had a role in, too. And I was no longer just a nobody: I was partnering with Janine Wood. The world would soon know about this. Congress would be all over it. Headlines everywhere.

"What do you want?" she asked.

"I want you to drop whatever it is that you're pursuing against me and Pam."

Weiss nodded. Faster than I expected. "I will do what I can. But there's more at play here than just me, Michael."

I stared at her and nodded that I understood. "I want you to release Nicole Wilkerson and Hannah Gottlieb."

Weiss nodded again. "That I can do."

"And I want you to be ready to arrest Robert Montrose and the three other Knights of Liberty this afternoon. And I want asylum for those three kids that they want to use to kill a lot of Americans."

Weiss nodded again. She didn't speak.

"Great," I said. "I'll be there, too. And Janine Wood will get it all on film. So you can atone for your sins. So you can look good, Agent Weiss."

She nodded again.

"If you do it right, Agent Weiss, then you won't be a traitor. You'll be a hero."

CHAPTER 51

SATURDAY, JULY 9, LATER.

I had copied all the documents that Bo and Kerry had found for me onto another flash drive. I popped the flash drive into my laptop, and then I texted Janine Wood.

"Janine, are you there?"

"I am here."

"Can you talk?"

I waited another minute, and then my phone rang. "Hi Joe," she said.

"Everything is looking good here," I said.

"That's great," she replied. "We're on our way."

"I need to send you some local maps. Detailing security issues, where cameras are, to keep you safe." Then I paused and spoke very slowly. "I put them together from documents I found in Armor Security." I paused again. "What's the best way to get them to you?"

She said, "Thanks very much, Joe. In a few hours we will be celebrating the success of today. Emails will be flying. It will be all over Google."

Then she ended the call. I thought that was an odd ending. Why didn't she just say it would go viral? Maybe Montrose had closed in. Maybe it was some kind of signal. I needed her to have these documents if we were going to win this war.

How could I get these documents to her so she would have the ammunition that she needed? Without getting her killed?

Then it struck me. Maybe she had just told me how. I could put them up on Google Docs and send her the link. I had her email: jwood@gnc.com.

I loaded them up and then clicked the settings so that only the recipient could access the link. Then I typed in my message.

"Here are some documents that will be of use to you on your journey. Fair winds, sis."

I hit SEND. It was the evidence that was going to help take down a president.

CHAPTER 52

SATURDAY, JULY 9, LATER.

Even though martial law was still in effect, or maybe because it was, Wolfgang's Beer Garden was overflowing on this hot Saturday afternoon in July. The evening curfew was still hours away. The patio was crowded with people, young and old, in bright-colored summer clothes. Kids were squealing with delight as they went down the slide and swung high in the swings on the playground Wolfgang had attached to the beer garden so that the whole family could enjoy the day out. Music was booming through the speakers. It was as if the city had decided to forget the war for the day.

I was sitting with Nicole and Hannah outside a shuttered Mexican café about one hundred yards down the street from the beer garden. Waiting. Watching. Weiss had released them as promised, shortly after we met, and they had showered and rested, but they were still shaken by their time inside.

"Public Protection Center Number Eight," Hannah said, cool and controlled. "Same one as Pam. It was only two days, but it was brutal."

"In Whiteland," Nicole added, anger in her voice. "No further comment necessary."

The feds had treated them like any other prisoners, so that meant a tiny cell with nauseating 24–7 lights on and the plastic basin that was the sink. They had two meals in plastic boxes of bread and soup.

"After we get rid of Davis, I'm doing everything I can to get rid of prisons like this," Hannah said.

Nicole nodded and turned to me and asked softly, "Now, what's our plan for today, Michael?"

I explained to Nicole and Hannah what I had found, and they listened skeptically. So I showed them the goods.

Like the good lawyers they were, they carefully went through the evidence I had produced. I told them that I had sent it all to Janine as well, via Google Docs. I wanted to label the file heading "Breaking News" but in the end opted for the less conspicuous "Security Issues," which was accurate.

"Wow," Nicole said, as she thumbed through the documents. "Clay and Steve are behind all this. That's means Davis is too. We can sue the government for a lot of money after he leaves office."

Hannah smiled at me. "More than enough to make up for how your stock options tanked after the Armor hack."

I knew that I could probably sue the government and win, if all went as planned and Davis was gone, but that journey would be long and expensive. What I wanted now was to get my wife safely home, the kids and Janine to safety, the Knights of Liberty in prison, and the footage we needed to get Janine's source to give her the Davis tape.

"I spoke to Janine a few minutes ago," Nicole said. "She had several updates. She said things are scary up there but she keeps getting really good footage. The kids are hanging in there and Montrose is letting them eat twice a day. She and her GNC colleagues have been doing some investigating of their own, too, and found a few things we will find helpful. She also talked to her source yesterday, the one with the tape of Davis and Clay talking about the immigrant bounty program. Janine thinks if everything goes well today and we get what we want on film then her source will give us the tape."

I smiled. "So it all comes down to the very thing that Davis loves so much," I said. "Television."

CHAPTER 53

SATURDAY, JULY 9, LATER.

At 1:35 p.m., I was seated next to Agent Jo Weiss in an empty office on the second floor of a building across the street from Wolfgang's, which was still packed with people trying to forget the soldiers parked in a Bradley just down the road. Nicole and Hannah were there with me, just in case Weiss tried to insert any kind of wrench in the works. Like sending me back to prison on treason charges. Or deporting Pam to Iran. I still didn't know Weiss's true intentions.

The tension between the three of them was thick. I could feel the shales of hostility sliding from the lawyers toward Weiss and the waves of professional fear emanating from the FBI agent. Weiss needed a win badly. Even after everything she had done to me and Pam, I needed to give her one.

Weiss had deployed a team of snipers around the perimeter of Wolfgang's. I told her that Montrose wasn't going to show up at the scene of his own crime. He'd be calling in to blow up the kids from nearby but out of sight. His three henchmen—Zeke, Travis, Pablo—would do the dirty work. And the way to find Montrose was to track my wife's phone. Pam was going to be in the burgundy Dodge Caravan with him. So were Zeke and Travis. Pablo would be with Janine and the kids in a white Jeep Cherokee.

I knew they probably had other ways, like the drones flying above, to get eyes on everyone. I had to tell myself that if the feds had eyes on Pam, then she would be safe. It was a terrifying irony that I felt deep in my midsection, but I had to believe it. I had imagined life without her twice now in the past month, and what kept me going was that I could imagine her coming back and us resuming our quiet life together.

Agent Weiss had her team of agents sitting in front of a bank of computers at a table behind us like some FBI geek squad. They were all wearing fancy headsets and staring at screens.

"You remember my team of special agents," Weiss said to me.

I did. "Agents McGarvey, Ortiz, and Cole." I paused. "Thanks for doing my gardening."

McGarvey's face reddened, and Ortiz and Cole looked down.

"They're on our side, Mr. Housen."

I didn't add "today."

The Special Agents were working from three computers, and three monitors were following Pam's progress into the city in the Caravan as if they were following Find My Friend on an iPhone.

"She's fifteen minutes out," Weiss said.

"They'll stop soon, I bet," I replied. "Where's Janine?"

Weiss turned to the table of geeks and asked.

"She's parked just around the corner on Morton," said the young woman. "Just south of Tenth Street. She's with Pablo and the three kids."

Weiss spoke into her wrist microphone. "The bombers are on Morton . . . just south of Tenth. In a white Jeep Cherokee. I will provide instructions once we have confirmation."

"You have to let Janine follow the kids when they get out of the car and start walking toward Wolfgang's," I said. "She needs to get that footage."

Weiss shook her head. "Can't risk it with the army sitting a block away in their Bradley. The second they see those kids in the Iranian clothes and vests, they will pounce."

"Can't you tell them what we're doing?"

Weiss shook her head again. "About half the army is with Davis. We have to assume that they all are. We can tell them some things about what we're up to, but say too much and we could wind up in cuffs. And the kids could wind up dead. We have guns. They have bombs and tanks."

Weiss had identified half the army as being with Davis. In drawing that distinction, I surmised that she was not. For the first time I saw what Weiss was up against. Her world was complicated in its own way. I had come to believe that maybe she had been working in the name of the law, as she saw it, even if that law was stacked against me and Pam. With the commander in chief the biggest criminal of all, the rule of law was anything but black and white.

Weiss turned to Team A. "Okay, we have a female friendly and three male hostiles in a burgundy Dodge Caravan, just coming up on North Crescent Road, at Seventeenth."

Pam in shotgun. Along with Montrose driving and Zeke and Travis in the back seat.

My pulse started racing.

"They've stopped, ma'am," the young woman said to Weiss.

I knew that where they had stopped was close to I-69. If Weiss and her team didn't get to Pam, then the Knights would escape with her. After everything was revealed to Montrose, he would eventually kill her.

"Team A, let me know when you have eyes on the Caravan."

A silence hung over the room. A silence that was way too long.

"Team A, do you read me?"

"Copy, we are looking for the vehicle."

Weiss turned to the geek squad. "They can't see the Caravan."

Cole fiddled with the keyboards. "Says that they're there. Still. Right on the southwest corner of Crescent at Seventeenth. They aren't moving."

Weiss cursed. "They dumped Pam's phone."

My heartbeat accelerated even more. It couldn't go any faster without exploding. The feds had lost Pam. I didn't think Montrose would be that smart, but I now knew that it sharpens the mind when you plan to kill a lot of your fellow citizens and make it look like the enemy did it. Now I had reached a level of fear I didn't know I could reach. I had to keep breathing, keep thinking.

Keep breathing . . . keep thinking.

Keep breathing . . . keep thinking.

"Get on the drones," Weiss said. "I want to see."

"On it, ma'am." Special Agent Ortiz tapped the keyboard and spun the screen around so we could see what the drones saw. There were three of them, one above College Avenue, looking down on the Jeep Cherokee with Janine and Pablo and the kids. Another drone was over the highway, looking at traffic. The third was on the move, looking for my wife.

"Take it down Crescent and then follow," Weiss said.

The drone started to move on the route she had commanded.

"Zoom," she said.

The drone's camera zoomed in.

"There!" I shouted. "There, to the right, along Seventeenth."

There was the burgundy Dodge Caravan with Pam and the Knights, heading toward College Avenue.

It was 1:55 p.m.

"Team A!" Weiss shouted. "We have eyes on them and we're transferring you the feed."

A wave of relief flooded through me.

But it lasted only a moment.

Suddenly, the screen went fuzzy—and then black.

"What the fuck?" Weiss said.

"We've lost the feed. Trying to get it back," said Special Agent Cole. He tapped something into the keyboard and scowled in frustration, pointing to what he saw on screen. A black hole of nothing.

"We've been jammed," said the white Special Agent.

Weiss looked like she was going to explode. "How the fuck did that happen?"

Then her face went hard, and her eyes shone. As if she had just answered her own question. She turned to her trio of agents, fierce urgency now in her voice. "Can we get any of the teams?"

Special Agent Ortiz tried to call up the teams on the computer, and Agent Cole tried on the phone. There was nothing.

"The army, right?"

The trio of Special Agents nodded.

"It was a risk," Weiss said to me, suddenly calm. "Telling the army we had drones in the area, which we had to do so they didn't shoot them down. But we knew they could do what they just did. This was always a possibility."

Why would Weiss tell the army anything? Was she trying to let madness ensue and make it look like she had tried to stop it? And when she failed, well, it would be my fault.

I felt like I had four minutes to save Pam. To save my life. But if the phones and the drones had both been jammed by the army, how was I going to do that?

"What are we going to do?" I said, my mouth as dry as if I'd run a marathon through the desert. I needed to know if Weiss was for real or just playing me.

"We need to find your wife," she said. "And we'd better do it fast."

CHAPTER 54

SATURDAY, JULY 9, LATER.

The people at Wolfgang's were glad to be out on a summer day, as if pretending to be normal for a couple of hours would make it so. The drones overhead were the jammed drones. Seeing nothing. And the people I saw as Weiss and I ran up College Avenue to Seventeenth were the ones who would die if things went sideways and a shoot-out followed. Men, women, and kids. Innocent of all that was happening.

We had lost our eyes when the Army jammed the drones, and we had lost our ears when they jammed the phone signals. This left me with one choice, the old-fashioned choice: face-to-face. If it wasn't already too late. We needed to find Pam. And we needed to reach Janine Wood before she let those kids loose.

I knew from the last drone shot of them that Janine was parked with Pablo and the kids on Morton, below Tenth. They needed to stay there until Montrose gave them the signal to go detonate. I ran faster than I thought I could, up the route the kids would likely take if Montrose gave them the go sign.

I rounded the corner on to Morton and saw Janine in the driver's seat of the white Jeep Cherokee, with Pablo and the kids in the back. I ran up to the driver's side and she powered down the window.

"Thank God, Janine," I said, breathing hard as I approached the car. "The Army has jammed the phones and the drones. They are on College in a Bradley armored van, and as soon as they see the bombers in

Iranian clothes wearing the vests, they're all dead. We need to tell Montrose we have to wait until the army moves."

She knew I needed to buy time. "Okay, Michael. But if the phones are jammed . . ."

"We're not fucking leaving this spot," Pablo shouted at her.

"Montrose needs to change the plan," I said. The kids were in the back seat in their costumes and vests, with Pablo holding a gun on them. They looked terrified.

"We have orders," Pablo barked at me.

"Okay, I'll get to him," I said, fear surging through me that it would be too late. "Do you know where he is?"

"He's planning to be on Seventeenth. Near College," Janine replied, her eyes cold with fear that this was all going to end in the very way we were trying to avoid. Everything was spiraling out of control.

I found another gear in my speed box and ran ever faster. I found Weiss around the corner, breathing hard. Good thing she had dressed for the mission and worn jeans and sneakers. "I found Janine," I told her. "She's right around the corner. Montrose is going to park on Seventeenth near College."

Weiss looked up the street. We were at Fifteenth. Two blocks away. The street was especially busy today. There would be carnage if this went sideways.

"Where's Team A?"

She shook her head. "Too far even if they could know what was up. And we've lost contact with the other teams. It's just you and me."

I looked at my phone. We had two minutes. I tried to call Montrose. Nothing happened.

"We're still jammed," I said.

Weiss looked like we might have just lost the battle. But then I said, "I have to go tell him. He'll believe me." She gave me a look that said both our lives were on the line. I knew it. And I wasn't going to die.

I ran as fast as I had ever run, up to Seventeenth and around the corner. I saw the Burgundy minivan. I saw Pam. She was sitting in the front seat next to Montrose. Travis and Zeke were in the back seat holding shotguns.

I waved to them and Pam saw me. Montrose looked startled, but he understood when I told him to roll down his window.

"What the fuck are you doing here?"

"You need to hold fire," I said, breathing hard. "The army has a Bradley parked right in front of the beer garden. The bombers won't get within one hundred yards before they'll be shot."

"You could have just called me."

I didn't tell him the phones were jammed, because that's how he was supposed to blow up the kids. With a phone call.

"Too many ears listening in, with the army around," I said. "Don't say anything on the phone."

Silence. He said nothing. I used every ounce of strength to stay silent myself. I needed him to come up with the idea himself, so he felt like he was in charge.

"Make the army move," he finally said, and I felt a touch of relief wash over me. As I caught my wife's eye, she winked. It was all going to be okay, she was saying.

"Great idea. Yes. It's going to have to be you guys," I said. "You need to send Travis or Zeke further to the south on College, and they need to let loose with their guns. Into the air." I turned to them in the back seat and they looked confused and nervous in their red helmets and black vests. "The army will head for the sound of gunfire. Then you can let the bombers loose."

Montrose thought about this plan. "Get in the van."

I hadn't expected that. I couldn't get in and have this end well. I needed to stay mobile.

"I need to watch the Bradley and signal to Pablo when it starts moving. I need to be on the street. He's going to need a visual once you have taken care of the Bradley."

Montrose nodded. He looked haggard and hungover, but there was a strange confidence in his bloodshot eyes. Then he rolled up the window of the van and motioned for me to get the hell away. The car skidded as they drove off.

I ran back to College and found Weiss where I had left her. "You have to get to the bombers," I said. "They are two blocks away from

Wolfgang's. In the Cherokee. Follow them and Pablo and Janine. Let Janine get the footage of them approaching the beer garden at gunpoint, and once she has it you can take them all in."

Weiss nodded, then turned and ran back up College toward Janine's Cherokee, her pistol now in her hand.

Then I turned and ran as fast as I could down College Avenue, toward the beer garden and toward the army's Bradley. It was sitting there. Waiting for trouble.

As soon as I got close to Wolfgang's, I slowed to a trot, trying to avoid any attention.

I heard a burst of gunfire about a block ahead and to the west. Then there was another, and another. Travis and Zeke were shooting their guns into the air. I heard the Bradley's engine gun, and the army was on the move.

I stood there near Wolfgang's for about thirty seconds. Then I saw Zeke and Travis sprinting down the street to the Dodge Caravan, which I saw was about fifty feet away.

"Hey guys!" I called out.

They both turned, weapons aimed at me, then they smiled.

"Fucken A, Weiss!" Zeke hollered.

Montrose put the van into gear and did a U-turn to meet Zeke and Travis in mid-block. I couldn't let that happen. I couldn't let them escape with Pam.

"Guys!" I ran up to them. "You don't want to go that way, the army's coming that way."

The van approached at speed, and Travis waved his gun at the driver. Montrose wasn't stopping. He was speeding, and next to him was Pam. She had his gun. She had it aimed at his head.

Travis raised his AR-15 to take aim at the van, at Pam, and I tackled him. We hit the ground hard, and his rifle clattered to the side.

"What the fuck?" Zeke said, standing above us in shock.

It was the last thing he said as the van plowed into him, sending him airborne into a lamppost, and then the van went up onto the curb and slammed into an SUV parked in the lot adjoining the street.

I grabbed Travis's rifle from the ground and smashed him in the head with the butt. Knocked him out cold. I ran toward the van. The airbags had deployed, and I yanked open the door. There was Pam. She had Montrose's gun in her hand, looking dazed. But Montrose was gone.

I pulled Pam out of the van. "Mikey," she said, wrapping her arms around me and dropping the gun.

The Bradley armored vehicle roared around the corner, and I put down the AR-15.

Half a dozen soldiers in camo and body armor jumped out of the vehicle, their rifles aimed at us.

I raised my hands, and Pam did the same. "We're friendlies," I said, as a soldier, just a kid, really, put hard steel cuffs around our wrists. "That guy on the ground is not a friendly."

"We'll sort that all out," a burly sergeant said with surprising calm, taking in Travis's red helmet and black vest.

We sat on the sidewalk for a couple of minutes as the army guys tried to figure out what had happened. Were we going back to a Davis prison? I looked at Pam, and she smiled and gave me a look that said she loved me no matter what. I loved her more than I ever had before, sitting on the curb together in handcuffs. I leaned over and kissed her.

At that moment, Agent Weiss came running around the corner, gun in hand, and the army guys swung their rifles at her. She flashed her badge. "FBI," she said.

Then she turned to the oldest solider, who looked like the boss, her chest heaving. "Let those two go. They're with me."

CHAPTER 55

SATURDAY, JULY 9, LATER.

Agent Weiss brought me and Pam to her temporary headquarters across from Wolfgang's. Nicole and Hannah were still there, looking as if they'd watched a horror film, which in a way they had.

All I could think about was whether Janine got the footage of the kids walking toward the beer garden at gunpoint. If she didn't, this whole thing was in vain.

"The feed came back up once the army started to move," the Latino Special Agent explained.

"We thought they were going to shoot you guys," Nicole said, looking shaken.

"How did you get the guy's gun?" Weiss asked Pam.

She was trembling. "He took it out and put it on the center console. When Michael appeared at the bottom of the street, after Zeke and Travis shot their guns in the air, he was surprised. And he looked away, and I grabbed his gun. Then he sped the van toward you Mikey . . . I thought you were going to die . . ."

Pam looked at me with tears welling in her beautiful, brave blue eyes, and I held her close.

"You two saved those kids," Hannah said, and Pam held me tighter.

I looked over at the three Latino boys, wrapped in Mylar blankets, drinking bottled water. They looked at me as if they should maybe be afraid again, but I raised my open hands and smiled at them. Then I picked up one of the suicide bomb vests and looked over at Agent Weiss.

She smiled. And I could tell that it was genuine. She knew what I was going to do.

So I pulled out the C4. I unwrapped the plastic and took out a piece of modeling clay. Then I twisted the clay like a pretzel as the kids stared at it, wide-eyed. Then smiles crept across their faces. They understood.

"*Son falsas*," said the older one. They were fakes.

"*Sí*," Hannah responded. Then she told them in Spanish that Pam and I had made these fake suicide vests and then delivered the fake vests to their captors so that we could save them.

The youngest kid started to cry. Then Pam started to cry. I held her in my arms again, and I held back tears myself. She was safe. But the country was not safe. Not yet.

The FBI had snagged Pablo and Travis on the street, and they had caught Montrose pretending to be just another patron at the bar at Wolfgang's. Zeke was dead. I was glad that they were all in custody. "Leave them to me," Weiss said. I had firsthand knowledge of what that was going to be like.

I called Janine Wood. "Hey Michael," she said. "You all okay?"

"Yes, all is well. With Pam. The kids are safe."

"Very good."

"And how are you?"

"Couldn't be better," she said, unfazed. "I just filed everything. Thanks for your email. Got it all."

"That was fast," I said.

She laughed. "These phones can do in a minute what it used to take editors a couple of hours to do. It should be up soon."

"Did you get everything?" I asked her, deeply worried that she hadn't gotten the footage of the kids we wanted and this whole harrowing extravaganza had been for nothing.

She paused. "Everything. What I saw, and what you're going to hear. My source came through. Are you near a television?"

The techies dialed up GNC and spun the screens so we could all see it.

And there it all was just a few minutes later. I recognized Janine's genius for capturing drama as the video unfolded. The kids in captivity, and the Knights abusing them with their voices and their fists. And then me and Pam, delivering the vests. And then the operation that we had just been part of. The kids in Iranian garb, weeping, tears streaming down their faces, being forced out of the Jeep at gunpoint by Pablo. Walking down the street toward the innocent crowd at Wolfgang's. Then Agent Weiss showing up like a force of good and her agents tackling and arresting Pablo. Janine took home the rest.

"These self-proclaimed defenders of liberty were kidnapping immigrants and dressing them up as Iranians and trying to use them as suicide bombers to kill innocent Americans so that President Davis's fledgling attack on Iran would gain domestic support. But they would not have done it had they not had President Davis's support in the first place. In this exclusive audio obtained by GNC, you will hear him lay out the crime with his unofficial adviser on foreign policy, Christopher Clay."

On-screen, photos of Clay and the president appeared. And then we heard the audio.

"It has to be on the DL," Davis said. "Paying the boys to capture and turn in illegals won't go over well on the hill or the press."

"Not too on the DL, though" Clay replied. "You want to not just get the scum back below the border. You also want to create fear."

Davis laughed. "Oh, I want those fuckers to be covered in their own shit with fear." He savored that scenario and said, "Okay, so we pay the boys a bounty, and give them the green light to . . ."

Clay chuckled. "To do what they see is in the best interests of protecting the United States of America. Against this perilous threat from the ragheads in Iran and the criminals to our south."

Davis laughed again. "We can get this message out to the boys?"

"We don't even have to use Davis Truth to do it," Clay responded. "Our ground ops among the base will take care of this easily."

Davis laughed again.

"Okay," he said. "Make this happen Chris. Get it done."

Then Janine came back on screen. In the same clothes she had been in for a week.

Exhausted.

Fierce.

Proud.

"But there's more. The alleged Iranian cyberattack on the United States—that justified this unjustifiable war to begin with—was a false flag. It was engineered by the very same Davis adviser Christopher Clay and Steve Velarde, the number two man at video-camera company Armor Security and Clay's longtime friend. GNC has obtained the forensic evidence establishing this, including detailed confidential internal files at Armor Security. We have posted it for our viewers on gnc.com/news/armor. President Davis's war on Iran was based on a fake premise from the start: Iran did not hack into Armor Security and then the US Treasury Department, as Davis has claimed. A rogue cadre of NSA hackers, under Clay's direction, hacked into Armor and then Treasury. The rogue unit posed as Iranian hackers by setting up servers in Iran and using unique hacking techniques known to be used by Iranian cybercriminals."

I was blown away at how Janine powerfully tied all the pieces together and added a few more with her own investigating.

"It was all a scam," she continued, "a scam for Davis to finally get Iran. And thousands of people have died because of it. Why did he do it? Why did he lie and say Iran attacked the US first? Because he needed to deflect the country from his own impending implosion in the courts, in Congress, and on Wall Street. As for Christopher Clay, he has been advocating to invade Iran for decades. Davis and Armor were his vessels to finally do so. And Steve Velarde, an ardent Davis supporter, we can see by the stock in Armor Security that he sold short before Armor imploded, that he did it not just to please Davis and Clay, but for the money. Tens of millions of dollars. We will be bringing you more in the coming hours and days, but my message to the Cabinet, the House, the Senate, the courts is this: Davis's time is finally up."

Images of the three young kids walking down the street dressed as Iranians, in tears and at gunpoint, came on the screen. The human faces of Davis's war.

Janine's presentation was brilliant. Stunning. Powerful. She explained how Steve and Clay worked together to fake the hack into Armor to give Davis his pretext for invading Iran. But one huge question loomed in my mind: Why me and Pam? I couldn't figure it out. Why were we set up? Were we just collateral damage, easy victims because of Pam's family? Or was there something more going on? Even Janine Wood couldn't explain it.

We all looked at each other after GNC went to commercial, as if maybe, just maybe, there was a fighting chance that the world as we had known it—before Davis was president, before Armor imploded, before Pam and I went to prison, before the Knights terrorized those kids—might actually, finally, return.

CHAPTER 56

MONDAY, JULY 11.

Agent Jo Weiss summoned Pam and me to meet with her on Monday at her office. As we drove downtown, NPR summarized the government's reaction to Janine's breaking story forty-eight hours before. The attorney general had appointed a special prosecutor to investigate Davis. Both the House and Senate seemed to have sufficient votes for impeachment and removal from office. Davis hadn't posted a Truth since the story broke—his longest break since his platform launched. We didn't know if the momentum would continue, but America seemed to be passing this test of its conscience.

I noticed that the air felt different. Fresher. Free of drones and sirens. There were people on the street, walking with more purpose and less fear. Several shopkeepers were taking the boards off the windows of their stores. And there wasn't a checkpoint in sight.

It was my first time inside Weiss's office, as our previous meetings had been in prison, on the street, in a café, and at Armor. I found the room spare and efficient. No photos of family on her desk, just a laptop computer and an FBI field manual. The beige walls were bare other than a small, framed picture of her winning some FBI medal and shaking hands with some old guy in a suit. There was a long table in the middle of the room with six chairs around it and a large flat-screen television bolted to the wall at the far end of the room, just above Weiss's desk and computer. It was like the whole office had been set up to be quickly taken down.

Weiss said she wanted to do an official debrief with us. I knew that was because she wanted to turn the dial on her own story. She made sure that Nicole and Hannah were there with us. And so, too, was another guest, one who had been there when Weiss first interrogated me what seemed like years ago. But it was less than a month. Either way, I never expected to meet with this guy again.

When Agent Weiss said we had a special guest joining us via Zoom, I thought it might be Zahra beaming in. We had not heard from her since she left Grant Woollard's house four days earlier, but Nicole told us not to worry. Zahra had sent a text saying she was fine. And I had been occupied with other things. As had Pam, who sat down next to me looking as if she was lit from within. All the stress of the past week had washed away, and she radiated a pure goodness that seemed to cast a warm glow on the barren room.

Then Weiss launched the Zoom link, and on the other end of it was Christopher Clay.

Weiss introduced us all, and Clay said nothing. He just nodded. Weiss took command.

"I wanted you to join us, Mr. Clay, because you are implicated in some of the documents that Mr. Housen has collected. Some of them were made public recently as you know. Some of them have not."

Clay just stared, unblinking, into the camera on his computer. The flat gray wall behind him, with no revealing books or paintings or anything personal to reveal, combined with his gray persona to make it seem like we were looking at a man encased in fog.

"I will just pop those documents up on screen, and Mr. Housen can explain what they are."

And so I did, as Weiss put up the fake phishing email and its deletion time stamp, my browser history showing I never visited the site in the email, the voice log transcripts showing calls to Armor from Davis's prisons. And then there was the money: Steve's short sales of Armor stock, just before all hell broke loose. The screen showed the picture of Clay and Steve together in Puerto Rico.

"Thank you, Mr. Housen," Weiss said. Speaking calmly, her low voice detailed the Knights of Liberty's capture of the immigrant kids—from

Venezuela, it turned out—and their plan to dress the kids as Iranians and explode them in a crowded beer garden in a twisted attempt to galvanize support for the war against Iran. "They did this with your and President Davis's authorization," Weiss said. "As you know full well, this was reported by GNC." Weiss paused, then turned to our table. "Is there anything else?"

"Yes," Pam said. "You put my husband and me in prison for no reason. You hounded my friend Zahra out of the country. You've terrorized us for no reason." Pam was mad, but Clay still didn't blink.

"Do you have a response, Mr. Clay?" Weiss asked.

I could see thoughts forming in his head, and then the man who had been a player in all that had happened to me and to the world said, "Thank you, Agent Weiss, for coming to me with these issues. I believe that you will soon see results."

Then his screen went blank.

We all looked at Agent Weiss, who stared at the screen, then smiled at us. There was a real pleasure in her green eyes.

"I think we will see results," she said.

"What are you expecting?" Nicole asked.

"I'm expecting Clay to take action to save his own skin."

I was surprised to hear her say this. "But he's responsible for all these crimes . . ."

Weiss put a hand to her mouth. "He is, as you say, Mr. Housen, responsible, but there are other actors who are also responsible. And power is what matters most. There's a reason Clay has been around as long as he has."

CHAPTER 57

FRIDAY, JULY 15.

Pam and I sat on our couch and watched GNC as what had been unthinkable just a month earlier became our new reality. From the Pentagon, the Chairman of the Joint Chiefs of Staff, General Randall McCluskey, strode up to the podium, looking like an Irish boxer about to enter the ring where the fight was fixed in his favor. He was flanked by the same team who had stood there recently when he said that they would defend the United States against its enemies at home and abroad.

McCluskey, in his Back Bay bark of a voice, announced that the war against Iran was over. He went on to say that it was an unjust war and that the United States would be working with "the next regime in Iran."

Pam looked at me in surprise. "Wow, Mikey! That's a signal to the Iranians that the US will back their regime change."

It was. But I knew the Joint Chiefs couldn't dictate policy. That would have to come from the president.

Even so, regime change in Iran was already underway. Once the US had not killed the family members of the Supreme Leader, there was a kind of national reckoning. He'd been reprieved on one front but not on another. The people had been jolted enough by American bombs that they were in a state of war still. They were mobilized and angry. They wanted Rhouhani and his accomplices out, and now they were at war inside their own country, against their own leaders.

So were we. McCluskey went on to say that President Davis had lost the support of the armed forces, and that he was declaring an end to martial law and freeing all people arrested for political reasons during its existence.

It was stunning. Had we endured Davis and his crimes to become a military dictatorship?

No, we had not. GNC then cut to the White House, where Vice President Gus O'Neil was being sworn in as the next president of the United States. The GNC anchor told us that an hour earlier, President Brian Davis had left the country. Davis was rumored to be heading to Russia, where he would doubtless fit in with the oligarchs, though they wouldn't be so generous as to let him get in on their crimes. He'd have to find his own space.

Christopher Clay, the guy who for so long had been hiding in the shadows, was now on camera inside the White House. He was leading the charge for a Cabinet cleansing, to replace those who had lied to the American people. He acknowledged that he held no elected office, but that his position as an insider who had tried to stop the war gave him credibility in the "corridors of power" and he would use his political capital to make sure we never went down this road again.

"I can promise you, in my capacity as adviser now to four presidents, that we have learned what tyranny can look like. And it is not us."

So Davis was finally gone and yet Clay—Steve's longtime friend—was still in power. Those must have been the "results" Clay had promised.

CHAPTER 58

FRIDAY, JULY 15, LATER.

I decided to go back to the office and clean out my things. Pam wanted me to wait until next week, but I was done with Armor Security and wanted to get anything that was mine out of there before someone could mess with it and get me into trouble again.

The place was like a ghost town without the tumbleweeds. It was crazy how quickly an office that had been busy with life could now seem as if it had always been a husk. The power was cut, but the front door was wide open, and I wandered past the empty reception desk to my office just like I had so many times before, yet without seeing another human face.

Everything was quiet and still.

Until I switched on my computer to offload files onto my flash drive. There on-screen was a photo of Zahra. She was staring at the camera with terrified wet eyes. Her face was dirty, her hair a frantic mess. Someone was holding a gun to her head. You could see the tip of the gun pressed hard against her skull.

I called Pam. She listened in silence. Shocked. Shaken. Then she said she would call Foad and see if he had heard anything.

I wondered how the hell this photo had wound up on my desktop. I looked around, half expecting Bo to walk up. But he wasn't here.

Pam called me back. She had reached Foad, and he said to see if I could find the photo file on my computer.

"You mean the actual photo?"

"Yes. If someone popped it up as your screen display remotely, they might have stored it on your computer first. Check in your Pictures file. Foad says that's where it might be stored."

I checked. And there it was, the image of Zahra.

"Okay, I have found it," I said to Pam.

"Great. Now right click it and then click on the Properties tab."

"Done."

"Now open the Details tab."

"Done."

"Do you see the GPS coordinates of the photo?"

"I do." 39°09'55.19" N 86°31'35.00" W.

"Load them into Google and see what comes up."

I popped the coordinates into Google.

"The photo was taken here in Bloomington, Pam. It looks like right by our house . . . wait . . . yes . . . at Grant's."

Pam gasped. "What's the date?"

It was July 7, the day that Zahra left town.

"So she didn't leave Woollard's voluntarily. She was forced to leave. Someone else wrote that cryptic note—or forced her to. Do you think he had anything to do with it?"

I didn't think so. He had been protecting her. Who would want to put a gun to the head of Zahra? And why did this person go to the trouble of letting me know they did?

CHAPTER 59

FRIDAY, JULY 15, LATER.

Grant Woollard was watering his garden when I pulled into my driveway. His smile faded as he saw the purpose in my stride as I hustled over to him.

I brandished my phone like a gun and showed him a photo of what I had seen on my Armor computer screen. Zahra with a gun to her head.

"Oh my God," Grant said. "Oh my God." He dropped the watering hose. He seemed genuinely shocked.

"This photo was taken here in Bloomington, Grant. In your house."

He looked at it again and closed his eyes in pain. "I knew I shouldn't have left her alone."

"Why is that? Had she been threatened?"

He shook his head. "No. But I saw a car parked outside that I didn't recognize. Not from the neighborhood."

"What kind of car?"

"Classic. Real eye-catcher. A white Mustang. It had a blue stripe down the middle"

My heartbeat accelerated. The only person I knew who had a white Mustang with a blue stripe down the middle was Bo. Had I told him Zahra was here? Had he followed me? Why would Bo kidnap Zahra?

"And I can tell you another thing," Grant said. "That's not my gun."

I called Bo, but he didn't answer. I sent him a text, but he didn't respond.

CHAPTER 60

FRIDAY, JULY 15, LATER.

Pam and I forced ourselves to go out that night to the spontaneous party that had been planned by Nicole. She, Hannah, Kerry, and Janine would all be there. The message sent to me about Zahra might be followed by another. But clearly, she was worth something to her captor alive, and it all somehow connected to me. To us.

"We just have to wait for the next message, Mikey," Pam said. "And in the meantime, we have to live. That's what Zahra would want. This is a nightmare, but it won't get any better by us just sitting around waiting for the next clue."

"Should we at least tell the police?"

"Not yet. That runs the risk of things getting worse. Davis is gone but his loyalists are still throughout law enforcement. Let's see what comes next. Let's go to the party and try to relax."

Nicole thought the best place in Bloomington to go to celebrate our freedom that night was at Wolfgang's. Who could say no to some bratwurst and sauerkraut and spaetzle, washed down with tankards of pilsner, after a month like we had just had?

Janine had delayed her flight back to D.C. until the next day, and she was sitting next to Nicole, their shoulders touching. They were smiling. Maybe out of all of this, they had found a way back to happiness, too. Janine was the one to raise the first toast. It was to me.

"Thanks to Michael Housen, Brian Davis is gone, and we are once again a free country."

"More or less," Hannah added, and we all laughed. Things were much better than they had been.

"The thanks are to you guys," I said, and my voice started to break. I took a sip of beer. "We all did this together."

We clinked our tankards and drank.

"Yeah, but that fascist Christopher Clay is still eating babies in D.C.," Janine said.

"How could he survive?" I asked.

"That's what he does," Janine said.

"That's what Weiss knew when she invited him to our meeting," Nicole said. "She was looking out for herself by making sure he knew what she had, because she knew he wasn't going away. He could only, in the end, be grateful to her for giving him a heads-up. And giving herself a head start on whatever is next for her."

Janine almost jumped out of her seat. "What do you mean Clay was at your meeting?"

We explained that he joined us via Zoom and that Weiss had led him through the crimes attached to his name. She wanted us there as witnesses.

"What did he say?"

I smiled. "He thanked Weiss for detailing 'these issues' to him and said we would soon see the results. And so we did. Davis is gone yet Clay remains."

Janine tapped notes into her phone. "You guys are the gift that never stops giving," she said.

That's when Pam told her that we had one more gift to give. "And Zahra Nasseri is being held hostage."

"By who?"

"We don't know."

I explained how the message had been delivered to us, and Nicole looked as if she was going to explode. "Why did she come back to the US?"

"To get footage sent to her house in LA, for our film," Pam said. "It was stupid but she's so passionate about her work."

"She was safe in Canada," Nicole said, shaking her head. "Who knew she was back here besides you guys?"

We thought about that. "We knew, and anyone watching might have seen her."

I stared at the Wolfgang pretzels that had arrived at our table. I had saved my wife and myself and yet had not protected Zahra. I felt, suddenly, like I had failed.

That's when Pam raised her glass in my direction and said, "Let us again toast the most wonderful man in the world, my husband, Michael. Without him, we wouldn't have had, and we won't have, a fighting chance."

And as we all clinked glasses, I knew that was Pam's message to me. The fighting chance wasn't going away. Because neither was the fight. And at that moment, I was ready to do it all again. Because I knew that I would have to.

CHAPTER 61

MONDAY, AUGUST 8.

The beginning of August saw the start of the "Senate Select Committee to Protect America." President Gus O'Neil had enthusiastically supported the committee as a way to throw the blame from the war and the gross attack on civil rights that had just happened as far from himself as he could. It was mostly Davis's fault, but O'Neil had been at his side the whole time.

Pam and I watched the proceedings on GNC. The first witness up was none other than Caleb Wagner. He sat at the table facing the committee, a nameplate in front of him bearing his name. He looked thin and pale. His vigor seemed to have disappeared along with his net worth. It had been quite a month for him too.

The seat to his left was empty. The nameplate in front of the seat was labeled: "Steve Velarde."

Caleb's usually booming voice was soft as he answered the questions from the senator from Vermont, who was the committee chair.

"Good morning, Mr. Wagner," said the senator, Caroline Coady. She was in her early seventies and had the air of the history professor she once had been.

"Good morning, Senator."

"Thank you for being with us."

Caleb nodded.

"Tell us about Armor Security, your company."

"I founded Armor when I was a teenager in my parents' garage.

We've been around for about twenty-five years. We sell internet-connected security video cameras. Before all this happened, we were one of the most successful companies in the country. We were in the Fortune 500."

"And one of your customers was the United States Department of the Treasury, is that right? You sold your internet-connected cameras to the Treasury?"

"Yes."

"Can you tell the committee to the best of your knowledge what happened with hackers entering the Department of the Treasury? They were not from Iran, were they?"

Caleb exhaled audibly and shook his head softly. Then he took a deep breath before speaking. "Well, there's still a lot of information coming in, but I have been informed that one of my longtime employees with detailed knowledge of our computer network worked with a rogue unit of the NSA to impersonate Iranian hackers and hack into Armor's computer network and create a back door into our software. Then the NSA hackers got into the Treasury's network through the back door in our software and caused trouble. The hackers set up servers in Iran and used known Iranian hacker techniques. So everyone thought it was Iranian hackers."

"But it wasn't Iran, was it?"

"No, it wasn't."

"Is the employee you referenced Steve Velarde?"

"Yes," Caleb said, looking at Steve's empty chair.

"What was his role at Armor?"

"He was my right-hand man."

"And you didn't know he was doing this?"

"I had no idea. Why would I have allowed him to ruin my own company?"

The senator smiled. "That's what we're trying to find out, Mr. Wagner. How long had he been with Armor?"

"Ten years."

"Did you trust him?"

"Yes, very much."

"And you didn't know he had sold short a substantial number of shares in your company?"

Caleb's face flushed with annoyance. "I had no clue."

"I see. So tens of millions of dollars is small potatoes to someone like . . ."

"It's a lot of money, Senator," Caleb interrupted, "but it wasn't on my radar. It wasn't public at the time and no one told me about it."

"Why did he do all this?"

"I don't really know."

"What's your best guess then, Mr. Wagner, about why Mr. Velarde did this to Armor, to you?"

"I've obviously thought a lot about that. And I think it's a mix of things. I think he wanted to help Davis and Clay get Iran. He's been friends with Clay for years. I also think he wanted the money. And, Senator, I think he wanted to hurt me."

"Why would he want to hurt you?"

The crowded room was silent as everyone waited several seconds for Caleb to respond.

"I think deep down he was jealous that I was the CEO and he was the deputy. I was rich and famous and he wasn't. He found a way to flip all that."

Senator Coady smiled. "Now he's rich and famous. And you're . . ."

Caleb nodded. "A lot less rich than I was before."

"Do you know where Steve Velarde is now?"

Caleb shook his head. "No, I do not. I have no idea."

CHAPTER 62

SUNDAY, AUGUST 21.

I was sitting on the sofa a few weeks later watching the A's, who were surprisingly good this season, when Pam came into the room and handed me an IPA. She gave me a bright, beautiful smile.

"What's up, sweetheart?" I asked her as she plopped down beside me, managing to not spill a drop of herbal tea that she clutched in an Armor Security mug.

She was silent for a couple of seconds, looking at me with a cute little smirk, and then she said, "Michael Housen, you're going to be a father."

I put down the IPA and turned to her with joy in my heart and a look on my face that must have read to her as "How did that happen?"

"It was the day I got out of prison."

I smiled. "I remember."

"When he or she gets old enough we can tell our child about our time in prison. If it's a girl, we can name her Justine. Take off the e if it's a boy."

I laughed and wrapped my arms around her, careful of the tea. "I love you more than life itself," I said.

She kissed me. "And Mikey, we have a better life to give our child than what we thought we might have."

And that was true. We had a new president who, despite his flaws, so far had not yet committed any public crimes against us or against humanity at large. The Iranian people had toppled the mullahs and were sorting out their country. They had an interim leadership that featured both a man and woman, both about the same age as me and Pam. We could not have been happier about it all, save for one huge problem: after six weeks, we were still missing Zahra. And no messages had come to us from her—or from whoever had her. We told Weiss she was kidnapped and did our best not to worry too much.

The cold chill of the Blair's IPA bottle felt nice in my left hand as I sat on the sofa. The warmth of impending fatherhood felt magnificent. It was as if all of the trouble and danger we had endured was so that we could emerge victorious, to produce a new life. Pam and I snuggled together, my right arm draped around her, enjoying a moment of peace.

We turned our eyes back to the big game at the A's new waterfront stadium at Howard Terminal in Oakland against the Kansas City Royals, who were really good. The A's were tied for first place. It was the bottom of the ninth. The A's were losing by two runs. Their top player, Tyler Soderstrom, was at the plate. There was a runner on second base. Two outs.

My phone was on the kitchen counter and the sound was off. No emails. No tweets. No alerts. Cyberspace had eaten me alive since June, but it didn't exist right now. No. It was just me and the things I love: my beer, my baseball, my couch. And, most of all, my wife. The mother of our child. There were times when I thought we would never be here again.

The Royals closing pitcher—a six-foot-five stud from the Dominican Republic—was throwing blazing ninety-nine-miles-per-hour heat.

"Maybe we can call our child baseball in Farsi," I said. "What is the word?"

"Baseball," she said, with a Persian accent on a giggle, gently digging her left elbow into my ribs. Her dimples sent beautiful little shock waves throughout my body.

"Ha!" I snorted and laughed, realizing I hadn't really laughed in weeks. It felt good.

Our laughter built. Her right hand reached up and gripped mine and she squeezed. I squeezed back, a little too hard. She winced.

"You okay?" I asked, letting up on my squeeze. I knew her shoulder was still a little sore from the slight sprain while being handcuffed by Weiss's henchman two months earlier.

"Yes. I'm fine." She paused, her eyes on the screen as the Royals threw another ball. It was a full count. "We could name our child after his or her month of conception."

"June might be an odd name for a boy," I said with a straight face that quickly melted into more laughter.

We laughed hard. I drank my beer. Pam's legs kicked up the blanket and it fell to the floor beside her as she sat up straight and looked hard into my eyes. We laughed more.

Swing. Foul ball.

We're home. We're laughing again. We're going to be parents. Our life has not returned to where it once was, but it has found a new level. It is still simple. And for now, it is quiet.

Swing. Crack . . . home run!

"Yes!" we screamed. We stood up with our arms raised and hugged. We kissed. "Yes!"

The game was now tied. The A's cleanup hitter strode to the plate.

Then Pam's phone rang. She looked at it. "It's a WhatsApp call. Where's 971?"

I shook my head. I didn't know. Pam answered.

A smile burst across her face when she heard the voice on the other end.

"Zahra!" she squealed. I felt a swell of relief rise in my body. Then Pam's smile faded as fast as it had appeared. She handed the phone to me.

"He wants to talk to you."

I took the phone.

"You need to keep your phone switched on, Mike."

It was Steve Velarde. My heart thudded and my brain buzzed with fury. But I knew I had to keep calm. "Why do you have Zahra, Steve?"

He laughed. "Because I need you to pay attention, Mike. I would have preferred to have your wife, but we take what we can get."

I wanted to kill him. Pam saw the look on my face and held up her hands. "Please. Save Zahra."

"What do you want, Steve?" I asked.

"I want to enjoy my life here in Dubai," he said. "You know, the nice thing about this country is there's no extradition to the US."

"Then let Zahra go. You don't need her."

"Oh but I do, Mike. I do. Until you do something for me."

"What do you want?"

"I'll tell you in good time. But for now, I want you to go back to Armor and turn the lights on."

"Why?"

"Because it has to seem like business as usual, Mike. Until I get what I want."

"What do you mean business as usual?"

"Just do what I say."

"What do you want?"

"You remember the Game Changer?"

I remembered Steve always suggesting he would eventually tell me what it was specifically. But he never did.

"Yes."

"Well, that's the road you're going to go down."

"What is the Game Changer?" I asked. "You would never tell me."

Steve laughed.

"You can ask Pam," Steve said.

"What? How would Pam know?"

"It was her father who gave us the idea. Her late great physicist father."

I felt like my entire body had been flash frozen. If Pam's father had given Steve—and Clay and whoever else was involved with them—the idea for the Game Changer, then it was probably these guys who had taken him and Pam's mother out of the game.

"We had one big missing piece to the equation, and we found it in your garage, in his notebooks."

Weiss and her agents, I thought immediately. They weren't snooping around in our house looking for evidence Pam and I were working with Iran, like we thought. They knew we weren't. No, they were looking for Pam's father's physics notebooks to find the missing piece to the Game Changer.

"So what do you want now? What am I looking for, Steve? Please."

"I will send you the codes. Bo can help you. So can that freak that you like from customer services."

"Bo is alive?"

Steve laughed again. A terrifying cackle. "I just took his car. I didn't take his life. Just put him under the weather for a while. He'll be happy to hear from you. In fact, you should probably get in touch with him today. He might need you . . ."

What had Steve done to Bo? What had he done to Zahra? What did he want?

"What do I do when I find whatever you need? I don't even know what I'm looking for."

"I'll be back in touch. For now just remember—keep everything at Armor business as usual."

"What does that mean?"

"Goodbye, Mike. Say goodbye, Zahra."

"Michael, I—" Zahra said.

But he hung up before she could continue. I called back but the phone just rang.

Pam looked deep into my eyes. "What was that about me knowing something, Mikey?"

I had traveled a thousand miles from happy to terrified. "It was about your father, Pam. He said they got the idea for something called the Game Changer from him. It has to do with defying quantum physics—that's all I know. They must have stolen his notebooks from the garage. Agent Weiss and her team must have grabbed them when they were snooping around the house."

"What about the camera out back?"

"It was a diversion from what they were really doing."

Pam's face then clouded with the same thought that I had. The car accident that killed her parents had been no accident.

"The accident," she said. "It must've been . . ."

"Yeah," I said, staring back into her eyes.

"What are we going to do, Mikey?"

I kissed her. Then I said, "We need to act like everything is business as usual, Pam."

"But what does that mean, Mikey? Business as usual?"

I didn't know. But we had only one choice. We were going to find out.

ACKNOWLEDGMENTS

The authors would like to thank each other, for the damn good time they had writing this book. They are also most grateful to Michael Campbell at Arcade for his strong commitment, insightful guidance, and skillful editing. And they'd like to thank Nancy Bell for her very helpful thoughts and comments.

ABOUT THE AUTHORS

William Cooper is a cybersecurity attorney and award-winning author. His writings have appeared in hundreds of publications around the world including the *New York Times*, *San Francisco Chronicle*, *Chicago Sun-Times*, *Huffington Post*, *Toronto Star*, *Jerusalem Post*, CNN, and *Newsweek*. *Publishers Weekly* calls his writings about American politics "a compelling rallying cry for democratic institutions under threat in America." Visit him online at Will-Cooper.com.

Michael McKinley is a journalist, author, and filmmaker. He has written more than a dozen books, and his most recent, *Willie: The Game Changing Story of the NHL's First Black Player*, was named in the Top 20 Books of 2020 by the CBC and nominated for a 2021 NAACP Image Award. His novel, *The Penalty Killing*, was nominated for an Arthur Ellis Award as best debut crime novel, and his Amazon Kindle thriller *Facetime* was a bestseller. Please see www.libertayo.com for a digital sampling of McKinley's work.